A DRAGON for CHRISTMAS

by Gavin Black

When the shot rang out, I ducked down into the wet paddy, scared out of my wits, the cigarette I'd come outside to smoke dropping from my nerveless fingers.

I peered quickly at the boathouse just twenty yards away. They must have heard the rifle go off, but none of my Chinese escorts came out to help me.

Who the hell was shooting at me?

Then I heard the rice squash as the sniper trod across the open paddy to finish me off at close range. . . .

"Potent excitement!"—*New York Herald Tribune*

A
DRAGON
for
CHRISTMAS

by

G A V I N   B L A C K

PERENNIAL LIBRARY
Harper & Row, Publishers
New York, Hagerstown, San Francisco, London

First PERENNIAL LIBRARY edition published 1979

ISBN: 0-06-080473-4

79 80 81 82 83 10 9 8 7 6 5 4 3 2 1

CHAPTER I

I went out on deck to look at the New China. It looked very much like the old China to me, the same few bare winter trees which had escaped being chopped up for firewood, and the same yellow soil where the snow let it show. The houses were yellow and so was the water in the river. The dogs were yellow, too, running along the banks yapping at us, the same as they used to. A new order can't do much about changing dogs.

The ship was moving up the Pei-Ho river, which twists across flat land for twenty miles from the Yellow Sea to Tientsin. It was certainly cold out on deck. The cold came from Manchuria and the terrible desolations of desert beyond it, from mountains scraped bare of trees by a million years of winds blowing. The cold bit at me, but with a kick to it, a little like the cold in New York, only harder. I could feel it getting through the layers of wool to my body in which circulated tropic-thinned blood. And I kept my breathing to the upper half of my lungs, not to let that cold really get inside.

"China closes about us," said a voice at my elbow.

I turned to Mr. Kishimura. He was a Japanese business man, like me no longer bright with youth, but with a face better polished up to cover this. Everything about Mr. Kishimura was polished. His glasses shone. So did his teeth.

"What are you selling them?" I asked.

I'd had four days from Kobe in which to ask this question, but hadn't, even one evening when we played

Japanese chess in the saloon.   Mr. Kishimura wasn't coy about his career.

"Shoeses," he said simply.   "Boots, also."

He smiled out at China.

"I am Okura Shoten Trading Company, Mr. Harris."

"With seven hundred million people waiting here for your shoes?"

"We hope, indeed."

"Have you been over before?"

"My first visit in some years."

"So you're after new business?"

"Not exactly.   Mr. Obata he come to China for my company.   He meets misfortune, maybe."

"How?"

"Perhaps throat slitted."

"I beg your pardon?"

"Mr. Obata not come back home. I find . . . maybe."

He didn't sound as if he really expected to find Mr. Obata at all.   It somehow put a curious emphasis on aspects of my mission which I had minimised to that rather small circle of people whom I can honestly claim love me.   It was a perfectly straightforward business trip, I had said, in to do a job and then out again.   Now, creeping into China, I couldn't help thinking about the out again.

"You expect to sell many Dolphin engine?" Mr. Kishimura asked.

"How did you know I'm selling them?"

"I am informed in Japan."

They are always informed, these little friends of ours, these allies.   Other people's business is also their business, or they mean to make it so.

"Okura Shoten is interested in engines?"

"No, Mr. Harris. Only shoeses."

On principle I never believe any straight-from-the-shoulder from them. I smiled at Mr. Kishimura and he returned the smile.

"You like to play Japanese chess, eh? Tientsin some time, I think."

"Delighted."

We went into the packed, seething heat of the passages and along to the little saloon where the chess had been left set out, waiting. I hung up my coat near the door. Mr. Kishimura had been out on deck without his, for a ritual hardening of the flesh.

"Ha," he said, sitting down to pleasure.

Mr. Kishimura beat me at the first game. "Go" is like chess but it was a long time since I had been in practice. As a boy I had sat on the porch of a villa at Gotemba in Japan and played "Go" with our hired man. He was hired to bring us water, for there was none piped in, and to take other things away, but he had plenty of time for "Go".

"You are long time not playing?" Mr. Kishimura said after his third win.

"That's right."

"But I think you are instinct of game."

"Thanks for the comfort."

"It means for me to watch carefully."

"Why?"

"To understand 'Go' is to understand Japanese mind. So I must watching."

"You're selling shoes. I'm selling engines. Remember?"

"So," said Mr. Kishimura. Then he giggled.

He beat me at the fourth game, but I took the fifth.

"Skill returning again," Mr. Kishimura said, as though this made him happy. "Why are you not speaking Japanese?"

"I'm rusty. Very."

"But you are listening to talks on ship?"

I got his point. It was a Japanese ship.

"I was sitting lapping everything up," I said.

"You are wiser?"

"Not much. Except that I know what a happy people you all are these days. Jolly."

"You think?"

"The world is a Japanese oyster, Mr. Kishimura. And you've got the wedge in. Poor old Britain is getting hungrier and hungrier."

"I not understand?"

"The direct point, Mr. Kishimura, is that the Dolphin engine manufactured under licence in Singapore by my associates is a very much better engine than the one manufactured in Osaka, which you are trying to sell . . . along with shoes."

"Ah . . ." he said. "Of engine I know nothing."

"Then let me tell you something. The Dolphin uses less fuel, very much less, than your Nishin. About a third less, in fact. It is ideal for Chinese river craft. And it has already been tested on something like eight hundred junks. Your Nishin has only been out for six months and if you want my opinion you haven't ironed out the wrinkles yet."

"Excuse?"

"The flaws. It hasn't been adequately trial-tested. The Chinese won't buy it. Stick to shoes."

"You hear many things in Japan, I think."

"The moment I get off a ship or a plane in your country, Mr. Kishimura, I get right down on the ground and put my ear to it. And this time I got the warning that Nishin had big eyes on the China market. It occurred to me that I might have a rival on board. Did you pack in a hurry?"

"My wife pack," said Mr. Kishimura. "You have wife in Singapore?"

"No."

"So?" He was genuinely surprised. "At your age you are not father many times?"

"At the moment my family ends with me."

The thought saddened him. It put him off his next game, which I won.

The door opened and the second mate came in, a young man who did judo exercises on the boat-deck every morning and who was clearly totally fit.

"*Tientsin da yo*," the mate said.

We all went and looked out of a forward porthole and there was the city all right, sprung on us out of flat China, the yellow country suddenly giving over to a place which smoked.

I wished now that I had flown in, though that isn't easy to do when you have an engine in your luggage. Coming this way was not only too deliberate, but it was moving into the past again, digging at memory. Tientsin was a lively town once, and there was a splendid hotel, the Astor, where at dinner there were always three amiable Chinese "boys" for every table, wearing felt slippers and breathing quietly. They were also psychic about your wants. It was luxury, imperialist, no doubt evil, but extremely pleasant at the receiving end. My father had been on the receiving end in the Orient all his life until his very last months, and some of the pleasures had certainly come off on his son.

Now, looking at the city swelling towards us, I thought of Mr. Obata. Okura Shoten shoes did seem an indifferent cause for which to have one's throat slit. But, of course, the Oriental doesn't hug the importance of his little individual life in the way we do. He has the comfort of a deep consciousness of race, and when he has to die for shoes he knows that another home boy salesman will come along to take his place. Our promotion men might get to work on this as a new keenness angle, but I suspect it's too late. It might have gone down with those first Elizabethans who were so steamed up over being British, but our crowd hasn't got the fire any more. We mostly plan for pensions.

I watched the tying up of the *Hashimi Maru* to that Tientsin quay with mixed feelings. We were being warped in against waiting China and I saw the Japanese sun flag blowing from the stern with more warmth than was my usual reaction. This little tub, billed in the brochure as "a floating palace of rest and recreation", was suddenly all the security there was in the world, neutral and immune to the vast and frightening immensity of the country beyond us. Tourists may romp around Moscow these days, with tea dances in the big hotels, but China offers none of this tolerance. It doesn't look as though it ever will, and on this grey morning all possibility of incidental pleasure was denied by winter. I had the sharpest feeling that the sale of a thousand Dolphin engines in a packaged deal just wasn't worth it. If that had been my only business in China I might have stayed on the ship and sailed back to nice, gay, polite Japan again. But it wasn't my only business in China.

"Ah," said Mr. Kishimura. "Reception committee, I think."

"Eh? Where?"

He pointed and he was right.

Down there on the dock were seven men in a row. They might have marched here in that formation, swinging around a crane in a Scots Guards swank parade drill. They stood now perfectly motionless, looking at us, up at the boat-deck, seven men all dressed alike, in a kind of uniform of blue serge, and without overcoats, even in that biting wind. The comforts of the flesh didn't concern them.

"They look like warders," I said.

"Please?"

"Prison keepers."

"Ah, so. Too truly. Even lady keeper."

"Lady?"

"End one," said Mr. Kishimura.

I don't know by what instinct he had identified sex. The end one was certainly a little shorter, and a little bulkier, perhaps from combies of knitted yak's wool under the tunic. But if she had more hair it was tucked away up under her peaked cap. And her expression was just as intent, just as passive as the others, who all waited for their moment soon to come.

"In Japan," Mr. Kishimura said, "lady now wear kimono again. I think good, no?"

"Very good."

"Lady in uniform is not pleasant."

I agreed with that sentiment too. I felt a lot closer to Mr. Kishimura in these moments. Rival he might be, and almost certainly was, but he was human, with a common denominator of the weaknesses and vices of our species. Those waiting didn't look as though they tolerated any kind of relaxing vice.

"We go to saloon now," Mr. Kishimura said. "They come."

And that was what happened. We went down to the saloon and sat waiting for Red China. We heard it first, and that was almost consoling, the ripple of the language, the curious rapid lightness of it, which is not unlike hearing French for the first time spoken by natives on a Messageries Maritimes liner, a kind of bubbling strangeness against which English seems prosy and dull. The voices swelled up outside the door to the saloon, and then the door opened. They came in, one by one, six flat-faced men followed, at the end, by Miss New China. They all had the same kind of eyes and noses and ears and mouths, except the girl, whose face was leaner, with cheek bones. And her eyes weren't dark, hidden in slits, they were wide and green.

Green! I couldn't believe it. I stared. Blue wouldn't have startled me so much, for there are blue-eyed Orientals, Siamese girls from north of Chiengmai with eyes like the cats of the country. But green, never. And yet the planes of this girl's face were Oriental. I could see now that under the padding she was almost certainly very slight, with the kind of body made for a *cheongsam*.

There were seven of us waiting in the saloon, four Japanese, two Indonesians, and me. We had our names called by number one warder, the Japanese names first, to which each of the island empire's business men answered with a polite little "*hai*" Then the warder said: "Hal-lis?"

"Here," I told him, feeling oddly back in school.

Warder number one was not an appealing specimen.

Smallpox had really hit him once, and his face was pitted. By the left of his nose was a small crater. While he had his head down, over that list, there was only a line for his eyes, two pencil strokes with no wrinkles on the lids or beneath. Then he lifted his head and looked at me, with his eyes showing, very black, very cold, with the iciness of a kind of permanent anger.

I was a lackey of murderous imperialism far from home but still dangerous. I knew then that it was a label I was going to be wearing for the whole of my time in the celestial socialist republic. Warder number one's eyes, fixed on me, said that. He would have enjoyed slitting my throat.

"Welcome to New China," he said.

The Japanese business men made a faint buzzing noise of appreciation, pushing the sound through their teeth. The Indonesians, both wearing round little hats above aquiline faces of burnished bronze, smiled and bobbed their heads. I moved in my seat a little.

"We now assist you in all difficulties," warder number one said, and it sounded like a threat.

I was conscious of green eyes fixed on me, staring harder than I had. The girl's look didn't waver when I met it either. I might have been a specimen on a slab on which she was going to be examined later. It was her job to dissect me out so carefully that there couldn't be any unpleasant surprises. She was getting the all-over picture now before she took out her scalpel kit.

Miss New China had certainly thrown away charm. She stood with her legs apart, like an "at ease" on parade, but waiting for the order to come to attention. She wore boots which were only a slightly smaller version of the boots of her fellow-warders. If Mr. Kishimura had more feminine-looking footwear amongst his samples he was carrying useless deadweight.

It was no surprise to me when warder number one began a series of introductions and I was assigned to the girl. He was People's Guardian Yang Yi and she was Miss Mei Lan, which seemed to me something of an old order hangover, an oddly flowery name for a lady hatchet-woman not to have got rid of. She was apparently an apprentice People's Guardian, and I was sure a new one, keen to prove herself. Given a choice I would have plumped for a woman warder, but not this one.

Eurasian, there wasn't a shadow of doubt about it. A touch of the West somewhere in her family history which had left her with those eyes, and probably a burning determination to work hard to overcome this natural disadvantage. She would be a letter-of-the-regulations girl all the way, and then some, trying to work out of her probationer status with a triumphant success over me.

I wondered, under observation from those jade eyes, just what Miss Mei Lan's idea of success involved. And I found myself digging then for all those arguments I had used earlier in Singapore about the essential simplicity of my mission. I wasn't a journalist likely to burst into print with impressions of three weeks in China. Nor was I an undercover man for the British Foreign Office, just a simple business type bent on the capitalistic end of stuffing my already overflowing warehouses with more gold sweated out of the proletarian workers of the world. It seemed to me then important to establish this clearly and soon. There was, of course, the nasty little fact that I had a certain history of private anti-Red activity, but that had been a long way from China. And if it was in my dossier . . . well, after all, it was exactly what they expected from us. We were enemies doing a deal under the cover of a kind of economic truce.

"You have Miss Mei," People's Guardian Yang said, making this quite clear.

He caught hold of the girl's arm and brought her a bit closer to the western imperialist. I was aware then that the Chinese still like garlic cookery.

"How do you do, Miss Mei."

"Good day," the girl said flatly, using the permitted greeting from her instruction book, but even this with caution.

"You selling motor machine for boat," Yang informed me, and daring me to try and sell anything else.

"That is correct."

"Miss Mei your interpreter. You speak Cantonese?"

"Some."

"Very well, I think. No good in north China."

"I'm very ready to use Miss Mei's services," I told him, smiling.

The smile upset her. She glared and then, glancing at Yang's veneer of amiability, tried to apply a little herself. It wasn't a smile that came, only a certain lightening of the suspicious gloom. But when Yang turned away even that was switched off at once.

We were left facing each other. It didn't embarrass me that I was sitting and the lady standing. Any display of courtesy on my part towards her sex would have put her on the offensive even more than she was. And had I stood I would have towered over her. The Oriental tends to resent our size. They make a music-hall joke of it, but they resent it too.

"Are you a student, Miss Mei?"

"Please?" Then she understood. "No!"

"You travel to Peking with me?"

"Yes. I am always present."

This suggested a vista of intimacy which left me without any enthusiasm. I was also made aware of the fact that it wasn't Yang who liked garlic.

Some of the other guardians were sitting down near their charges and Miss Mei did so, too, quite suddenly, on her cue.

"You live in Peking?" I asked.

"Sometimes."

The American influence in China is oddly lasting. The girl's intonation was of the States, clipped. And I began to have the feeling that she had once used English a great deal, that her learning of it hadn't just been academic, though she was rusty now. I tried to assess her age, and it was difficult. There was simply nothing in her face to indicate experience or a lack of it, just a mask in which green eyes were wary. She had, I noticed then, a very good skin, the pale smooth skin which comes from a diet low in animal fats. In the West that porcelain-clear, faintly translucent look used to be considered a symptom of tuberculosis. As though to confirm the diagnosis Miss Mei coughed, quite heavily, trying to smother this, then having to put up a hand to her face.

It was the lifting of her hand which startled me, something totally out of character. The movement was positively stylised, elbow out slightly, fingers extended, head lowered to meet them. I had the feeling of having seen the movement a hundred times, perhaps in old China, a kind of practised delicacy of behaviour which was totally alien to the proletarian performance. It gave me the feeling of someone else under all that padding.

I noticed her hands too. They were red with chilblains

and broken nails were cut short. But it wasn't the kind of hand which suggested a long history of hard labour, it was too small for one thing, almost the tiny doll's hand once highly in favour.

The coughing brought colour into Miss Mei's face. And the suggestion of garlic was very strong indeed, together with something else, something remembered from Japan, a reek of camphor. The Japanese used to take camphor pills for a weak chest.

"You have a bad cold," I said.

"Not so!" Miss Mei swallowed and sat up straight. She looked at me with thin dark brows brought almost together in anger over those remarkable eyes. But it wasn't a hot anger. It was like a glimpse of the moving parts of some calculating machine through small glass windows.

Miss Mei had, I decided, an oddly photogenic face. Repellent in its set expression, but photogenic. In a London exhibition of camera craft from the New China a portrait of Miss Mei would certainly have taken a prize, posed as she was now. Everything about her said a great deal and some things shouted. One of the things which shouted was that a new order turning women into this had gone round a wrong corner somewhere. It wasn't a question of politics at all, but a plain fact about the human animal. When you set out to eliminate sex differentiation you eliminated a great hunk of joy from living. In fact nearly all joy. There was probably eating left, but from what I had heard of things up here the pleasure from that had been eliminated too.

"We go now," Yang said. "You return to cabins for luggage. You must carry."

We had been warned about this. The New China

didn't offer porters to carry bags any more, and I travelled with only two smallish airplane suitcases. I also had a Dolphin engine crated down in the hold, but they would have to find transport for that.

My two suitcases were on the bunk in my tiny cabin. I had booked this space back to Japan after the *Hashimi Maru's* turn around up at Dairen and Port Arthur. It would have been nice to know I was going to sleep here again.

"Excuse?" said Mr. Kishimura from the doorway.

I had to step back against the wash-basin to make room for him. He shut the door carefully, and smiled. He was using a Kyoto lacquer cigarette holder, very ornate, the only hint I'd seen of the possible æsthete behind the serious executive.

"I think to speak something to you, Mr. Harris."

"By all means."

"You like reception committee?"

"Not much. But I was expecting something like them."

"Mr. Harris, please listen. Before I come on this ship I have information about you."

I grinned at him.

"Don't say I didn't jump to it."

His face was set and solemn.

"This most serious thing. Into Japan comes little newses from China. Like small waves on shore. Whisper only. But we hear things not heard other places. You understand?"

"I do. Go on."

"For a man like you, Mr. Harris, to come to China now is most dangerous."

"Why now particularly?"

"Moment of crisis. Internal policy changing. Bitter

anti-West feeling. From this could come many things very dangerous to you."

"Your information about me has been incorrect. I'm not that important."

"My information quite correct, Mr. Harris. From what I know I say this . . . you go down from this ship to walk on China and you could quickly become dead man."

Japanese haven't very big eyes either, most of them. But Mr. Kishimura and I looked at each other then, for about half a minute, and I could see right into his. They were solemn. So was his whole face. He was a man doing his duty, but it could be his duty to the Nishin engine. I reached around and pulled one of those airplane suitcases from the bunk.

"I think People's Guardian Yang is waiting for us, Mr. Kishimura. Tell you what, I'll come behind you. Keeping close. Then maybe you'll get the first bullet."

CHAPTER II

MR. KISHIMURA turned and went out of my cabin. I was more than a little surprised at his gauche scare tactics, so totally lacking in the subtle Oriental approach. If he had wanted to play that kind of game he should have started to work on my nerves, delicately, while we were still cruising through Japan's inland sea.

And out on deck it was at once apparent that he had dropped me flat as a friend. He didn't even look at me, taking time now to be what I thought was somewhat too agreeable to the Chief People's Guardian. Then we were all herded towards the gangway and went down it as a kind of sandwich, shaggy socialist warders in layers between a lush filling of well-fed-looking imperialists with gold watches.

From my height I could look down on the rest, and it was an odd effect, the Japanese now polite and reserved and mildly expectant, immune to surprise. The two Indonesians might have been coming to their new Mecca, faces lifted to anything they could see, bright faces, believing. I looked for a sign that had once glittered out in lights over the dock area . . . "Gaiety Theatre" . . . and to my total surprise saw it was still there, though clearly with all the bulbs out of the sockets, just letters still on a wall in peeling yellow paint. I wondered if the Astor Hotel still functioned, but now as a People's Palace of Rest for Commissars and above.

"Mind the feet," said Yang loudly from the front, and the other warders took that up. Miss Mei, behind me, got it in last.

Then I was walking on China again, even if this bit was only concrete poured under contract by a British company long ago. As we were herded towards three ancient cars I turned and looked back at the *Hashimi Maru*. A nice little ship she seemed now, about four thousand tons, with the rakish lines of Japanese building, the sharp cut-away bow, the squat funnel, and gleaming white superstructure. Everything about her looked new and shining, a visitant from another world to this one of rust and crumbling plaster and paint forgotten. I had the feeling again of the ship as my world lost, and this was increased by the sight of the mate standing under the bridge watching us leave. He might have been waiting politely for our disappearance before having another go at his judo exercises.

I was put into the back of the middle car, with my legs straddling my bags. On one side of me was Miss Mei and on the other Yang. There were three in the front seat, too, another warder, one of the Indonesian pilgrims, and the driver. I had a feeling that we were a bit over-loaded with warders there in the middle of the convoy, and these seemed to be set rather obviously around me, though this of course could have just happened, in spite of the fact that Yang didn't give the impression of being casual about the things he organised.

I'll say this for a socialist republic, it's almost ideal for the motorist, there's so little competition. Our convoy rattled away from the docks and swung into a roadway I just recognised, roaring down it, with horns blaring. There was plenty of traffic of sorts in the road, carts, people, and bicycles, but all this dissolved away from under tyred wheels, just in time, and with no panic. Face after face looked in at us from close range, in fixed stares of curiosity. One of the back windows was gone and I smelled city China again, its winter smell, of stale sweat-soaked cloth, animal dung, and a peculiar mustiness that might be from old buildings. There was also a hint of cooking, though I didn't see any food stalls.

I've said I just recognised the road. This had been considerably altered, not by any new buildings, but by the Ministry of Propaganda, who had erected huge bill-boards to educate the masses. The lessons on those posters were quite simple. There was one in vivid greens, blues and reds which showed a massive Chinese peasant of the new day impaling on some sort of agricultural instrument a squirming Uncle Sam as well as a smaller John Bull, both in top hats. I didn't need to ask for a translation of the text underneath.

Those posters glared in at us and I had the feeling that Yang was looking at me for my reaction. The main smallpox crater was on my side of his face. I inquired about the once famous Tientsin carpet industry and wondered whether it was still functioning. Yang said output had quadrupled in the last five years. I said I didn't see the carpets for sale about the place any more and he said that they weren't being sent outside for the pleasure of imperialist buyers. I suggested that perhaps they were being used for rest-rooms on the communal farms, and he said nothing to that, angrily. Beside us Miss Mei had a fit of coughing from the terrible window draught which she tried, unsuccessfully, to smother, desperately damping down the paroxysm like someone in church determined not to set up a distraction to a par-ticularly good sermon. When I didn't have to look at her I was beginning to feel a little sorry for Miss Mei and her cough.

We were bound for the railway station but before we reached it, just before, I saw one of those pictures of China that I knew I would keep up in the lumber room of my experience like a lot of earlier pictures. The station was ahead, to our right, and the main road left it, going over a bridge across a river. The bridge was one of those steel things of a period, perhaps 1905, when a lot of metal work was allowed to show above the parapet level, with massive rivets. Beyond this superstructure was a pattern of junk masts and I had a flash view of river craft at a level below city life, with padded women cooking on deck in the hard winter sunshine, surrounded by children. One little boy was urinating into the water. Farther up a woman was washing rice in the flow. There was the Chinese din of living in the air, a vibration of voices, dogs barking, and somewhere a People's Democracy loud-speaker ranting out one of those marching tunes which these days are bullying us even as far south as Singapore.

Then brakes squealed us into the station parking area and the cars, which would never have passed their British ten-year test, slewed about to a stop.

We got out, our party a curious hybrid thing between a group of V.I.P.s and a huddle of closely watched con-victs. Yang assumed leadership again.

"Train leaves in one hour. Exactly. In New China trains always on time. We have arranged special tea for you."

The news of tea was greeted by little yips of joy from the Indonesians, as though to drink tea in China was worth all the pains of their travel. The Japanese made hissing noises of polite acceptance and I tried to look hopeful in spite of my spirits which had suddenly, and for no specific reason, become low.

The waiting-room didn't perk them up at all. This was clearly a place not in general use by the masses, reserved possibly for new citizens on the way to the top or those about to be liquidated. It was equipped with wooden benches and a scarred table and on the wall was an enamel sign no one had bothered to remove which said, first in English, "Spitting Prohibited", then the same in French, then a row of Chinese characters.

Tea was on the scarred table, to be drunk from railway porcelain, and there was a plate of biscuits to which no one had added the necessary dog vitamins.

"Mr. Yang," I said, "I'm a little worried about my engine. I meant to stay and see it unloaded. . . ."

"It is all arranged," he waved his hand. "Engine will follow to Peking."

He was plainly not liking me now. I wasn't contributing to the tone of this occasion, which was probably their version of a cocktail party. I noticed he pitched into the biscuits. The tea was good, weak as green tea should be, but with the aroma of the best Shantung. I had three cups and felt the warmth radiating out from my stomach even if it didn't quite reach my cold heart.

Without Mr. Kishimura for a pal I was decidedly out of things. I needed his company right then, but he had removed himself, staying tightly with the Japanese delegation. Miss Mei leaned against one wall, sipping her tea as though grateful for this luxury. No one had offered her a dog-biscuit and she hadn't come forward to the table. I picked up the plate and went over to her.

A kind of surprise came into her eyes then, slipping through a hole in the wall of caution. She shook her head.

"No!"

"Go on. The stationmaster will just gobble them up after we've gone."

Yang was busy talking to the Indonesians. Miss Mei's red, chilblained hand came out and closed about a biscuit. The way she took it reminded me of the way I had taken food as a prisoner of the Japanese, driven by the hunger of a wild dog. Was she hungry?

"Another," I said.

She took that, too, with a kind of daring, her eyes still not including me in a conspiracy. The second biscuit seemed to disappear, hidden, while she munched the first. I had the strong feeling that she wanted me to put that plate back quickly, before its absence from the table was noticed, and I did that.

I didn't go to stand beside her again, knowing she wouldn't want it, but she was suddenly in my mind. What kind of worlds had those green eyes seen? She couldn't be more than twenty-five, which made her a child when Mao took over his China. But a child can see and remember a lot, storing it away. Shanghai, perhaps? That's where most of the Eurasians were once, a whole community of them, grubbing a life out of what was left from a glossy world only lightly rooted in that soil. That world had gone, in panic flight to Formosa, much of it. Its death pangs hadn't lasted long. Only the buildings remained down there on a dirty river, tall skyscrapers that had once been hotels.

Mei Lan. A flower name. A hangover. And the girl in the padded clothes couldn't have known a time of blossoming. She looked as though easy laughter wasn't even something held in memory. I knew how it felt, for I had felt that way, after only three and a half years, having to come back to laughter slowly, as though too much of it was terribly indigestible. Maybe if I'd had to go on much longer the laughter would have died for ever. Mei Lan looked as though it had for her.

The journey to Peking over the flat, winter-dulled plain was relieved from boredom only by a discussion about graves. Yang sat beside me, in a comfortably heated and clean, if old, coach, where the seats were of cracked black leather. I missed the thing I had been looking for, the mounds in every field which marked the graves of ancestors, and about which respectful ploughs had once taken curved paths. These were gone.

Yang explained. The ancestors had been ploughed under. In a collective farm there was no place for memorials to the dead. The New China put the past away, looking only forward. It was a pity, Yang said, that I could not see the home-smelting plants in which the workers made iron. Everyone made iron now. Chinese production was greater than Britain's. Soon it would beat America. China was on the march.

We even saw a demonstration of that marching which might almost have been arranged for us. From the station outside the old walls we drove towards the capital, through new areas of building that would have slightly depressed even British Civil Service architects. We drove towards the *Hatamen*, the great towered gate which I could remember, as a boy, having approached once on foot, arriving at it together with a convoy of camels in from the Gobi Desert, camels still haughty at the end of a great trek, bells tinkling around their long, weaving necks. That could almost have been the end of a golden journey from Samarkand, with the weary, dusty merchants up high on their loaded saddles.

Now there were no camels. Instead we halted for a

procession of what looked like schoolgirls, wearing trousers and serge blouses, and marching to the time of a tune bellowed from their throats. They were carrying banners, the only traditional note, huge pieces of flapping cloth held up on poles and splashed with black hieroglyphs. Everything stopped for the girls who went surging under the massive stone arch with its tiered tiled roofs above. Once through this gate had come the wicked old Empress after the Boxer uprising, returning to her capital and to wave up at the watching Europeans whom she had wanted to wipe out of China. It had needed a later conqueror to do that effectively. These marching girls were an ultimate triumph which would have surprised an old woman with her long, gold-sheathed finger-nails.

The hotel surprised me, a new building, seven storeys high, like a celled beehive in ferro-concrete. The lobby struck an almost cosmopolitan note which took away some of my feeling of isolation in a vast strangeness. There were murals in poster colours of the new China at work, but not quite so aggressively anti-imperialist, muted for the sensibilities of visitors. Europeans were about the place, too, most unmistakably Russians in those suits which look cut for expected growth. I didn't see any women.

Yang's control of us seemed to slacken in here, as though the jurisdiction of People's Guardians eased off behind plate-glass doors. We stood unattended in a queue to register just as we might have done anywhere else, and the man behind the desk put up a great show of efficiency, knowing our names and rationing out welcoming smiles. That hotel lobby, except for the murals, could have been almost anywhere . . . the murals and the fact that there were no bellhops. I turned away with a key and a room number; located, with a cell of my own, but still carrying those bags.

A tall fair young man rose from a chair near an ornamental pine tree in a porcelain pot. His suit was as emphatically London West End as his haircut, and he moved towards me with a half smile applied over weariness. When he spoke his voice was as pale as the rest of him, a flat monotone which just floated above total exhaustion.

"You'll be Mr. Harris? How do you do? Watt-Chalmers is the name. I'm on the commercial side at our Embassy here. I've been sent along to see if you needed anything?"

"It's a little soon to say. But it's very kind of you."

"Oh, absolutely routine. Part of my job, really. We're so glad to see you in China. We don't get enough of our business men here. Not nearly. Did you have a good trip?"

"Slower than I like."

"Oh." His smile had gone. "Well, you'll have to put up with that kind of thing, I'm afraid. You're selling engines, aren't you?"

"That's right."

"Oh. Well, I hope you sell 'em. There's quite a thing about that just now. Selling things, I mean."

Watt-Chalmers didn't look as though he had ever sold anything in his life. He was well enough placed by birth not even to have to sell himself. There was a long history of self-assurance behind this boy, if little else, besides ancestors.

He was looking at my clothes. I was wearing an American washable suit with an open greatcoat bought in Tokyo over it. The outfit clearly made me slightly incredible. I've been in a lot of places where embassies ought to have been useful to me, but I never tried to use them, possibly because I didn't feel we spoke the same language.

"Cigarette? Look here, Mr. Harris, there's a fellow at the Ministry of Foreign Trade called Tsung Fa Chew. Quite amiable, really. Would you like me to put you in touch?"

"That's kind of you. But since I've come here more or less by invitation to do a demonstration of our product I expect my contacts have been arranged."

"Oh." He looked relieved. "You won't really need us then? Here's a card though. Do give us a ring whenever you like. There's always someone available."

He looked at me again, considering something.

"We've got a drinks thing on Tuesday at six. Would you be interested?"

"I haven't an idea what my schedule will be."

"Oh." He could almost like me simply for not threatening to be a liability. "Well, I'll push off. You'll be wanting a bit of a rest. And do remember that we're there, and so on."

My room was on the fourth floor and I went up in a lift, finding my own way down corridors. 157 wasn't much bigger than my cabin on the *Hashimi Maru*, but packed with the essentials. It had a telephone and a door that I thought was a cupboard, but turned out to be a tiny bathroom. There didn't seem to be a cupboard, you were meant to leave your clothes in a suitcase. There were however, two hooks on the door as well as a printed notice in Russian, English and Chinese telling guests to put out all lights not needed.

It was nice to close a door which could be locked.

I sat down on the bed after shedding my coat, and in a moment lay along it with my eyes shut. I found myself wondering about Mei Lan and couldn't remember whether I had seen her coming through those glass doors. Perhaps there was an interpreters' room off the lobby, somewhere in which they sat and waited. It might be interesting, a little later, to see whether I could get out of the building unattended.

The telephone rang. I could just reach for it.

"This is 157. Harris here."

"Good afternoon, Mr. Harris. I'm Humbold, the Peking correspondent of the London *Workers' Weekly*."

"Are you?"

"Yes." The voice on the wire was faintly cockney. "I thought there might be time before your evening meal to give me a little interview."

"About what?"

"Well, your mission to the People's China, for one thing."

"I haven't come on a mission to the People's China. I've come here to sell something."

"That would be interesting to our readership. Any commercial connections with Britain are news."

"I'm not in sympathy with your readership."

He laughed.

"I didn't expect you to be, Mr. Harris. But I'd suggest that it would be a good move on your part to have a talk with me."

"Go to hell," I said and hung up.

In a moment the phone rang again. Humbold's voice said:

"Your line is rather silly, Mr. Harris."

"It's my line and I'm sticking to it."

"Journalists can be quite useful, you know."

"Not your kind. Good afternoon, Mr. Humbold."

I lay on thinking how very quiet it was in my little room. The window was a double one, to keep out the winter gales, and the heating was extremely efficient. Not a sound came in to me to suggest China at all, only a faint gurgling of hot-water pipes. I got up and went over to the window. The bright day had gone, and now the sky was leaden, suggesting more snow. My window faced on to a back courtyard, three sides the hotel, as neutral and uninteresting as a modern block anywhere, but there was an opening to the roofs of the city and I thought I could just make out the great curving tiled sweeps of the Winter Palace.

A snowflake came past the window and then another. It was going to be fun, in this kind of weather, probably in a wind from Manchuria, fitting my Dolphin into a boat on some dreary canal, and then running tests. It would have been more sensible to come in summer for this, but my other business couldn't wait. And every now and then even the resident of the tropics gets the feeling it would be good to be cold. It looked as though I'd get enough of that.

Heat seemed to be fanning out against my knees. It was some kind of hot-air system from a grille directly under the window ledge, and looking down at that grille I remembered where I was, behind the bamboo curtain. The thing was of aluminised metal, held in place by four screws. It seemed the obvious, too obvious, place for a microphone, but they would be fitting these wholesale. I went over and turned the key in the door.

The back of a nail file turned the screws after a while and the whole grille lifted out. I didn't at once see the microphone for it was tacked on to the top board, just a small disc. The new hotel was certainly under government management.

I next tested the bathroom. When you switched on the light this set in operation an extractor fan which made so much noise that a microphone wouldn't really have been practicable at all. I looked carefully, but decided there wasn't one. Clearly the wise host in a Red China hotel invited his friends in to sit on the edge of the tub.

I put back the grille as noiselessly as I hoped I'd removed it and set about the business of unpacking. Then, at the dressing-table, I noticed a small switch with a cloth-covered circle above it, both almost half hidden by the window curtains.

Radio laid on. Suddenly my room was filled with the wailing screech of Chinese music, rather a jazzy half march this time, with a female vocalist who must have tortured her voice from an early age to get these falsetto effects. There was no way of turning down the volume, you either took local culture or you switched it off. And it struck me that at this strength the speaker must rather cancel out the effectiveness of that small mike.

I left the music on, because I admit to rather liking the stuff, an acquired taste certainly. I folded away trousers to that voice shrieking at me. . . . "Pai, Pai, Tsao, Tsao, Tsing Fa Tsu . . ." or something similar, which was probably the current top hit-number "Death to the Imperialist Worker-Eating Monster." Then I took a jacket on a hanger over to one of the two pegs on the door. While I was there I turned the key back.

The orchestra stopped dead. Chinese numbers are like that, they don't come to any recognisable finale, everybody just gives up suddenly. An announcer with a very wide-awake voice then spoke for about two minutes, probably exhorting us all to double our production rate. He cut out in favour of what sounded like a race between a battery of musical saws and flutes made out of converted lead pipes. Our vocalist came back, joining the fracas. I could just see the production belt in a thousand factories suddenly speeded up for an end-of-the-day spurt, like something in those early Chaplin films, bolts flying about the place and wrenches jerking. And here I was, a proper enemy of the masses, doing everything in slow motion half time.

I didn't hear the door open. I just looked up and there was a man in the room, leaning back against the door. He wore the regulation serge tunic and trousers, but these unusually neat, almost starched, and he certainly made an odd-looking Chinaman, with cropped ginger hair and eyebrows to match, with under them pale blue eyes. A slight man, nervous-looking, who held one finger to his lips, patting them, in a desperate bid to keep me from shouting out for help. When I didn't his confidence came seeping back. He came towards me then, pointing towards the heating vent, and mouthing one word, his eyes rolling a bit from fear I wouldn't get it.

"Mike! Mike!" He pointed.

"Oh!" I said roundly, keeping up the mime.

That turned him almost limp with relief. And it took him a moment or two to get up strength to indicate the bathroom. I shut the door and he sat on the edge of the tub. Above us the extractor fan roared.

"Thank God you didn't say anything. I was scared of that, sir. I mean coming in on you."

I recognised the accent all right, plain Lowland Scots.

"Where have you come from?"

"Kilmarnock, sir."

"That isn't any outer suburb of Peking."

"I mean . . . that's my home, sir. Before I did it."

"Did what?"

"Became a Chink, sir."

And then he burst into tears.

CHAPTER III

I WENT OUT and got the bottle of whisky from my suitcase. I poured him a big slug in a toothglass and gave it to him neat. He gulped over it, but it all went down.

"Thanks, sir. That's a bit o' the real stuff. I needed it. I'd be for the high jump sure if they caught me here."

"Just who are you?"

"I work here. In the hotel. A kind of cellarman, you could call it. I look after the drinks. I'm Tiny McVey. That's my name. I was a corporal in the army. Officers' Mess, most of the time."

"You were caught in Korea?"

"Aye. Me and my mate. He's a sergeant. They put the heat on us, sir. I can tell you it was bad. And then my mate said to play it their way. I just didn't know what I was doin'. Not then. Maybe I'm no hero type."

He didn't look the hero type, sitting there on the edge of the tub, still holding the glass in both hands, as though the drops of whisky in the bottom had a kind of warmth.

"They brought you to Peking?"

"Aye. Two years ago. Before that we was in Manchuria. That's a hell-hole, I'm telling you. What a place! You wouldn't think human beings could live in it. It's bad enough to freeze a bear."

"What were you doing?"

"Oh, I worked in factories. And then . . . they said they was going to educate me. Because I hadn't had a chance under . . . under the capitalist devils. I was an exploited worker, they called it. My mate said to go on playing it their way. But he's got a brain, see. I mean, he could take their education. I couldnae."

"Where's your mate now?"

Tiny shook his head.

"I don't know. Maybe he's at the University, or something. I don't know. I've been on my own since they brought me here."

"To work in the hotel? That doesn't sound too bad."

Tiny stared at the floor.

"Okay. It's not too bad. Not with what I've had. But it's being on my own all the time. I canny go out in the town. Not that there's a damn thing here to go out to. But I'm just cooped up. You know this, I've thought I'd go mad."

"I'd give you another shot of this whisky only I think it would show when you left here."

"Aye, you're right, sir. Better not. Thanks anyway. It's a helluva good thing, just talking to you. You know this, I don't seem to get their lingo at all. I just can't do it. I've no brains, you see. I could have been a barman in a nice wee pub, that's all. And here I am. And me a Chink!"

His bewilderment was no act. It had lasted for more than a decade.

"Why did you do it, McVey? Why did you renounce your country?"

He didn't look at me.

"It was my mate that said to. The others in the camp was dying, see. A lot of them. I was scared, that's all. That's why I did it."

He lifted his head then and said, with a terrible honesty.

"It meant more grub."

Maybe I shouldn't have felt as I did then, remote from

any indignation. I felt that Tiny McVey had served twelve years hard and then some. Though he didn't know it we had a shared experience. Mine was farther away, but I still had only to open a door to remember what it was like.

"Did you never think that you could go to the British Embassy here?"

"Could I hell! Excuse me, sir. But I'm a Chink. That's what I've made myself. They wouldn't have me in the doors at the Embassy. And if I was seen trying to get there I'd just be shot. Like that. If they thought I was here now they'd . . ."

"Haven't you been able to write home?"

"My folks is dead. My mother didn't live long after . . . after it happened. I got a letter from my sister saying it was what I done."

A hell for Tiny McVey, all right.

"And why did you come to me?"

He made a sound that could have been a laugh. At himself.

"Maybe I thought someone like you could help me. There's been British here before but they've been in parties. There wasn't a man on his own like you. It seemed like my chance."

"What can I do? I can't smuggle a man out of China."

"I know, I know. But you could do something for me when you're out of here. That's what I want. Someone who'll maybe tell them I'm here."

"I live in Singapore, not Britain."

"I know. It was in the paper. They've got an English paper and I get to see it. All about you coming on a trade mission. A lot of talk about it. Mr. Harris, the Chinks is funny. They think they can do what they like with me, that nobody gives a damn about me. And that's the way it is. No one does. But if you was . . . outside, and kicking up a fuss out there, well, something might happen. . . ."

"You could be shot, as you said."

"You mean they'd know I'd seen you? I'd risk that. And talk about me outside would put them in a spot. It would mean I hadn't just been forgotten. That some-one was trying to do something. Maybe I'd have a bad time for a bit. Well, I could take it. I've taken it before. But they might let me out. I just might be put over the border into Hong Kong."

"You'd have to face arrest."

"Gawd! Do you think I'd mind that? I'd do time outside wi' bells on. If I just could get outside. I'm dead here, sir, I'm dead."

He began to cry again, simply, like a child. And his lack of control disturbed me because it pointed to so much, the long road of surrender down which this man had come. I couldn't feel that there had been any point of resistance in Tiny McVey, not even secretly, just as he said, he had lost his identity. He wasn't the first prisoner to whom this had happened.

He looked at me again, his eyes markedly bloodshot even against that curious pinkness of his skin.

"If I could get to Singapore, Mr. Harris, I could do something with myself. I'm not wanting back to the old country. But Singapore. . . ."

A little dream that he had. I could remember my own dreams when the Japs had me. And perhaps because of this I told him I'd do what I could when I got out. He said "thanks", looking again at the floor. I was expecting him to break down again, but he didn't, he straightened

up on that bath edge as though hope he could clutch at
again was in some way stiffening up his body.

"I'd better be getting back," he said.

"Is there anything more I should know about you?
I won't write it down. I've got your rank and name. I'd
better have your unit."

He told me.

"Can you get mail?"

"I've had two letters."

"In twelve years?"

"Aye."

"I'll try and not let you down by giving away who is
working for you. That mayn't be easy, but I'll do my
best. Am I likely to see you again while I'm here?"

"It's risky. But maybe I'll chance it. If I've got the
nerve. Gawd, you don't know what it means just to
talk to you."

"How will you get back to your cellars?"

"The lift goes right down. If I can make it without
being seen. Will you just look out for me?"

I did that. There was no one in the corridor at all.
I didn't think any of the rooms were occupied by Chinese
spies, either. The hotel appeared to be pretty full. It was
likely the management counted on those mikes for the
information they wanted. Snoopers in the passages
would be a bit obvious and this place was a show window.

Tiny McVey went quietly away. And when he had
gone I sat down and had a cigarette, wondering just what
in hell I was going to do about him when I got home.
He had gone over to the enemy in war-time. And there
had probably been some publicity about his asking to
become Chinese. It made nice propaganda and that
wouldn't have been neglected. I could see official

reactions, the looks of distaste. It's not easy to sell mercy in some quarters. Still, I had to try.

The phone rang. I certainly wasn't being neglected in the New China. But the voice I heard made me stiffen, a woman's voice. I'd have known it anywhere. And I certainly hadn't been expecting contact so quickly.

"Is that Mr. Harris? Paul Harris?"

"How are you, Florie?"

"Oh! Oh, my goodness! The way you say that. As though . . . it was only yesterday." I could hear her draw in her breath. "Oh, Paul! I think I'm going to cry."

"Save it for later. How are you, my dear?"

"How am I? Oh, I'm fine. I'm just fine."

I couldn't ask if it was safe to phone me like this. She ought to know. But then again she mightn't.

"Where are you?"

"I'm at home, Paul."

"In your old house?" I had heard she was but could scarcely credit it.

"Yes. Part of it's a children's clinic now. But I have rooms. I'm sure you'll recognise them."

"You mean . . . I can just come and see you?"

"Of course. If you want to."

"Do I want to!"

"Well then, come to-night. Would that be all right? I can't really offer you a meal. It isn't too easy. We haven't got . . . well, you'll see. You'd be best to eat at the hotel. But come right after."

"What do I do, just whistle a taxi?"

"The hotel desk will lay it on, I'm sure."

My heart was doing a bit of a thump. Florence Yin had been my first girl friend, when I was eight and she was seven. The Yin car had stopped by every morning down there in Shanghai to take us to school together. And at recess we had shared sandwiches. Mine had usually been entirely strawberry jam, our indulgent cook catering to my passion for these. Strawberry jam was Florie's passion, too, only she didn't get it from her cook. I went to terrible lengths of youthful self-sacrifice over those sandwiches.

Florie had a face like a little heart, curved down to a pointed chin, with a Japanese doll haircut to a bang just above thin, neatly curved eyebrows. And even after she had graduated M.D. from the University of California she still went around with that little girl look. We had last met in 1947, just before the heavens fell for people like the Yins. I think in a kind of way that wasn't entirely fraternal I had always kept a compartment for that old feeling. And certainly when we met, back there in '47, my heart had thumped away as it was doing now.

She had married a young Chinese doctor who had been killed on active service with Chiang's armies. Florie had a job with the Rockefeller Institute in Peking when the revolution took over, something in research, but I knew she had switched to child welfare. Doctors were needed in the New China and she had appeared to be safe enough. That was all I'd known, or almost all.

When I rang down after Florie's call the hotel desk couldn't have been more obliging. I might have been staying in the Dorchester. Certainly a car could be ordered for me. I had only to indicate the time. Eight o'clock, perhaps? I was a V.I.P.

I went down to eat at seven. As I opened my bedroom door Mr. Kishimura opened his. He was in the next room to me. He bowed. Clearly diplomatic relations had been resumed.

"Snow falls, I think," Mr. Kishimura said, showing the glittering teeth.

"Yes, I noticed that too."

I looked around for the rest of the Japanese contingent, but none of them were in evidence. A couple of Russians came out of their rooms, however, both of them glancing at the capitalists, and then turning away quickly from contagion. They were big men and stood waiting for the lift, shoulder to shoulder, just in front of us. Mr. Kishimura and I didn't contest their precedence. We got into the cage and let the Russians do the necessary with buttons and we descended slowly, like delegates to the United Nations who aren't speaking.

There was even a head waiter in the dining-room. He wasn't dressed for the part, but he had the authority, and waddled between the tables in a kind of half compromise with bourgeois practice.

"You wish to have dinner alone?" Mr. Kishimura asked.

"I'd be delighted to have your company."

"So? Excellent."

We sat down together. There was a menu in Chinese and Russian, which foxed me completely, but not Mr. Kishimura, who could, of course, read the characters. He did a bit of staring and then said, seriously:

"Soup? Yes?"

Thanks to my friend I got a very palatable meal. The cooking wasn't *cordon bleu* but we gambled on the Chinese still being able to do things with pig and were right. Everyone ate very seriously, I noticed, and without much talk. There was more than a suggestion of feeding time at an evangelical conference, the needs of the body admitted, but not something to be lingered over. You put the food away as quickly as possible and then left.

It wasn't possible to be very quick, the waiters saw to that. There was no subservience about them, they were all comrades. It seemed to me that the Russians were more irritated by this than the rest of us and I began to wonder if Mao Tse Tung had a point when he complained of his allies slumping into relaxed Western ways.

Mr. Kishimura also belonged to a race who believe that the mouth can be used for eating or speech, but not both together, however he compromised and was mildly chatty.

"Much is written in to-day's papers of your visit to China, Mr. Harris. No mention of other missions. You are of great importance, it appears."

"As you suggested?"

"So."

"It makes it a poor look-out for your Nishin engine."

He smiled politely, then popped pork in his mouth. A moment later he said:

"You sample delights of New China entertainment this evening?"

"No. I'm going out to see an old friend."

"Oh, so fortunate to have old friend in Peking. I am only lonely here."

"What about the other Japanese?"

"Not intimate," said Mr. Kishimura, dismissing them.

"Any news of Mr. Obata?"

"Please, not speak!" Then he said: "Do you not feel truly sad to spend Christmas in Peking?"

"Well, I'm not expecting any decorated trees. But I don't hang out my stocking any more. And I'll be taking a signed contract out with me. That's a nice present."

Mr. Kishimura picked up the menu and studied it.

"Pudding. Is East Russian national dish. They call . . . Harbin Pie."

I can't recommend Harbin Pie. In so far as it could be subjected to analysis it seemed to consist of a bottom layer of wheat cereal, then a shelf of candied fruits, then one of cornflakes, then tinned mandarin orange sections, the confection topped off with a sugary crust and served tepid from an hour ago's oven.

"Delicious," said Mr. Kishimura. This seemed to me to be taking goodwill for co-existence rather a long way.

I left him still at the pie and went up for an overcoat. It was just eight when I stepped out into the lobby again from the lift. The place had a curiously dead feel for a pretty full hotel at this hour. Whatever evening delights New China offered there was no anticipatory bustle of people about to set out to enjoy them. You got the impression that after that national pie nearly everyone had gone back upstairs to lie on their beds. And certainly about the only one using the chairs out here was a solitary woman, flaxen fair and knitting. She was a mature Slav, which is to say no Mata Hari, and she looked at me with a plain statement in her eyes. She didn't like being where she was. She was counting the hours until her husband finished his engineering job and took her back to Smolensk, where she expected to go on being bored, but in a different way. Meanwhile she was knitting herself another woollen comforter. It couldn't be called a sweater if it was like the green thing she was wearing. I don't think I've ever seen anyone more bourgeois-looking than that damped-down Russian wife in the lobby of a Peking hotel.

I have a private theory that the thing which will defeat Communism in the end is not the united effort of the Free World, but plain boredom. Communism which has worked through its birth pangs, and past its purges, just bores everyone to death. Once you've stopped being afraid of that midnight knock on the door a kind of terrible greyness descends. But then total security is a terrible thing. Even in the West more people die of it every year than cancer.

There was no one at the reception desk. I rang a little bell and the young man who had signed me in came out from a back room, still chewing. His smile showed part of his supper, but I was glad to get a smile in China. The car was waiting for me. Would I just go and stand in the entrance?

As I crossed the lobby I said good night to the knitting matron. She dropped a stitch, looked around her, and then smiled. China was warming up for me, or so I thought until I happened to look left. The lady warder was approaching.

Somehow I had forgotten all about Miss Mei in spite of her promises to stick close. There must have been some kind of accommodation for interpreters laid on in the hotel and Mei Lan emerged from this looking somehow different, as though she had been through a wash and brush up. Then I realised that she was wearing a new uniform and looked thinner in it, perhaps because layers had been peeled off underneath. The effect still left a lot to be desired and there was still a cap into which all her hair, if she had any, was still tucked.

"Good evening, Miss Mei."

I must have seemed too jaunty in manner to please her. She nodded. She reached the glass doors just as I did, and I realised then that the last thing I had considered was an evening with Florie supervised by my guard. But perhaps Florie wouldn't be surprised at all.

"Have you no coat, Miss Mei? It's snowing out there."

"I don't need."

We went out. I needed my coat. The wind was a sickle from the north. It was five yards to the car but I reached it breathless. There was a driver and another man. The second man was reaching back, holding open the door, and Miss Mei made me get in first. Then the door slammed. All the windows were steamed over and there was the suggestion of air used up by people suffering from digestive upsets.

I made a round peephole in my window with a clean linen handkerchief at which I caught Miss Mei looking. I had shaved earlier and used a face lotion of which I became a bit conscious then. It set me apart in my distinctive decadent odours.

The street from the hotel was wide and lit by globes on poles, which showed the snow coming down. Once or twice we crunched on it where it was piling up and there was no mass of traffic to turn it into slush.

Soon we were in lanes, the China I remembered, narrow, with sewers down the sides and people packed in the middle. Our driver hooted and once turned down his window to shout. The proletarian masses over on this side of the town still didn't seem terribly well disciplined. I could see into open shops, too, and there was a food place with a glowing brazier in the middle. What I missed most were the rickshaws. They had been part of this setting of heavy tile roofs sweeping down to lean over peeling walls, and carts and bicycles and children and dogs. Everyone was padded up for winter, but not kept in by it, and there were a lot of bulky fur hats. The car, with its fugged-up windows, seemed to cause more irritation than interest. We went slowly, honking.

"Will you be coming in with me to see my friend, Miss Mei?"

"Yes."

This was certainly going to make the reunion memorable.

"What about the car? Does it wait? Is there a time limit?"

"When you wish car comes."

She sounded slightly resentful over the red carpet laid out for me. Maybe she had put in the time reading in the papers about how important I was.

And then we stopped. The wall and the gate were on my side. I recognised them with a pang for the years which had rushed away from me. The Yins had moved to this house in the capital when the old man retired. It had once been a mandarin's town residence, a sprawling one-storey house built about courtyards and entirely enclosed by a ten-foot wall. There were blue ceramic griffins on the ridge-pole of the gate roof and I looked up somehow expecting to see these gone. But they were there. I could just make out the shape of them.

The driver leaned back and opened the door on my side. I got out first this time to stand in front of the massive, iron-studded doors I remembered. There was even the old bell-pull, and the small inset door, as well as the peep-hole with the sliding panel. The only new thing was a plaque of what looked to be white porcelain set in the wall by the gate. This was covered with characters.

I rang the bell and we heard a clanging beyond. The car didn't move and I had the feeling of eyes on me, of a kind of wary curiosity about what would happen now. The small door opened and Florie stood framed in it, an inside light shining down on her.

She was wearing a long *cheongsam* that reached to her ankles and after Malaya and Hong Kong looked dated. But it was of a lush, creamy silk brocade. She wore her black hair still in the Japanese doll cut, but the bang much shorter now, only a small fringe on her forehead. This left more of her face showing, and it wasn't a young face any more.

"Paul!"

I didn't give a damn about the watchers. I kissed her. Florie drew back under her gate and I knocked my head on the low lintel.

"You always used to," she said. "You idiot!"

Florie sounded near tears. I heard the car put in gear and Miss Mei climbed through the hatch after me. We all stood in front of the carved stone devil-screen in the white light from a naked bulb, Florie and I looking at each other. I thought again of years spent and was sure she did too.

Miss Mei began to cough. She put out a hand and pushed the hatch shut behind us, against a crowd of people who had replaced the parked car. Then the paroxysm took her and she had to give way to it. We waited, both of us trying not to look at my warder and not looking at each other either.

"This is Miss Mei," I said. "She is my interpreter."

It was a nice euphemism. But the explanation wasn't

really necessary. I could see that Florie hadn't been expecting me to turn up unaccompanied.

"Come out of the cold," she said.

We went left around the devil-screen and there was a light burning at the house which showed me that the courtyard had been halved since I'd last seen it. Once it had been a spacious and rather formal affair, with a lot of those crumbling rocks as an æsthetic end in themselves which the Chinese like so much. Now there was a raw-looking concrete wall down the middle, slicing the place in two.

As we walked up a paved path, with Miss Mei stubbornly behind us, a position she'd taken up herself, Florie told me that she had four rooms now in their old family house. The rest was the clinic, in which she was the chief doctor with two assistants. And I was aware, even before we stepped into a pleasantly warm hall, that if Florie had lost youth she had gained something else, poise and authority. Somehow this was a little surprising. I had thought of her as a kind of victim of the new order, disciplined into it, perhaps achieving a kind of compromise, but it was clear she had done more than this. It must have had something to do with her status as a doctor.

And Miss Mei was clearly sharply surprised, too. She stood in that hallway looking around her, as though she couldn't believe that there were little nests as comfortable as this tucked away into the New China.

"I've been able to keep our old drawing-room," Florie said and opened the door.

I remembered the room. It was thirty feet long, about twenty wide, with courtyards on both sides, and cross lighting in daytime. There was a fireplace in one wall and a small wood fire burned in it, as well as the central heating. Wood in China! The furnishings seemed to me as they had been, not those dreadful dragon chairs of black ebony and the inevitable cabinets which clutter the retirement of every old China hand, but deep armchairs and a couple of sofas. The rugs were thick pile Peking and the lighting was from tall lamps of blue and white porcelain with white silk shades. The room certainly suggested a cosy little hide-out of reaction. That was in Miss Mei's face as she stared at it.

"You must be frozen, both of you," Florie said. "Come over to the fire. I can only offer tea and biscuits, I'm afraid. I haven't a permanent servant, only help from the clinic staff."

The lighting in here suited Florie, erasing all lines from her face. She was comfortably the hostess in her own place, a setting in which she had every confidence. It gave her a tolerance which could be extended towards my warder who had sat down on the only straight chair.

"Cigarette, Paul? I've just remembered. I have some Shensi wine. I think you used to like it."

"Don't open a bottle for me."

"Oh, it's all right. I can always get it."

She went out. I sat down on the sofa at right angles to the fire, very conscious of Miss Mei bolt upright, an uneasy spectator at a little tableau vivant of bourgeois décadence. Florie came back with a stone bottle on a tray, together with three pale yellow cups. She was smoking now, using a holder, and poured the wine carefully. There was something almost exhibitionist about all this, as though she was laughing at me, knowing that I had come expecting to find someone cowering in a

corner of a new world.   Instead she had been able to
cope all right.

In fact, Florie had always been able to cope, an inde-
pendent little girl who liked to organise things for herself,
only rarely taking advantage of the fact that she was
born a Yin.

She offered wine to the girl in the straight chair.

"No."

I took my cup and held it.

"Why don't you take off your hat, Miss Mei?" Florie
suggested.

There was a moment's total silence during which this
suggestion was bitterly resented.

"No!"

Florie smiled and sat down, crossing her slim legs under
the *cheongsam*.   She was wearing silk stockings and her
slippers had spike heels.   They must have come from
Hong Kong and certainly weren't pre-revolution.

"Why didn't you write me, Paul?   I just couldn't
believe it when I saw in to-day's paper that you were
here."

It wasn't possible to say that I hadn't written to her
because I was frightened to, that I thought letters from
people outside could sometimes lead the recipients on to
a death sentence.   So I asked her about her father.
Florie became almost formal, with heavy overtones of
the filial piety which is supposed to be so much out of
favour.

"I'm glad to say that he died in this house, as he
would have wished.   As you know, Papa was most
devoted to Peking.   It was his hope to spend his last
days here.   And so it came about."

Almost as though little things like revolutions were

something you could manage to keep beyond a high wall if you were a Yin. Somehow Florie had worked it, and all on her own, against a new order that was alien and bitterly hostile to the easy patterns of her own youth. I thought of richer peasants in country villages forced to confess their capitalist sins and then given public executions. The old families, the ones with power, should have been prime targets. But had this always happened? After all there was a daughter of the Soongs in Peking as well as the one who was Chiang's wife on Formosa.

A telephone rang in the hall. Florie excused herself but a moment later she was back.

"It's for you, Miss Mei."

Miss Mei didn't like that at all. But Florie did. She closed the door behind the girl, carefully, and then held out her hands to me.

"Paul! Oh, Paul, dear!"

CHAPTER IV

THERE WAS THAT old thumping in my heart again. We met half-way across the room, and when we had kissed she put her head on my shoulder. But all I could think about was Robert. I was sure she didn't know.

"Oh, Paul . . ."

"We won't have much time. Florie . . . do you know about your brother?"

"What?"

She drew back from me, staring.

"Robert's dead."

She didn't say anything, she just shook her head, denying it.

"I'm sorry. I had to tell you when I got the chance. I didn't think you would have heard. Canton's a long way off. And the thing was kept quiet."

"Canton? Paul, what are you talking about? Robert could never have been in Canton! He could never come back to China!"

"He came to China all the time. On junks. Up river from Macao and Hong Kong."

"But . . . why? Paul, what is this?"

"He was helping people out, that's all. People who couldn't just walk over the border into the Kowloon territories. People on the run, Florie. A lot of them your kind."

"My kind?"

She was believing me now. Her eyes had the brightness of tears held. She was fighting shock.

"What do you mean by my kind?" she asked, not really wanting an answer. "I don't understand what that means."

"People like the Yins, who had position once. And money. Robert knew he'd be caught sooner or later. He told me that."

"How do you know all this?"

"He was a business associate in a sort of way. I was agent for his firm in Singapore. He had built up his business. He had the Yin flair, starting almost from scratch in Hong Kong too. Robert and I got to know each other pretty well."

"I feel sick," Florie said then.

"I didn't know how I was going to tell you. And, of course, no one could write. I wasn't even sure I'd find you here . . . in your old home."

"What do you mean?"

Her head came up. She took a slow deep breath.

"Robert was your brother. It mightn't have been healthy for you."

"I heard nothing. Did you say that Robert was working against Red China? Is that what you meant?"

"He was helping people escape. Who were down to be liquidated, or had reason to think they might be soon. Yes, I guess he was working against the Reds all right. Full steam. He had a kind of network in the south. But of course he couldn't do anything up this way. Too far off. And even if he had been able to he'd have been afraid of repercussions on you. That was in his mind a lot, I know."

"Was it?" she asked, with sudden control. "He never wrote."

"But you must see why. You were here, part of Red

China. It was better that the family seem to have no connection with you. Until they got you out."

"They shot him in Canton," she said as though she hadn't been listening to me. "How long ago?"

"Two months."

"That girl will be back in a minute. Paul, do I look all right? Do I look as if I . . ."

"No."

"I so much . . . want to cry."

"Please don't, Florie."

"I know. I mustn't. What's happened to Robert's wife?"

"She's safe in Hong Kong, with the children. They so much want you to come to them."

"No! Don't talk about that to-night. Don't talk about my coming away. Talk about something else, Paul, anything so that we can be . . ."

"Yes."

I began to talk about my engine. It seemed the only topic handy. And how well it would do on the Chinese rivers. Florie sat down and folded her hands in her lap and pretended to listen to me. She kept her head up and a slight smile on her lips that could have been painted there. We were like that when Mei Lan came back, my voice producing a kind of sales patter packaged for the drawing-room.

My interpreter sat down again on her upright chair, and whatever the reason for the call to her here she remained buttoned away behind that flat calm. Florie's house had surprised her briefly, but she had recovered from that quickly, climbing back into her aggressive neutrality. She made talk about as easy as it would have been in front of the warders in a death cell.

But Florie was fighting back. She was even able to rescue me from my engine, telling me about her work. And after a little a note of real interest crept into what she said. She kept moving her long, beautiful and well-cared-for hands and I saw Mei Lan staring at those hands.

This house was mostly clinic, which I knew. It was a sort of combined crèche and medical centre, where mothers could leave ailing children for attention and treatment during the day, though they were all taken away again at night. It struck me as a curious arrangement that sick kids should be carted in and then out again. But the sick in China have always had a remarkable mobility, patients walking about who with us would be on their death-beds. I could remember seeing a well-dressed middle-aged man at the peak of a virulent attack of smallpox taking a caged bird out for its daily airing.

The car arrived about eleven. Just before that I had noticed how pale Florie had gone and suggested the move. She didn't protest, and Mei Lan went out to phone, this time with the door open behind her.

There wasn't much I could say to Florie. I was terribly conscious of her loneliness and isolation in it. She had told me that no one spent the night behind the walls of her little compound. She was the caretaker, she said, and laughed. And it was a little like that, too, the caretaker in a house in which she had lived another life and known another world. The drawing-room was still the same, a kind of museum setting for the echoes of old laughter.

Florie was coming out of China! I knew I could work it. There were Robert's contacts. It would take time, but it only needed the initiative from her, the decision. Once she had taken that she could take her own first steps towards freedom. There would be a point at which she would be met. I could tell her about that. And I was going to.

I knew the decision wouldn't be entirely easy. It was perfectly clear from what she said that she had work here, and work she believed in. It might seem a kind of running away to desert that work. But Florie didn't belong in the New China at all, she wasn't made for its patterns and I was certain hadn't really adjusted to them. She had accepted, that was all, at first because the acceptance was necessary while her father lived, then it had become a kind of routine. There was plenty of work.

Robert had said that Florie wouldn't budge from Peking while her father lived. The old man was settled in China, whatever changes might come to it, and his daughter had let him live out his days there, building about him a kind of screen, doing her duty in the old way. Well, the duty had been fulfilled.

Florie went out with us to the car, and in the hall she picked up a fur coat from a chair. Somehow that coat put her a chasm away from Mei Lan. We stepped out into a surprise of moonlight glittering on an inch of snow, the courtyard a surgical white, our steps on it a violation. The air was frigid, but with a tonic crispness. There can be nothing fresher than an old city suddenly rendered sterile by snow at night, squalor wiped away. And when we went through the gate hatch there was only the single track of car tyres down the lane, not a sign of people now, as though they had been wiped away by a curfew.

This was the old Peking and the new things didn't matter for the moment. I was sharply conscious of being in one of the places that had my heart, and just then change wasn't important. There was no evidence of it here, just the curving roofs, the closed gates and silence. I was in a walled city which is one of the oldest on earth and which has seen new violence often, other upheavals quite as devastating as the Communist one.

The Manchus had come here, ruthless invaders with new patterns that must have seemed to sweep away all the old certainties of life, but something of the old had remained, a small leaven. I wondered in an odd way whether Florie Yin was a kind of leaven remaining from a conquered living, unconsciously so, perhaps. She certainly looked no part of the new order standing there with that fur coat pulled about her.

She didn't seem to notice the two men in the car at all. She lifted her face to be kissed.

"Good night, Paul dear. See you very soon."

When she shut the gate she'd be alone, with grief, and maybe a little fear too. Fear must always be around people like Florie adapting to strangeness.

::   ::

Mei Lan came into the hotel lobby with me. She was frozen from the unheated car and her red little paws stuck out from the sleeves of her tunic, only just showing, as though she would like to pull them right out of sight. Inside the doors she began to cough, fighting it, but having to fold herself over in the spasm. She waved one hand at me, as though sending me off to my room, but I waited.

"Are you living in the hotel?" I asked when she had straightened up.

She looked at the empty chairs, then towards the desk, as though considering whether an answer was dangerous. It might, of course, violate top secret priorities. She didn't have a private life that I was to know anything about. I was quite certain she was hungry and sure that whatever supper she had been given hadn't come near mine for solidity.

"Yes, I stay here."

"I want something to eat," I said. "Do you think we can lay it on?"

"In your room."

"No, down here. And with you."

"I am not hotel guest."

"But you are my interpreter. And I'm sure that your service expects you to be gracious to important foreigners."

Something flashed in those green eyes.

"Supposing we sit over here."

There wasn't a soul in the lobby, but a stranger behind the desk was watching. We went towards him to a table beside an ornamental pot garden. I waited until Mei Lan, with great reluctance, had sat down and then walked over to the desk.

"I'd like some meat sandwiches and cocoa. For two. Room 157."

"Meat?" He seemed astonished. "Not meal hour."

"There's a notice in my bedroom about room service. I just want it down here. See what you can do, will you?"

He didn't want to do anything and certainly didn't commit himself. He disappeared, probably for consultations. I sat down and Mei Lan shook her head at my offer of a cigarette.

"You don't smoke at all?"

"No."

"But you'll enjoy some cocoa. Made with milk, I hope. How's the milk position in China these days? Plenty of cows?"

"Plenty!"

"There used not to be. And they used to add rice water to the bottles."

"Old China perhaps."

"Yes. Bad old days. Half the people hungry all the time. Not like that now, is it?"

Mei Lan didn't say anything. She wasn't a girl it was easy to stir into conversation. But she was beginning to thaw out and that was one of the things I wanted. I didn't put it past the designers of this hotel to omit, for economic and disciplinary reasons, any heating from the quarters assigned to the guards. She could so easily be going to a cold bed soon. There wasn't a single reason why I should care about that but somehow I did. Maybe it was those little red paws.

Our sandwiches and cocoa arrived. The comrade waiter who brought them looked as though he was going to write personally to the great Leader about treating foreigners too well. And since I wasn't allowed to tip him all I could do was smile. This wasn't returned. He shot us both dark looks, it seemed to me the darker to Mei Lan.

The cocoa was made with powdered milk and the filling of the sandwiches was thin slivers of Yangtze mud ox, but still protein. I held out the plate to Mei Lan. She would have given a great deal then to say no in her usual manner, but just couldn't. The paw came out from its cave. She chewed for a while like someone desperate to show that what was in her mouth didn't mean anything. Then she gave up and had a second. Both her hands closed about the mug, clutching its warmth. When the mugs and plate were empty I wished her a good night and said I looked forward to seeing her in the morning. She left me with a quick look from those green eyes.

In the slow-moving lift I stood waiting for my floor with a kind of deep thankfulness in my heart that I hadn't been privileged to be born a Chinese, and particularly into this time of the Great Stride Forward. It was hideous to see a human being reduced to a frightened shell of obedience. And I was sure Mei Lan was frightened. I was most curious to know why in this assignment to watch me.

The passage along to my room was dead still, though I did hear snores and fitted my key very quietly into the lock with the slight feeling of being one of the night hawks of Peking, back from what was probably the pretty terrible dissipation of not using allotted rest time for rest. It was your duty to do that, so you could jump up at a loud bell and crash on with your task for China, to the sound of loudspeaker patriotism.

I switched on the light and at once saw something. It made me shut the door and push myself back against it. And I sucked in a long breath.

There was a man lying on the floor just beyond the end of my bed, crumpled legs, a bit of a tunic, and one hand. I couldn't see his head but I did see that hand. And there were ginger hairs on it.

::   ::

Slowly I pushed myself up from my knees by Tiny McVey's body. His neck was broken. There were other marks on him, too, a great weal down the side of his head. But no blood. The bleeding might be internal. He had taken some rough stuff before he died, and his eyes were almost strained out of their sockets. Some deaths are uglier than others. This was very ugly indeed. He wasn't quite cold.

There wasn't a sound anywhere. I was conscious of the mike, a kind of wary ticking in my brain. I got up, a bit late, and went and looked in the bathroom. It was empty. I was locked in here with a corpse.

I didn't feel sick, just miserable. I had meant to help this man if I could. And now I was mocked by that tiny good intention, perhaps realising that in the end I couldn't have achieved much. Back in Singapore, having made the gesture, I might have reached the point soon enough when I would have stopped trying. I wondered how long Tiny would have gone on clutching at that little hope derived from one contact with me. Not too long after what had happened to him in China, not too long at all.

But I was thinking of Tiny then, for a moment, before the ticking in my head brought attention back to me. I'd made a little room for the dead man even if fear pushed that out soon enough.

It was real fear when it came, a pulsing surge of it, driven on by the sure feeling I had then that he hadn't died here in my room. Tiny had died from violence, but all around his crumpled body was an impeccable neatness, a hotel room ready for the night use of a transient. The bed was turned down. I could see the switch of the electric blanket which was so thoughtfully provided for the thin-blooded in this icy land. On the dressing-table sat my brushes and shaving things, everything tidy. Quite near his head was a chair which seemed to me in exactly the position it had been when I left. It was a light chair. A touch would have moved it. You can't break a man's neck and leave the setting for murder so strictly neutral.

He had been brought here!

I was glad the whirring from the bathroom light switched on covered the sound of my breathing. There had been no other sound. Wherever they listened they must be sitting tense, leaning forward, waiting for noise, made by a man finding this when he came back after an evening out. They weren't getting any noise. Damn them all!

Tiny McVey had been brought here, planted in my room. And they hadn't even bothered with the trimmings, pulling out a few drawers, kicking things about. Probably there hadn't been time for that, or they hadn't wanted to risk noise in these thin-walled cubicles for the sleeping. They mightn't need more for their purposes than just this body found in my room.

They were on to me all right, a few moves ahead in a little game I had come to China thinking I could start when I had tested out the ground. They had a game of their own. Maybe Kishimura, sleeping next door, knew more about it than I did. Or guessed. I was very conscious of Kishimura in those seconds, and of his warning. Maybe he hadn't been thinking of engines.

China was the spider's parlour for me, and I had walked right into it. It seemed that the spider was hungry and had decided to pounce at once. And the situation wasn't pretty at all. A foreigner here in Peking with a murder charge pinned on him, even badly pinned on, could squeal maybe, but what sort of help would be forthcoming? I remembered the kind of help that had been available for some western business men caught in Shanghai by the Red take-over. This had rated as nil. They had been prisoners without any real charges against them and, in spite of questions in a very distant British

Parliament, no one had sprung them. They had stayed in China for years, most of them. Some had died there.

Who was going to spring me from a murder rap, even a pretty gauchely organised murder rap? I got the answer to that with remarkable speed, and it was simple . . . no one. McVey was a Chinese subject officially and his alleged killer would be tried in a Chinese People's Court. And almost certainly, long before that Court convened, the prisoner would be brainwashed into a kind of zombie state.

I was certain, in my mind, that McVey hadn't been party to anything, that he was only the small-scale man that he had seemed. But he had been seen coming to me. And that had been used, probably after a quick top-level conference while I was sitting with Florie. Maybe they hadn't meant to rope me in quite so quickly, but the opportunity had seemed too golden to miss.

My first night in China. That warm little room with its electric blanket and illusion of privacy seemed very cosy then. It also seemed extremely impermanent in my schedule. It didn't look as though I was going to get a chance to test out that mattress.

Down somewhere the listeners were waiting. They wouldn't wait for long. They'd come up. I had to be discovered with the corpse and these people worked fast, they liked to get the job tied up. I wouldn't have many more minutes alone.

I remembered something then, the set of three lifts up from the lobby. You operated them yourself and they came on a call button from the floor to which they had last travelled. At this time of night it seemed more than possible that the cage I had used was still sitting there on this landing, empty and waiting, with the light on.

The corridors outside were empty too. I looked down at McVey. He was a small man. I bent down and pulled him up by the arms, hauling the body up on to my shoulders. It wasn't pleasant to feel that lolling head against my neck for a moment, and then jerking sideways. But I got him in an easy hold, easy to carry.

If I was nabbed in the corridors it couldn't be worse than being nabbed in my room. Only different. It would be nicer evidence for them, of course, but I didn't really feel that niceties of evidence would bother them much. You don't really need to be fussy about evidence in a People's Court.

I got the bedroom door opened and looked out. About fifty yards down a carpeted passage a red bulb glowed over the cage I had used. It was waiting.

Except for shut-away snoring the hotel was held in a deep night silence. I'd noticed before the emptiness of these corridors. In old China there would probably have been an attendant in a cubby-hole somewhere, waiting to serve insomniacs. But the comrades didn't run to this kind of service. I walked to the lifts in the soft glow of economy bulbs set at not too frequent intervals in the ceiling.

There were double doors on the lift. It wasn't easy getting them open with the one hand I could spare from hanging on to the body. But I pushed my foot into a crack and forced them back, the outer lot first, then the inner, both with hydraulic pressure on them. The doors shut themselves with a small hissing, and I was in the bright box in which they apparently wasted electricity all night.

It was only when I put the body down that I realised how much I was sweating. The palms of my hands were slippery. And I was shaking, too, in the way which indicates that you haven't got your nerves completely under control. I knew I hadn't. It took me a second or two before I could press a button.

The lift began to move, with a small rumbling, and very slowly sank to the next floor, where it came to what seemed to me a noisily creaking stop. Without looking back, I pulled the doors open and stepped out into a corridor exactly like the one above, and quite empty. Behind me the doors sealed McVey away again.

The stairs were just beyond the lift shafts and they had a well, right down to the ground floor. I had to look over, perhaps to confirm that feeling of emptiness around me, of no one about. The feeling didn't get confirmed.

Two flights down, but climbing, were three Chinese, in a row, each with hands out on the metal polished railing. They made no sound, and the leading man was People's Guardian Yang Yi.

I ran then, up the flight to my level, not making any sound on the thick carpeting, but when I looked over again the three weren't plodding on after me. They seemed to be in a huddle down there, waiting for something, leaning back against the railing. Waiting for orders, maybe. It could be from the listening post.

It was high time they heard something from my room, I knew that. It couldn't be more than ten minutes since I had walked in on that body, but ten minutes of total silence on an issue like this would make the boys in the hotel listening service decidedly restive. They had to be fed the sound of the human voice.

What I really wanted to do then was get that bottle of whisky in my hand, but I went past my door, to the one beyond, pleased to see a light from a crack beneath it, but no light wouldn't have stopped me. I knocked, waiting, thinking about the judo hold that could break a man's neck with one jerk. There was a slight cracking sound and you had done the job. Of course a lot of Chinese might have studied judo during their neighbour's occupation of the country.

If there is one thing which makes the Japanese look a race apart, which they are, it is formal native dress. Mr. Kishimura opened the door wearing heavy grey-black silk robes, with the *hakama* over-garment. Even his spectacles didn't hint at the go-getter shoe executive any more. I might have interrupted him at a private and curtailed tea ceremony for the refreshment of spirit in times of uncertainty. He looked at me for a moment, from behind glinting glass, as though he had to come back from somewhere, doing a kind of conscious mental focusing on this time and place.

"Ah! Mr. Harris. Pleasant evening now over?"

"Not quite." My voice sounded oddly pitched to my ears. "I was hoping you'd round it off with me. In my room. With a bottle of whisky. I think you like whisky, don't you, Mr. Kishimura? I can recommend this bottle. I import it myself direct from Scotland. From a distillery I know there. Pure malt. I'd like you to sample it."

Perhaps he thought I had already been at that bottle. I could see him hesitating for a moment, wanting to return to what he had been doing, which on second thoughts might well be the composition of the day's little poem. But in a sudden charity he came with me.

It was only when we were in my room that I realised that my face was damp with sweat still, and he must have seen the glistening.

"Please sit down," I said loudly, for the mike. "You take the chair. I'll use the bed."

Mr. Kishimura sat down, waiting for me to come out of the bathroom with the toothglass and a carafe of water.

"Snowing to-night, I think," Mr. Kishimura said.

It was like dialogue out of a play written by the producer of a local amateur dramatic society for a one and only performance.

"Yes, snowing," I said, doing things with the bottle. I also wanted to laugh, with the feeling that it was in the script in capital letters.

"You have agreeable meeting with friend, Mr. Harris?"

"Absolutely delightful," said my loud, echoing voice.

"Lady?"

"Yes. A school friend. We talked about old days."

"You are in company of warder? Miss Mei?"

"She came along, yes. After a time you don't notice."

Mr. Kishimura had his whisky with a little water. I was wondering how long it would be before there was a knock at the door. Somewhere curiosity would be bubbling about whether all this was going on with a corpse under the bed. They would certainly send a man to find out. I didn't see them waiting, either, until Mr. Kishimura had retired. I hoped they wouldn't wait. I had an intense desire not to be alone during the next phase.

My guest smiled at me.

"You are surprised that I wearing Japanese dress on business travels?"

"No, Mr. Kishimura. I know that all you people like to relax wearing it."

"Oh, truly. We put on clotheses of native place and return in spirit to homeland. China is strange to feeling. Not warm to heart, you think?"

"Not to my heart, no. Not at all warm. You know where I'd like to be right now?"

"Singapore?"

"Actually not. Nearer. Just a little hotel I know at Chuzenji up above Nikko. Room service is splendid."

He looked at me solemnly for a moment, then his laughter was a little explosion. He rocked gently over his whisky.

"Oh! You explore Japan greatly, Mr. Harris. When we return in safety you will please come to party?"

"With the greatest of pleasure. . . ."

There was the knock on the door. I don't think what I was feeling then showed. I put down my glass carefully and laid a cigarette in the ash-tray. Then I opened to People's Guardian Yang Yi.

CHAPTER V

YANG BELONGED to a generation which had spent a lot
of time under the old China. He had probably known
home and mummy and daddy. But he didn't look like
it. He looked as though he had come out of a bottle,
been weaned in a state crèche and caught his smallpox
playing anti-imperialist games with a lot of other rowdies.

He was angry now, and though there was a need to
put a veneer on that anger he wasn't in training for this
and politeness was so thin a film it didn't cover anything.
He came into the bedroom without an invitation and
moved down it to stand by the bed. Three people in
there made the place crowded, and Yang's eyes were
doing a quick check around for the remains of a fourth.
I knew then that no one had pushed the button for that
third lift. Yang was in the midst of an unsolved mystery
which made him more than peevish.

"Mr. Kishimura and I are just having a nightcap," I
said. "Would you like a whisky?"

"No."

Mr. Kishimura got a look which would have frozen
anyone but another Oriental. As it was that look just
bounced off a spiritually repatriated Japanese who was
armoured against it behind a smile of infinite gentleness.

"Your passport," Yang said to me.

"I beg your pardon?"

"It is needed. For checking."

I may be in some ways a dubious British subject but
I cling to that passport. On the ship it had been checked

and returned to me. It was sitting in my inside breast pocket now, very snug, and very close to me. When you hand over your passport you hand over your identity, certainly in China.

"You want to see it?"

I bent over and pulled out a suitcase from under the bed. There was room down there under the cover for two airplane cases but not for two cases and a body.

"Where did I put it?"

I flipped through the case, then shoved it back, right back. The same with the second case. Yang was attentive. I wondered what excuse he would make to look in the bathroom.

"Oh, it's in my pocket all the time."

"I take," Yang said.

We looked at each other.

"I'm afraid not, Mr. Yang. You see, this is on loan to me from the British Government. I'm not supposed to hand it over."

"For inspection!" Yang said loudly.

"Are you inspecting Mr. Kishimura's, too?"

"No. Not necessary."

"In that case I'm afraid you can't have mine." I put it back in my pocket. "To-morrow I'm willing to have anyone who wishes look at it again. In my presence. But I'm not surrendering it. Would you perhaps like to get in touch with the British Embassy about this?"

I was living in the wrong age for mention of the Embassy to strike any terror in a Chinese heart, but Yang had no instructions beyond this point. He had been sent up to find out what had happened to a corpse. So far there wasn't the hint of an answer to that. There was also a witness to everything done here. Yang was greatly troubled. Indeed there was now a moisture on his face just like there had been on mine a while back. Someone big was waiting for Yang's return, waiting impatiently, too, and not much enjoying the little audio-drama we were sending down the wires.

When you have your man rattled it's a good time to move on to the offensive. Yang's wasn't an easy face to smile at but I did it.

"While you're here I wonder if you would report something for me? The hot-water tap in the hand-basin is dripping slightly. It seems a waste. You might get someone to fix it in the morning."

He didn't like being offered the freedom to inspect the place from me, but when I pushed back the door he went in for long enough to see the tap, which did drip, and the tub, which was empty. He came out again and gave me the kind of look designed to produce insomnia in a victim. Then, with a terrible reluctance, said:

"I report."

When I had shut the door I turned and found Mr. Kishimura standing at the window.

"Snow now cease, Mr. Harris. Perhaps to-morrow sun shining brightly."

I was sharply conscious of my Japanese friend playing his part in the ham drama we had cooked up, and not innocently, either. He might have been a frustrated actor.

"Scottish whisky very encouraging to strength of feeling, I think. Most pleasant flavour in palate."

"I'll send you a bottle when I get home."

"Oh, please. Most kind. And now, good night. Many thanks for nightcaps."

Mr. Kishimura opened the bedroom door, closing it

again somewhat noisily, but without going out. Then he nipped into the bathroom, where I joined him. The fan hissed above us.

"Where did you find your mike?"

"Same place as yours, Mr. Harris, I think."

"It gives one an exposed feeling, doesn't it?"

"Truly."

"Later I must remember to snore. Thank you for coming. I like having a witness in China."

"I come most willingly. There is someone in your room earlier. Walls very thin."

"A routine search, I expect. After all, we must expect that kind of thing. It will probably happen to you to-morrow when you're out selling shoes."

"Maybe. But attention on you very close."

"It's not the first time in my life."

"Mr. Harris, I think perhaps you brave man."

"You're wrong. It all comes out of that bottle in there. I started on the stuff at sixteen. When I can't get it I'm scared."

"So. You are not scared now?"

I remembered the sweat glistening on my face as I stood by his door.

"Just a bit jumpy, Mr. Kishimura. After all, it's my first night in China."

::   ::

A little later I put a chair under the door handle and went to bed. But I didn't snore for the mike, I lay and smoked in the darkness. It seemed likely that this night was going to pass with no new developments of high drama. Somewhere they were in conference again, on precipitate action which had misfired, deciding not to be so slap-happy next time, preparing the ground carefully, not just seizing a convenient little opportunity which had cropped up. But I was still down to be alone in the centre of a stage when they were ready to ring up the curtain again. It was me they wanted, not the Dolphin engine.

I could reach out now to the phone and demand to get the British Embassy and I was certain I'd get through. There was a road out of China that way if I took it to-night, quickly. I had only to ask for official protection and to move out of this hotel over to the new legation quarter outside the city walls. I could conduct my business, possibly, from the Chancery and then clear out. Or better still, from the official point of view of First Secretaries, get out without conducting my business. This would deal with Yang's bosses before they had time to get their second wind. Right now they were totally surprised at their failure, not conditioned to having failures. Briefly I held the cards while they took time out for a more subtle approach.

It would probably be a very subtle approach, and take a bit of doing. After all, they had been challenged to-night. They must see that I was now fully aware of the game being played against me, and that from this moment on I would be walking around in their China seeing only my enemies. In this way it could be said that I held quite a good hand, for the present, and briefly.

It wasn't likely I'd be holding that good hand for long. I couldn't assess the time factor at all. The sensible thing would be to run whimpering for protection to my own people. They would know about McVey in Peking and believe me. I could choose right now to become a fugitive from the China in which I had just arrived, and get shipped out of it again under a kind of sealed bond. The Embassy could do that for me. And I could just see their faces when I asked them to.

I remember a consul saying to me once: "Three-quarters of the pain in my life is getting nitwits out of trouble."

I'd have earned the nitwit rating all right.

The phone went off almost in my ear, and the sound of it scraped along my nerves. I had begun to feel shut away for the rest of the night in a small space of safeness.

"Humbold here," the faintly cockney voice said. "Remember me?"

I took a deep breath.

"It's nearly half past twelve. Is this the kind of hour you choose for your victims?"

"A journalist never sleeps. Especially when he thinks his victim isn't either. You don't sound like a man who has just been woken up."

"If you're one of the hazards of trade with China it's no wonder trade isn't flourishing."

Humbold laughed.

"How about me coming up?"

"Just like that? At half past twelve at night?"

"Sure. Another British face in a strange land. Do you good. Got any whisky?"

"I have."

"I thought you would. That'll be worth it, even if I don't get a story for the British masses."

"The British masses don't read your weekly."

"Don't be too sure. The ones that matter do. I'm in the hotel. Shall I just walk up?"

"Yes."

I had to get up to take away the chair and unlock the door. Then I got back into bed and put on the reading light. I couldn't see him when he came in, but he soon moved to a position where I could.

I don't know what I'd been expecting, perhaps a little ferret of a man. Humbold was no ferret, well over six feet and in spite of an overcoat with a fur collar looked not unlike a British police detective turning up after a cat burglary. He took off a battered and very un-Oriental-looking black felt and dropped it on my quilt.

"You look cosy," he said, sitting down. "Got the electric blanket on, too?"

His hair was going and when it did he would have one of those heads which is nearly all vast face, with the wrinkles of his forehead continuing on up into his scalp. Even now he looked like a sardonically mournful bloodhound and he stared at me with frank curiosity from eyes that might have once been a bright blue but had gone dingy.

"Nice of you to see me," he added. "What made you change your mind?"

"Insomnia."

He grinned.

"You keep the bottle locked up, Mr. Harris, or can I reach for it?"

"In the case nearest you . . . under the bed."

"The hospitality of you capitalists is one of the nice things about you. And a used glass, too. Still, I'm not fussy."

He poured himself a triple and didn't bother about any water from the bathroom. He held up the glass and sniffed, which somehow pleased me. It showed he hadn't wasted all of his life.

"You live in the hotel?" I asked.

"Far from it. My finances don't rate the show-place. No, I live with my wife."

"How does she like China?"

"She took it with her mamma's milk. She's Chinese."

"So you're really out here?"

He looked at me.

"Now what do you mean by that? If you want to know whether I'm committed to China the answer is yes, friend."

"And you just happened to drop by?"

"No, I was called in on a story." His eyes stayed on my face. "About an ex-fellow-countryman of ours. Died to-night."

"What do you mean ex?"

"Oh, he saw the light during the Korean war. Stayed with us, you might say. Worked in the hotel here. Fell down the lift shaft. Broke his neck."

"Poor devil," I said in what I thought was the right tone.

"Yes. And not much of a story either. A lift shaft. Still, I'll send it in. One of our brothers working for the New China, and all that. A fraternal obituary."

Humbold didn't seem to be worrying about all this going down on tape somewhere.

"What did this man work as? A waiter?"

"Kind of."

"I don't think I've seen him about."

Humbold raised his glass and drank. His eyes still remained stuck on me.

"Well, you haven't been here long, have you?"

He lit himself a cigarette.

"Now about this engine, Mr. Harris. Dolphin. Made

by you and your partners in Johore Bahru under licence from Sweden."

"You're well informed."

He brought out a little notebook and looked at it.

"You've sold about six and a half thousand Dolphin already and now you want to get rid of another thousand up here."

"You can write your story without me."

"I want more than the factual angle. I'm interested in your motives, Mr. Harris. Why China for a market? Doesn't . . . ah . . . principle come into this?"

"What do you mean by that?"

"I mean selling to the Reds."

"Mr. Humbold, my company has a good product which has saturated the markets immediately around us. But if you know anything about business you'll know that even the best product has a limited life. Someone comes along with a newer model. Unfortunately my partners and I are not a production empire, or anything like it. We can't evolve improvements of a fundamental kind ourselves. When we want a new machine we'll have to buy another licence. And in order to be able to do that I must sell as many of the present model as quickly as I can."

"Lucid and to the point," Humbold said.

"I try to be. Is anything given to you likely to be used by Chinese papers?"

"On occasion."

"Well, I've made a clear statement of my purpose in being in China which I'd very much like to have given the maximum publicity."

"For this whisky I might just try to do that. You see,

you ought to take the Press into your confidence right away, Mr. Harris. It's good policy."

"Sometimes."

"All the time. Is it true that you were responsible for the death of General Sorumbai in Sumatra?"

I felt then as though I'd had a moderate electric shock.

"What has Sumatra to do with my present mission?"

"Oh, just background. Shall I say you declined to answer?"

"No, I'll answer. I was not in any way responsible for the death of General Sorumbai. Though I was in Sumatra when it happened."

"As a saboteur?"

"I have never been a saboteur anywhere."

"You left that to the people you hired?"

"None of my employees have ever engaged in sabotage."

"Isn't gun-running sabotage, Mr. Harris?"

"Not when there's a revolution going on."

"And when you are supporting reaction in that so-called revolution?"

"What I supported was not reaction."

"You would call them freedom fighters, I suppose?"

I was angry enough to forget about the mike.

"Yes, I would. Just that!"

Humbold smiled.

"Thank you, Mr. Harris. You've been most co-operative."

I knew then what the bastard meant. He'd got his story all right, and down on tape, where he wanted it. He sipped my whisky, looking at me. He wasn't smiling, but I had the feeling he wanted to. And I was certain that Humbold had been summoned to this hotel as soon as someone had pressed the button which had brought McVey's body down to them. This man was committed to China, he had said so.

"Are you a Stalinist?" I asked.

I could see the total surprise in his eyes. He had thought me too winded to rally. He moved a little in his chair, to put the empty glass on the table.

"That's an odd question, Mr. Harris?"

"Not odd at all these days. Fundamental on your side of the fence, isn't it? I mean which camp you play for?"

He didn't like that one little bit, being very conscious of the mike. And I was suddenly almost enjoying myself.

"A little difficult to be committed to China and not be a Stalinist, isn't it? I wonder what they think about that in the *Workers' Weekly*'s offices in London? I have a feeling that the British party roots for Moscow. Is that right?"

"I haven't been home for a long time."

"But the situation must complicate your dispatches? Having to keep a weather-eye open for the London reaction, I mean. It puts you rather up on that fence, doesn't it?"

"I don't sit on any fences!"

"Which means that you think they shouldn't have moved the old boy's body from Red Square? Perhaps they ought to have sent it out here, to be placed in the Temple of Heaven?"

He hated me then. I didn't mind that. Before I'd had a kind of contempt from him, and that mild. The more aggressive feeling gave me an odd confidence. I wanted to be dangerous, to Humbold and the boys behind him. I wanted them to feel that they had to take a deep breath and think about their planning for my future, not just go jumping into things with casually planted corpses. I wasn't going to serve their purposes except as the star turn in a widely tub-thumped trial which would demonstrate that China has long arms to reach out for the people who stick pins in her old hide.

Humbold had goaded me. It was my turn.

"You could be in a bit of a spot," I said, "if your London office decided they wanted a fresh slant on China, and a new man here. Someone who makes his obeisance to Moscow."

He stood. He plucked his hat from my quilt.

"Good night, Mr. Harris. Sleep well in your cosy little bed!"

I got up and locked the door and put the chair under the handle again.

CHAPTER VI

THE NEXT MORNING I continued to rate V.I.P. treatment. After breakfast, which was brought up by room service without a squeak of protest . . . the comrade waiter almost solicitous . . . I was driven to the Ministry of Foreign Trade in a larger and newer car than I'd had for the Florie visit. It was a black Russian commissar's delight with slightly scuffed upholstery, and it had two men up in front, sealed away beyond what seemed to me a shockingly unsocialist plate-glass window. I was alone in the back, Miss Mei not along, which was interesting. There had been no sign of her in the lobby at all at the moment of my departure, as though I had been passed on to other hands. The cushions were soft enough and I relaxed against them, almost feeling that I ought from time to time to wave graciously towards the available segment of China's toiling masses out there beyond my heated cell. It was a bitterly icy morning, in spite of sun, and most of the populace didn't seem to be striding about gulping in the health-giving air in the way I'd seen them doing in propaganda films. They just looked damn cold.

We were in a part of the city behind the walls which has been largely reconstructed by the new régime, the old torn away and the new uniquely hideous slab blocks of building, some of them with some pretty nasty trimmings of Marxist *chinoiserie*. There were banners on long poles, tattered at the bottom, but these added no real gaiety. Everything in this area had the aseptic sombreness of bureaucracy triumphant, a kind of imposed architectural hygiene. I was sure then that even if the

new conquerors didn't last they had destroyed Peking
for ever. And this was very sad because in its curious,
stinking way the world's oldest city had once been its
most exciting . . . yes, and beautiful. Much more so than
Paris. Though I've never heard even a drunk French
chinophile admit this.

The last bit of our run in to the doors of the Ministry
was gravelled and the tyres crunched. We also slewed
about a bit on those granite chips which could have
been laid as an obstacle to a quick getaway. One of the
boys up front got out and came round to open a door for
me, and as though on signal someone else came out
from the building and stood. I handed over a slip of
paper I had been given at the hotel desk and went into
a lobby which was warm and where I was met again,
this time by an English speaker.

She was a girl, but very unlike Mei Lan. A Hong
Kong import, this one, I was sure of that, who had
brought her clothes with her and had the nerve to wear
them. After my less than twenty-four hours in China she
seemed to me madly well dressed for her *cheongsam*,
though of winter thickness, only came to below her knees,
with a slight slit above that. She was poured into it, too,
and was obviously a top level confidential assistant. The
girl's hair-do suggested that there were still bourgeois
stylists hidden away for the people Mao really liked, and
her stiletto heels would have surprised, and perhaps
heartened, Mr. Kishimura. She wore two little family
heirloom diamond ear studs which she hadn't had to
hock yet. She held out her hand to me.

"My name is Feng, Mr. Harris. Mr. Chow will see
you right away. Will you please come?"

Her English was faintly British. We have had our

influences in China, too. And as we walked together across stone slab floors I saw from the corner of my eye that she waved her behind around in a manner that would almost certainly have startled all those drab emancipated hordes out beyond the steam heating.

"The sun shines for you," said Miss Feng in the lift. "I hope it's a good omen."

"So do I."

Her smile was definitely provocative.

"You know Peking, Mr. Harris?"

"Not now, I don't."

"Oh. The new changes? You prefer the old way?"

"Yes. Probably I'm a relic."

She laughed. I was twinkled at as though she could do quite a line with relics if there was the right provocation. That lift didn't seem the place to start anything, though, particularly so soon after breakfast.

Mr. Chow surprised me too. He was keen, one of the hustlers in the Bright New Day. He got up from behind his desk with a Rotary smile and a held-out hand.

"Welcome to People's China, Mr. Harris. I'm sorry not to have come to meet you, but I only flew in from Nanking late last night. Please forgive me. You must have felt that your arrival was scarcely organised?"

"On the contrary, Mr. Chow, it was highly organised. I had an interesting evening."

He didn't blink, and the smile stayed, together with the near top executive's terrible air of juvenile eagerness. I was assigned a chair and told that tea would arrive presently. Miss Feng arranged herself with a pad on her knee and her legs crossed, showing a progressive amount of nylon. Everything, in fact, was being done to make me feel right at home. It was my fault that I didn't, quite.

However, I have to be a long way off form to be unable to sell. It's almost instinctive, at least something that I started to learn practically at my father's knee. In his day my father sold an extraordinary assortment of things to China, with only one point of high principle to hold his income down. He wouldn't have anything to do with the Chinese War Lords who at that time were the best market, keeping munition firms in Europe trundling along on full time even when large chunks of the rest of the world seemed to have taken to the ploughshare. I've hung on to a portion of my father's principles and I've always declined to act as agent in an arms deal unless I approved of my customer's cause. On the whole it isn't a bad amount of principle to have kept by me in rougher times than my daddy's.

For nearly an hour I sold the Dolphin engine on paper, from documents in my case, with all the time Chow's rice-rounded face opposite me, his mouth a little open, and his cheeks slack from concentration. He asked intelligent questions which showed he wasn't only a desk man, and I began to acquire for him a kind of reluctant respect. There are some bureaucrats who would have done well in private enterprise if they had been given the chance. And Chow was the type that my Chinese partners in Singapore would have liked doing business with. I almost enjoyed it myself.

"When will my engine be here, Mr. Chow?"

"To-day."

He had the answers ready.

"And a demonstration? I'd like at least a day to supervise a fitting in the boat you are going to use. Where's the water, by the way?"

"A canal near Peking. I have the boat fixed. It is now in a boathouse. You could visit to-morrow."

"I'll certainly do that. I'll need an interpreter, of course. Miss Mei?"

"You find satisfactory?"

"Neutral is the word. She doesn't talk as much as most women."

Miss Feng made a noise in her throat then. I looked up and smiled at her. This was returned. The Chinese so often have beautiful teeth. There was a hint of lipstick on two of Miss Feng's.

We all drank tea from handleless non-utility cups with an embossed gilt design on eggshell porcelain. Those cups were little exotics in an austere utility setting, rather like Miss Feng.

"Are you running the Nishin engine trials along with mine?" I asked, quite suddenly.

"Pardon?" Chow's eyes had reached their widest.

"The Japanese think China ought to be their market, even with an inferior product. Mr. Kishimura and I are friendly business rivals."

"Is that so?"

"Yes. I'd welcome a comparison test if you wish it. I don't suppose Mr. Kishimura would, however. He is a little uneasy, as well he might be. His only advantage may be price. But I would suggest, Mr. Chow, that you look at price from a number of angles. One is maintenance. The Dolphin isn't going to require a crew of resident engineers to keep it running."

"And you think the Nishin would?"

"Their products have improved, of course. Enormously."

Chow laughed. It was short and explosive.

"You have for Japanese respect but not great enthusiasm, Mr. Harris?"

"On the contrary, I'm extremely enthusiastic about some of them."

"Remarkable people. Highly industrialised. One day not so long from now they fit neatly into the new pattern of Asia."

"You mean a Communist Japan would serve your ends nicely?"

"It will happen, Mr. Harris."

"A lot of us will do plenty to try and prevent that happening."

"You cannot block solid advance of natural history."

Mr. Chow wasn't, after all, just the keen executive type. Something about him had gone cold and still. And I suddenly didn't find that fleshy face on a relatively lean body attractive. I found myself wondering again, after having forgotten for a time, just how important the Dolphin engine was in the little game we were playing.

It appeared to be important enough. We spent another three-quarters of an hour on it and then I was driven back to my hotel in the black Zis.

My room was just as the paying guest expects to find his room, neat and tidy, with no corpses. But I was scarcely in it before there was a knock on the door. Mr. Kishimura had come to call. He looked solemn and formal, with something on his mind.

"Shall we please go to lunch, Mr. Harris?"

"Yes, I'm just ready. I've had an interesting morning at the Trade Ministry. Everything is going quite smoothly."

"Excellent." It committed him to nothing.

"I expect the hold ups will come later. Getting them to sign on the dotted line."

This time he didn't comment at all. We went down the hall to the lifts, using the middle one by my choice. And when we were in it, with the doors shut, Mr. Kishimura said:

"Elevator is without microphone, I think."

"You've checked on that?"

"No evidence of instrument. Safe to talk."

"About what?"

He handed me a small revolver, a little beauty, a tidy Colt-type automatic, but clearly made in Japan, with mother-of-pearl laid into the handle.

"And what's this for?"

"You to keep, please."

"Mr. Kishimura, I came to China unarmed. For a very good reason."

"I know, I know. But please take. You may need."

"Look, if anything happened to me and I was found with this . . ."

"It make no difference," he said grimly. "If you are in trouble it make no difference. Gun may assist to keep from trouble."

"I don't see that. A business man selling engines doesn't need a revolver."

"You need."

"Do you mind letting me know why you're so damn sure?"

"I can't. We are now ground level. We must open doors, Mr. Harris. Put into inside pocket. Very small. You not notice."

He began to open the doors. I couldn't then force the gun back on him. We went out together to face that menu which had to be translated for me.

I didn't like this development at all. I didn't like Mr.

Kishimura's emergence as a kind of watchdog. It gave me the uneasy feeling of being overlooked all the time, as well as listened to. He was going to get his revolver back, at the earliest available opportunity which would probably be right after lunch in the lift again.

We came out of the dining-room together, fed if not well fed, and Mr. Kishimura stopped for a moment by an illuminated case near the reception desk.

"You like to smoke cigar, Mr. Harris?"

"Ask the price first."

"No, no, expense account. International business men."

He liked that. The price, when the surprised desk clerk had checked on it, turned out to be something near a pound sterling for each cigar, and with these symbols of our international expense account status in our hands we sat down in wicker-chairs in the exact centre of the lobby, as remote from any concealed mikes as possible. I sniffed at my present. It smelled much more like Java leaf than Philippine or Cuban, and a pound for this junk was certainly robbing the imperialists. The thing didn't draw well either. Mr. Kishimura, working up the cloud of opulence that was to surround us, inflated his cheeks like a boy with a balloon.

"So. You like?"

"Mr. Kishimura, it was a gesture from your heart, but it's stinking horrible."

"Cut in two and use like cheroot. I smoke much cheroot in Java."

"During the Greater East Asia War?"

"So."

"Rank?"

"Major. At end Colonel. I am in Java, Borneo, Philippines, Tarawa."

"Fighting your way back, in fact?"

His expression didn't change. He nodded. He patted then the slightest swelling of his stomach.

"Time like dream now to fat business man. You also?"

"Me also."

"Oh . . . !" he said.

I looked up. A woman had come through the plate-glass doors. She wore a long grey squirrel coat and hat to match and snow boots, and she came in out of the afternoon winter sunshine as she might have done into a London hotel looking for someone, assured, and walking even in those boots, like a model. It was Florie.

And only when she was close to us did I see that she wasn't so assured, only moving in the manner. Her eyes sought mine and I knew that something had happened, something unpleasant.

We both stood. I introduced Kishimura. Florie looked at the Japanese business man and then dismissed him.

"Paul, are you doing anything this afternoon?"

"Not so far."

"Then will you go up to your room and get your coat. Without asking questions. Just do it. And wrap up warmly."

When I came out of the lift again ready for outdoors, Florie and Mr. Kishimura were sitting together, but they didn't seem to be making any conversation. Florie just got up and left him. She met me, and with her hand on my arm turned me to the doors.

"What is this . . . ?"

"Don't talk now, Paul. Just walk through those doors and out!"

And that's what we did. It was all rather sudden. In

so far as I could see no one came out of the interpreters' corridor.

We went down the steps and turned west into the sun. I could feel that sun on my face penetrating even the stinging of the cold. Florie was walking fast.

"I don't think there's anyone following," she said, without looking.

"This was a manœuvre to shake off the watchdogs?"

"Yes. I was lucky to catch you in the lobby. It mightn't have worked if I'd had to phone up or get you out of the dining-room."

"Florie, what's happened?"

"Something rather nasty. When I was in the clinic this morning the secret police came and turned out everything in my rooms. I came in an hour ago to find the place an absolute shambles. I've never seen anything like it."

"You're new to the attentions of the local gestapo?"

"Yes."

"Then it must have happened because of me. Because of last night."

"That's what I'm furious about. I phoned the Ministry of the Interior. I know the principal secretary. I said a few things."

"And what did he say?"

"Nothing really. It wasn't his department. Obviously."

"Look, Florie, I'm going back to the hotel."

"Why?"

"Because you can't walk away from snoopers in China to-day."

"We'll have time enough to talk. And there are no microphones on these trees."

"You know about microphones?"

"Of course I know about them. They're everywhere. Though not in my clinic yet, not that I know of."

"Florie, where the hell can we go?"

"The Winter Palace. It's not far. It's a public place now. Paul, don't leave me! I've got to be with you just now. I don't care what the risk is. And . . . and I won't be bullied."

"What do you mean by that?"

"I've done my best for China. I've tried to for years. In my job. But I won't crawl to them. They can do what they want with me, but they're not going to beat me down. I'm a Yin and I'm not forgetting that."

"Robert was a Yin too."

"They can't tie me in with what Robert did. I knew nothing about it. I've served them, that's all. Then they come and tear my house to bits. Looking for letters, I suppose, something you might have smuggled in. A plan for my escape, perhaps. I told them that at the Ministry, that I had no plan to escape, and I'd be interested to hear what they found in my house."

"I hope you weren't quite as blunt as that?"

"I was and I'm glad."

"Look, Florie, whether you like it or not you've got to take cover. And stop thinking that being a Yin is some kind of insurance. We'll walk down to the end of this street and then turn back. I'll be in the hotel again before they've got the posse to come after us properly organised."

She stopped dead, looking up at me. Two schoolgirls in winter drab came by staring with disapproval at the fur coat. And out in the broad road hordes on bicycles, all going one way, turned their heads, holding us in their eyes as long as they could. Somewhere, distant on the crisp air, a factory hooter sounded.

"Something's happened to you, too," she said.

"My trip to China mayn't turn out as simple as I thought it was going to be."

"What do you mean?"

"I could soon be the worst man in Peking for you to know."

"All right! I tell you I'm not frightened. And I'm staying with you now. Do you hear?"

"It isn't a question of me hearing, Florie. A good section of Peking will soon."

"Are you coming to the Winter Palace?"

We went to the Winter Palace. We didn't talk in the crowded streets, where eyes looked at the Chinese woman not dressed drably walking with a foreigner. I began to feel that Florie was suddenly realising what she was doing and the fear, which she had defied, wasn't too far off. But it was peaceful in the first courtyard of the palace, with the snow glittering on a vast expanse of flag-stones, outshining the white marble of the balustrades. In a loose circle pigeons were eating crumbled rice and they looked as plump as ever, blue-coated and pompously bustling. It was suddenly very still. We were the only people on the long strip of swept walk leading up to a terrace where huge bronze lions sat waiting. Even the pigeons were quiet.

"I want to know what's happened to you."

So I told her. There might be reasons not to, but there were plenty why she should know. Fear began to come into her eyes. She waited until I was finished.

"It just doesn't make any sense to me, Paul."

"I find it makes a lot of sense. I haven't been exactly

a friend of the New China. And I've obligingly walked in here. They don't mean to let me just walk out again."

"How can they stop you getting out?"

"Easy enough. They can arrest me on a criminal charge."

"But what's the point of . . . of framing you?"

"Well, it could be a nice little propaganda trial. Imperialist saboteur nabbed for murder in China. Make good reading in the Red Press, wouldn't it? And the Press outside, too."

She tightened the collar of her coat with one hand. I saw her eyes go to the emptiness about us, the huge square edged by galleries with heavy tile roofs.

"Give me a cigarette," she said.

I didn't throw down the match to mar the almost terrible neatness around us, I put it back in the box, a gesture to the Manchus, in this their museum. And then I saw a movement down by the gate we had come through, quickly covered by shadow, but there. It could be Yang, on duty again.

CHAPTER VII

I DIDN'T TELL Florie we were being followed. We couldn't be overheard in this emptiness, and I wanted her to talk. She needed to.

"Get out of China, Paul. Now!"

"I've got a business deal pending."

"You're still thinking about that damn engine?"

"It's a good engine. China needs it. My partners and I need the money. I think there's a chance the contract will be signed."

"Even after what happened last night?"

"Yes, oddly enough. It could be that someone boobed last night. An underling with a bright idea. But the people higher up are not thinking it so bright to-day. What I did must have rattled them a bit. And this morning at the Ministry everything was sweetness and light, with much politeness and tea drinking."

"I think it's horrible cat and mouse."

I smiled at her.

"I've played things this way before, Florie."

She stared at me.

"I believe you quite like things this way!"

"That's making it a bit too strong. But I don't think it's a time for a panic retreat. I've got a feeling that there was a high-level conference this morning or last night. On policy with regard to me. They want me, and they want my engine. But they've reversed the order, getting the engine first, me after. And I think that in spite of last night I'm safe enough until I sign the contract."

"And then?"

"Then they may pounce."

"But . . . it doesn't make sense! Your partners in Singapore wouldn't go through with the engine deal if you were arrested on some trumped-up charge."

"Oh, I think they would, you know. They're Chinese, too. They'd be terribly sad about the news of me up for murder and sabotage and possibly spying as well. There might even be a two-minute silence at the Board Meeting. After that . . . well, there wouldn't be a thing they could do. And I should think that before too long those Dolphins would start coming north. Business must go on, you know. Particularly when the price has been paid in gold into a Hong Kong bank."

"You'd be a write-off?"

"And a fragrant memory."

I smiled at her. Little Florie was very serious right then, thinking about what I had said in terms of local probabilities. She may have been tucked away in her nest but she had heard things. The Eastern mind can seem tortuous, but once you get on the beam it's not too difficult to stay with it. I was sure I was on the beam, and that Florie believed this too.

"Why did you come to China really? Was it to help me?"

"In a way. I thought I might carry on where Robert had to leave off."

She shivered. It wasn't the cold.

"It was madness to come. With your record."

That brought me up with a little jerk. It seemed unlikely that the Chinese papers would have said much about my anti-Red activities down south. How could she have heard? It wasn't the sort of thing her old friends outside now would chat about in letters home.

"What's my record, Florie?" I asked gently.

Her head came up at once, her eyes meeting mine.

"You're surprised that I know? I didn't until this morning. A man called Humbold rang me up. He said he was interested in our old friendship. I didn't like his tone at all, I must have shown that. So he prodded me a little for a reaction. He asked me if I knew my old friend had fought against the legal government of Java. And a few other things. He made out you were a kind of bandit. Paul, how much of this is true?"

"Any truth in it is highly coloured."

"But there's some?"

"You could say that. When did Humbold ring you?"

"Just after the search of my rooms. He probably knew about that. He's greatly favoured in Peking, from all I hear. And he probably thought he could catch me off balance. But I wasn't chatty, Paul."

"I didn't think you would be. Still, you were a fool to come running to me like this."

"I had to. After you went last night I thought about Robert and what he had been doing, while I kept myself safe. Hiding behind my job. There may have been an excuse for it while Father was alive. But not any more. Paul, I've come out of hiding."

"A bit too soon. And in the wrong company. It looks as though they may have marked you down too."

"Let them!"

I put out my hand and she took it.

The Yins had all been fighters. They were the kind who either came out on top or got killed.

We began to go up the steps. There was a change in Florie. I had the feeling of her being committed to me now and making quite a thing of that. She would end up being flamboyant about it. It was a family tendency too. I could remember Robert telling me of one of his excursions into Red China, when he had got as far north as Hangchow, simply disguised as an Inspector of Railways. He said it was much safer to go about in China as someone people are naturally afraid of than dressed up as a peasant. Humility never pays, Robert had said. He had created some particular kinds of hell all along that road to Hangchow amongst the station-masters who were unlucky enough to be minor party members. No one had ever questioned him in that role of a big-shot snooper. But he said that as a tiller of the soil he would have been searched twenty times and probably grilled in police cells.

Florie and I walked through another courtyard talking about Robert. He was in both our minds. She asked a lot of questions and I gave all the answers I could, about his home in Hong Kong and the wife Florie had never met. I told her about his children and his business and how we had come to meet up again.

"He sent me food parcels while Father was alive," Florie said. "I didn't really like it. And when I was alone I wrote and said I didn't need them."

"A Yin on her own feet."

"Well, he did try to organise me. You remember?"

"I remember."

"We didn't write after that. There's nothing you can really say in a letter that is going to the censor. And I see now that he mightn't have thought it a good idea to write to me."

"He meant to get you out, Florie."

She made no comment on that. I had the feeling that she was well past the shock of her brother's death, and the way it had come about. She was thinking of him now as a Yin in action, and the kind of action it had been. At any rate what she said next didn't surprise me.

"The night after to-morrow is Christmas Eve, Paul. Have you any plans for celebrations?"

"None."

"I hadn't either. But I've got one now. Let's go to the opera, you and me. The Kiangsi Opera is just ending its season here. It's supposed to be marvellously good, and if you ask your hotel for two seats you'll get them all right. The Kiangsi are culture for export. They do tours abroad."

"And it would be a good idea for us to be seen together in public?"

"It would be good for me to get out of my hole!"

"Now you remind me of Robert."

"I hoped you'd say that. . . ."

"I'm not going to the opera with you, Florie."

She didn't argue, she just took my arm.

"Let's see more of the palace."

Our feet were loud on the marble flags which had taken on a dark veining and I noticed that the veining was matched from one slab to the next. A long time ago slaves had built this palace for the artificial peace of the rulers. And the sweeping emptiness was haunted. We were intruders into an area frozen in time, breaking the spell which was always broken by alien footfalls. But, when we left, the static picture would round out again, the mandarins would be back in their robes of burning colours and a vast ritual of ceremonial would take up its ponderous, unceasing movement. The Winter Palace feels like that, that it can't be dead. The design is even now too flawless not to be completed by the movement of life it was meant to contain.

We stood perfectly still by a rearing, stylised bronze dog, six feet high, both of us as though listening for something, but here were no pigeons and the sound of the city didn't reach us.

"Let's go into the women's quarters," Florie said.

These were much smaller and though that first courtyard still had the perfection of line in tiled roofs and colonnaded arcades, under them was a suggestion of new frivolousness. Colour was back for one thing, a deep maroon lacquer on the uprights which must once have been bright red. There was carving, too, about the pediments, touches of stylised fuss for the less austere taste of court ladies. The centre area was gravelled, but I had the feeling it had held flowers, and probably caged nightingales and the companionable croaking of cicadas hung up in little gilded bamboo boxes.

"A pretty prison," Florie said. And then: "My great-grandmother must have walked here."

I was surprised, for I had thought of the Yins as rich business, not aristocrats. But great-grandmama had apparently brought tone to new money. And it was escape now to talk about her, a kind of switching off of the present which Florie needed right then.

"She was a lady-in-waiting to the Empress Dowager. I can just remember her when I was a child. She had no teeth at all, but her gums hardened up and she could chew anything. She was very grand. And used to scare me stiff. I don't think she thought a lot of the Yins. Tiny bound feet and the peony-swaying-in-the-wind walk. It was really quite pretty, you know. People say it was a hobble, but it wasn't. They walked like creatures not of this world at all, and not very far ever, because they didn't have to. With a kind of fluttering. Even when she was very old Madame Yin walked like that. And she would never let anyone take her arm. She always wore full Manchu dress and had eyes like a hungry hawk. When she came to our house she put a kind of stillness on it, and we children walked softly, I can tell you. You see, Paul, I can jump a long way in my life. Back to an echo from the wicked old Empress."

"And chopping off foreigners' heads," I said.

"What on earth do you mean by that?"

I didn't get time to answer. There was a creaking of wood. On our right was a long wall with arched windows, shuttered now on what must be empty rooms. But one of the shutters wasn't quite closed. There was a hand pushing it out.

Two men were suddenly five yards in front of us. They were dressed for a rough-house, tight pants in blue and some sort of heavy shirt. And I was trussed up in a greatcoat. One of the men had his arms folded on his chest, in a kind of posture of waiting. He was smiling. The other was a little in front, his arms down, his fists closed, a big man, a trained bully boy.

I looked at Florie. Her mouth was a little open in terror.

"Get back against the wall."

"Paul . . ."

"Get back!"

The first man moved. He had sized me up. The movement was one step, a tensing of the body, almost leisurely. Then he sprang like a big cat.

He was watching for my hands but not my feet. Before we went down he got what he didn't expect, where he didn't expect it. The weight of him threw me back, at the same second as a yowl filled the courtyard, shattering, loud with pain, animal.

The marble wasn't a good fall even in a greatcoat. It jarred every bone in me. I was a cushion, too, a groaning heaviness on my legs and stomach. I hadn't much breath, but I got two punches in, not playing by any rules either.

Florie screamed.

The second man was there, over us. He kicked at my face. I only just got my head away, taking it below an ear. There was a cracking noise in my head. I couldn't see. I was pushing myself up, palms flat on the cold stone, when I got it again, this time in the kidneys. The greatcoat was some padding, but not nearly enough and it was my noise that went out then to echo in the courtyard.

They both had hold of me, hauling me up, their breathing spitting in my face. I started to heave about, but without much snap in the movement, my body muffled down under all that wool. I saw the big one's closed fist and a clean professional right coming to the jaw. All the rules in that one. It made contact and the rules were in the way it lifted and sent me whirling back over slippery marble.

I nearly caught my head on the balustrade, but missed that, falling in front of it. Something was battering in my head, but I had my eyes open and I could see out of them. I could see the way those two were breathing, taking their time now.

I couldn't allow them time. My right hand went under my coat. It wasn't there long. It came out with Kishimura's gun. I pointed it at them and shoved myself back against the railing, a little frightened by the dizziness that had started to come. I think I was grinning, too, but not from the fun. I didn't feel I could risk bringing my jaws together. They didn't seem to be fitting as neatly as usual into my head.

The two were looking at me, just standing there doing that now, as though for all their training some reactions came slowly to them. A gun produced this dulled reaction. A knife wouldn't have worried them, but the gun did. Maybe there isn't the ammo in China to train thugs in this form of field sport.

I could see Florie as well, breathing as though she had been in the fight. Her coat had fallen open and was a little off one shoulder. It made her look a bit like a model displaying a good piece of workmanship in top-grade squirrel. She wasn't looking at me, she was staring down the gallery.

So were the bully boys. They seemed to have gone passive, as though letting the initiative slip from them. I got that then . . . a bit late . . . someone else joining us. I couldn't jerk my head around, it wouldn't do that on my neck any more. But I got it round, to a shadow, to feet and legs and then a face.

"*Kura!*"

The man dropped on me, for my gun. I did the only thing I could, kept it low and sent it slithering on marble, straight over to Florie. It reached her before the man had me.

We were threshing about when I heard the first shot. There were hands on my throat when I heard the second.

The hands came away. Florie was shouting in Chinese. A weight suddenly wasn't on me any more. I heard running feet and felt my dizziness coming back. But I could see all right. I saw the model in the fur coat busy with that revolver. She was making a noise between shots, and I don't know now whether it was her bullets they were running from or what Florie said. There are great reserves in a Chinese girl. It's part of her mystery.

I hauled myself up and looked out into the courtyard just as Florie said, in English:

"It won't fire any more."

"You've used up the bullets. They don't . . . when you have."

The gun dropped out of her hand. She came towards me in the peony-in-the-wind tottering step.

"Paul . . . ! Oh, Paul . . . !"

"Florie, don't faint. Just at this moment I couldn't hold you up."

"Paul, they've gone."

"Yes. But I wish we had a bullet left to see us out of this place. Just one."

"Paul, you're hurt! Maybe I can do something?"

"No, I'll do the first assessment. Right now I want to lean a moment."

I waggled my jaw and something clicked in my head, so that was all right. Florie took hold of both my hands suddenly.

"Thanks for the gun play," I said. "Very deep thanks. Did you hit anything?"

She shook her head.

"Just one of the posts. Nowhere near them."

She sounded regretful and quite self-controlled.

"Still, they heard the bullets whining. You saved the day, Florie."

I began to straighten up. I've learned that if I can walk I'm not in need of immediate medical attention. The kidney part hurt worst, but I didn't have to stay bent with it.

"What do you think it means?" Florie asked.

"I haven't begun to think yet. I'll do that in a hot bath."

Her hands were fists.

"It makes you want to fight!" she said.

"That's a good reaction to rough stuff. Come on, I'm taking you out of here, back to the hotel for a drink."

"Are you going to report this, Paul?"

"No."

"You mean . . . it wouldn't do any good?"

"There are times when I just let things unroll. This is one of them."

"If you hadn't had that gun they could have killed you. And I wouldn't have been able to stop them!"

The odd thing was I couldn't see that happening. I couldn't feel that the party just over had been designed for a killing at all. It made my head ache to try and work out what it had been designed for.

Going out of the Winter Palace we met a conducted party of schoolgirls coming in for a bit of indoctrination about China's great heritage. The girls were giggling just the way they would have done in a free society. Maybe they knew time was on their side and the Great Stride Forward would be history before they were called on for any active participation. It would have been interesting to hear how teacher tied in the glories of the Manchus with the doctrines of Marx and Joe Stalin, but I didn't ask Florie to stop and translate for me. She had the look on her face now of a Yin going places in anger.

::   ::

I lay on my bed in my room talking to Florie on the phone. There wasn't a lot we could say, without informing the listening service about an afternoon of slightly off-beat sightseeing, so all we did in the end was reassure each other that we were fine now. Florie stated that an evening at the theatre was on. I didn't argue.

When she hung up I closed my eyes. I felt a lot better after the hot bath. There was probably a bit of internal bruising as well as the pretty marks outside, but I wasn't bleeding, except for one knuckle. My big toe was sore. It's one of the things that always happens to me after a round of Malay boxing, I get a sore toe. Maybe I should wear heavier shoes.

I lay there thinking until I heard Mr. Kishimura come back to his room. Then I pushed myself up rather slowly, as though I had put twenty years on my age that afternoon. I went out into the empty passage and tried the next door handle, hoping Kishimura hadn't locked it.

He hadn't. He was sitting in his one chair, not then going through a ritual of spiritual refreshment, unless working on teeth with a long toothpick could be counted as one of them. He put the toothpick down but refrained from any cry of joy at seeing me.

China was forcing on us some peculiar habits in social relations. If you just wanted to be cheerful the room was all right, but business meant the bathroom. I went in and sat on his tub. He didn't seem terribly pleased about this when he joined me, but he did all the right things and closed the door.

"So? You have pleasant entertainment with beautiful Chinese lady?"

I watched him. He had the kind of face with built-in insulation against shock. I wondered if I could break through that insulation.

"I wouldn't call it a perfect afternoon. We were jumped by thugs. Three of them. I'm not quite sure what the object was, but I think it was to beat me up pretty thoroughly. I don't think I was meant to die. . . ."

"*Ara!*" Kishimura's astonishment and apparent distress were rather beautifully done, if artificial.

"Your gun came in handy," I said. "I didn't get a chance to use it, but my friend did. I've brought it back, though. I don't think it's a good idea for me to be carrying one. Particularly now."

"But this terrible thing, Mr. Harris. You are wounded?"

I laughed.

"Walking wounded. Mr. Kishimura, one of the three thugs was a Japanese."

CHAPTER VIII

NEVER BEFORE had I seen so much of Mr. Kishimura's eyes. They seemed to be pulled wide by a tightening of skin back against bone.

"Japanese? Impossible!"

"I agree, it's odd. The most remarkable coincidence. Here we are with seven hundred million Chinese round about us and I'm jumped in the Winter Palace by one of your countrymen."

"How can you know surely?"

"He said '*kura*'. I've heard at least fifty Japanese use that before they moved into action, and from anger. Is there any Chinese word that sounds like '*kura*', Mr. Kishimura?"

He didn't try to suggest that I had been mistaken, I gave him marks for that. I was certain he wanted a cigarette then and I took out my case. His hand trembled just a little as he used my lighter.

"The other men?" he asked, not looking at me.

"Chinese. Your countryman came on the scene after the first action. I had the feeling he was the boss."

"Mr. Harris, this is so difficult to believe!"

"Yes, isn't it? Unless, of course, my attacker was your missing Mr. Obata?"

"Eh?"

"I merely put it up as a theory, Mr. Kishimura. I shouldn't imagine there are many Japanese missing in China these days, with no record of what happened to them. The idea it might be this Obata occurred to me only a few moments ago. I wanted your reaction."

"But . . . impossible!"

"Why? If the man has gone missing and you don't know what he's up to? You don't know he's dead. He might be very much alive. Just how much do you know about your ex-salesman?"

"Only letters."

"To Japan?"

"Yes. Suddenly stopping. To wife also. No more newses. No business report."

"And you're over here to look into this?"

"So."

"You don't have a picture of your man, do you?"

Something flickered in Kishimura's eyes. He did have a picture. And he saw I guessed this. He turned and went out of the bathroom, back in a moment with what was clearly a reproduction of a passport photo blown up to postcard size.

"What you say?"

I couldn't really say anything. I hadn't been able to stare at the man in the courtyard and this was a posed portrait, full face. It could be, but I wasn't sure, and I said so.

"He was about your height."

"Many Japanese my height."

"Yes." I stood. "Well, I thought I'd let you know. And here's your gun back. Whatever you say I don't think it's a good idea I keep it. I nearly used it this afternoon. When you're in a corner and have your finger on a trigger the temptation is to pull it. I'd be properly in the soup now if we'd left a corpse behind up in that museum. You get my point?"

He didn't say anything. I smiled at him and suggested he give me a knock when he was ready to go down to dinner.

Back in my own room I was glad I had resisted the

temptation to move in to the attack with my friend next door. It had been a real temptation. There were grounds enough. Mr. Kishimura didn't want me to land in China. There was nothing to tie him in with the corpse in my room except that it had been a judo kill and he was next door. Certainly some other people in the hotel had been in on that little deal. But that didn't rule Kishimura out. He wasn't ruled out this afternoon, either. He had given me the gun, stuck with me after lunch until he saw how I was going to put in the time, and was witness to the fact that I had left the hotel without my usual posse. If he was playing hard against me, with accomplices, it would have been a golden opportunity.

I wished I had been able to identify Obata. Kishimura knew that I hadn't really, that I wasn't just pretending uncertainty.

There was another thing, too. The Japanese thug hadn't joined the party until there had been plenty of time for me to use a gun against one or both of the Chinese. It could be argued that this delay was because he wanted me to use that gun, and had taken a hand when it didn't look as though I was going to. The general situation could be said to be pregnant with possibilities, too damn pregnant.

I reached for the phone and asked to be connected with the British Embassy, giving the name of Watt-Chalmers. I was offered a lot of other people, as alternatives, but plumped for the man I knew, and waited, receiver to my ear. He finally arrived, sounding irritated.

"Hallo? Watt-Chalmers here. Who wants me?"

"Paul Harris at this end. Sorry to disturb you."

"Oh, Mr. Harris. That's all right. I was playing squash actually. Damn all else to do in this place."

"You're finding China dull? I'm not."

"You would if you'd been stuck here for eighteen months. Now how can I help you?"

I told him how and he was most amiable, but instead of sending the messenger I had suggested he came himself, at the time I'd arranged, when Mr. Kishimura and I were having an after-dinner cigarette in the lobby. There were polite introductions and we all drank whisky, talking about international trade until Watt-Chalmers, a little pointedly I felt, looked at his watch. We were taking a possibly valuable chunk from his evening. In charity he ought to be allowed to go. I pulled a plumpish envelope out of my pocket.

"It was good of you to come yourself. But as you'll see a messenger would have done perfectly well. I only want you to put this document in your safe at the Chancery. Is that all right?"

"Why . . . certainly," his eyebrows elevated. "Any instructions with it?"

"Yes, just this. Lock it away. Hang on to it while I'm in China. When I've left, I'll send you a wire asking you to burn this without reading it."

"Well, I must say this is rather odd."

"I suppose it is. Business is sometimes rather odd these days. You can call this a kind of insurance policy if you like. Against accidents."

"To you?"

He wasn't slow, this pale young man.

"Yes. A remote eventuality, but I'm a cautious type. If anything unusual should happen to me while I'm in this country what you would find in there might help you in the necessary action you would take for a British subject."

"I see. This letter is really for us?"

"Yes, in certain circumstances only. I'm hoping the letter will never be opened."

"I'll lock it up as soon as I get back," Watt-Chalmers said.

And then for some reason he looked at Kishimura. So did I. My friend's face showed nothing at all, but his eyes had almost disappeared behind slits. He picked up his glass with a steady hand and smiled suddenly. Watt-Chalmers left us after having again assured me that he was there to give any help he could. I was beginning to like the man, but I couldn't see any suggestion that this feeling was returned. As far as he was concerned business men, especially slightly eccentric ones, were a damn nuisance. And if he had any real curiosity about my somewhat unusual request he concealed it behind a professional politeness.

I walked with him to the door and then returned to Mr. Kishimura. We were sitting in seats I had chosen, this time near a pillar with floral decorations at the bottom which was the perfect place in which to set a mike.

"Two birds with one stone," I thought. Or was it only one bird?

"Another whisky, Mr. Kishimura?"

"No thank you, please."

"Oh, well, I suppose there's nothing much left to do but go up to bed. I've a good book. Or would you like to watch Chinese television?"

"To me not enjoyable."

"My feeling, too. Look, isn't it time we became less formal? My first name's Paul."

He cleared his throat.

"My name Taro. But friend call me Kishi only."

"We want to be friends, don't we?" I said.

::   ::

The next morning at nine-thirty there was a car waiting for me and already in it was Mei Lan. She was sitting tightly into her corner of the back seat and produced the usual minimum reaction to my greeting. I nearly said "long time no see" but didn't.

We drove out from the walled city and through the suburbs beyond it. The sunshine was crisp and I could see all the way to the Western Hills which rose up blue from the yellow plain. Once these had been the resort of bandits and Europeans on holiday, an odd mixture. You hired a temple up there for the hot weather and hoped that your cook or your wife wouldn't be carried off for ransom during your stay. It added a certain spice to the season and made even picnics bearable. Now those hills were almost certainly free of brigands, and the agreeable dilapidated temples would be standing empty. I remembered living in one for a time which had its own private pagoda at the foot of the garden, tiny, only about twenty feet high, and made almost entirely of chipped, pastel-coloured ceramic tiles. You looked past the pagoda and down at what had seemed all China, turned summer green then, with a suggestion of vast, limitless space, but all of it with people fitted in somewhere.

There were even more people now. We never got away from evidence of them on our drive, the sprawling suburbs thinning out into stretches of drained paddy packed with clean snow, and on this, like yellow patches, were the villages. There was scarcely a tree in sight.

The road roughened, jolting us about. No one paid any attention to the car except the dogs. In one village we were practically surrounded by them, and they weren't friendly. But they were beautiful. I suppose they must be mongrels but they don't look it. It is as though the whole of north China had kept a pure strain, part long-haired collie, part wolf. The brutes out beyond us were probably half starving, but they had a kind of rough-coated, snarling elegance and I remembered as a boy wanting a Chinese village dog and being told by my father that you couldn't train them easily for pets. At Crufts, as a new breed, and polished up a bit, they would have been a sensation. But they'd have bitten the judges.

One thing did jolt Mei Lan out of her unapproachable self-containment. The car slowed for a column of marching men and then began to creep by them. Faces looked in at us and they didn't seem indifferent faces. I realised, with a little shock, that they weren't all men either, a lot of them young women, dressed rather like Mei Lan, but in even rougher drab. They looked pretty dirty, most of them, and their faces didn't have the passive indifference of the peasant. They looked in at us with a kind of anger, and there was comment out there at this spectacle of plutocrats tucked into the comfort of a closed car. It wasn't a chronic anger we saw then, but something that flared up, and Mei Lan was huddled down in a private retreat from it, as though from accusing eyes.

"Prisoners?" I asked, with more indifference than I felt.

"No! No, not prisoners! They . . ."

"Yes?"

"They are workers for good of the people. Volunteer workers. For a time only."

"Intellectuals, you mean?"

"Perhaps." She seemed to have caught their anger and to be beaming it at me. "They do this to help China."

"I see. Willingly and with happy hearts. Where's the laughter?"

"What?"

"The export films show the laughter. That should have been laid on for me."

"Do not speak this way!"

One of the men up front had turned his head. I had the feeling that the girl's protest was for him. And she had to go on with a spiel, too. I got it hot and fast for a few minutes as we pulled away from the column, all about the urban workers wanting to keep in touch with the land, which was their great heritage. They did this voluntary labour as part of the great sharing which would make China the most powerful country in the world. It all sounded like something off a record, delivered in too high a pitch, with a suggestion of hysteria in the way it was put over.

Then she saw that I was watching her closely and suddenly shut the sound off. I had the extraordinary feeling that Mei Lan wanted more than anything in the world to cry right then, but didn't dare. She gave me one angry glare instead and switched her eyes out.

I waited a little.

"Are there many of these work camps near Peking?"

"There is a big one here. New irrigation. They are digging huge ditch, to move canal."

"I see."

And I could, too. No bulldozers on this scene of operations, just a stream of the thing China has so much of, people, long chains of them carrying mud up a bank from the diggers. Soul-restoring, no doubt, for the office worker or the university lecturer. How they must all look forward to this periodic escape. I thought then of Miss Feng, with her spike heels, and wondered whether there was, perhaps, a class already emerging in the new China which contrived to avoid this kind of spiritual rejuvenation. I had the feeling that Miss Feng would pretty certainly want to avoid it, and probably belonged to a safe minority which managed to do this. That would account for the anger sent through car windows at us. And Mei Lan's sudden fear might be because she hadn't yet earned her own immunity ticket.

The canal chosen for my demonstration purposes had a bend in it like a boomerang. It was apparently dammed up now at both ends and was clearly a piece of water cut off by the new workings. These were only about a mile beyond, pyramids of soil up which toiled the silhouettes of figures, a long line of them against the sky. We got out of the car by a shed that looked new and was built like a boathouse out over the water. Inside was the boat and my engine sitting on a covered wharf ready to be lifted down by a primitive derrick arrangement of iron chains powered by what could have been a two-cylinder bicycle engine set on a box. There were four or five men inside who had been running the putt-putt motor and hadn't heard us come. They were caught in attitudes of inaction which they somewhat dramatically tried to cover at once by a good deal of running about. The gaffer started bellowing.

All this was clearly my baby, and I was left to get on with it. It would take some doing. In the first place the boat was far too light. The Dolphin is meant to power junks up to a considerable size, and fitting it into what was little more than a sampan was like squeezing a truck engine into a mini-car. It could probably just be done but the results, for demonstration purposes, would be odd in the extreme.

I made a fuss about this at once, through Mei Lan, and everyone began shouting, including the girl, to make herself heard. I took time out to examine my diesel, leaving them to it. The Dolphin had arrived in excellent condition, the remains of its case all about. It sat glistening in a Chinese shed, a lump of evidence about Western know-how which gave me a certain feeling of complacence, a beautiful baby which I had watched come off the production line. I had my hands on it when Mei Lan said at my elbow:

"It must be this boat. No other one is available."

I didn't look at her.

"Too bad. We'll have to take the engine to a river somewhere."

"But this place is arranged for testing."

"We'll unarrange it. I need a junk, not a row-boat."

"These men obey orders only."

"Precisely. There doesn't seem to be anyone here who can give orders. Except me. We'll go back to Peking now and see them at the Ministry."

"But the car has gone. You were to be here until evening!"

"I love my engine, Miss Mei, but I still don't want to sit by it all day. Someone has got to ring up and get the car back. I can do nothing here. And I'm not going to try."

"There is no phone!"

"Then send a runner. We're all unemployed around here this morning. My engine isn't going in that boat!"

More shouts, rising to a kind of wailing. The gaffer, who was pocked, swaggering and confident of advancement, came up to me and started to say something about Imperialist trouble-makers, or so it looked from his unappealing expression. I smiled at him and he stopped, winded. I cupped my hands and did a mime of the engine in the small boat and then the small boat going off like a rocket, finally disintegrating. It was a good mime and the gaffer watched with his mouth open. At the demonstration of an explosion he suddenly laughed.

The whole atmosphere changed. Everyone began to laugh except Mei Lan. There was no one of importance around and they could afford to. You could see that they were indulging in a luxury, but the Comrade Gaffer had started it and a lead from him was usually ideologically sound. Laughter echoed in that shed, making me feel a star turn.

Mei Lan didn't like it.

"We must wait until evening," she shouted into the first lull.

"My time is money," I said.

"Mr. Harris, we cannot go back to Peking. There is no car."

"Then we'll all have a picnic. I hope you've brought your lunch? The hotel gave me mine."

Mei Lan began to cough. It was a quite horrible spasm and before it ended she was the centre of our attention, waving those tiny imitation worker's hands at us in protest. It was bitterly cold in the shed, with a kind of added clamminess off the water, and I couldn't believe that we had been dumped down here for the day without some means of keeping warm. There was the need to impress the foreigner for one thing, unless, of course, they had given up trying to impress me because I wasn't going to be able to take any messages to the outside.

With this uncomfortable thought right at the front of my mind I opened a door to be hit by a reassuring blast of warmth from an eight-foot square cubby-hole in which, neatly centred, was an almost red-hot iron stove with a huge bucket of coal beside it. I still rated the V.I.P. touch. It was a relief.

"In here," I said to Mei Lan.

The whole party moved into comfort. The girl leant against a wall recovering, while I passed out cigarettes. Gaffer, the laughter over, was beginning to be conscious of the enemy in the midst again, and he took this seriously for a moment, reflecting. No one lit up until he did, and by that time I had sat down, on a box, my height reduced and with it my menace. I kept on smiling to restore tone.

About an hour later no work whatsoever had been done and everyone, except Mei Lan, was eating my packed lunch. I had the feeling that food would be a success and it was. They accepted my indications that I wasn't hungry at face value. They were. There may be plenty of food for everyone in China but I don't think so.

I've learned to wait when I have to. I didn't press the idea of sending a runner to call our car back, but settled down instead to write the day off. A little hard for an executive of some years' standing to do, but it only requires a relaxed attitude of mind and you snap up after it keener than ever. To-morrow I would make a big fuss. To-day I'd put my feet out towards an antique but efficient little stove, and put a big zero opposite this date in my mind.

For a zero day it offered a considerable number of

surprises after the slow start. The nothing doing and acceptance of this produced a torpor on the part of my fellow-workers. They lay down on the floor and were soon snoring. Mei Lan was propped up against the wall, watching me, quite silent, working on the report she was going to put in later. What was happening was a kind of sabotage and it worried her a lot.

Other things were worrying her too. She looked ill, and possibly in pain. Pallor had made her skin quite waxy, there was no colour in her face at all, scarcely a hint of it on her lips. It made those green eyes, lifted to me, more startling. And my curiosity about her suddenly became almost obtrusive. I wanted to ask a lot of questions.

"None of us are to blame for this," I said softly, above the sleepers. "They should have sent a man from the Ministry down with us to start the ball rolling. I can't think why they didn't. It's scarcely polite to me, is it?"

Mei Lan made no comment. The Gaffer rolled about a little on his stretch of boards and made smacking noises with his lips. Then he groaned.

"Were you born in Shanghai?"

There was suddenly anger in those eyes, as though she knew I was trying to take advantage of weakness. She didn't want to rally to fence with me, and took the only course open to her, dropping her lids. Long black lashes lay on her cheeks. I had then a feeling of waste for Mei Lan, a waste of life from the accident of having been born in this particular time. I knew that the enduring thing about her was that she didn't belong to this time and never could. And that all she would ever achieve was a kind of performance in it, a performance which mocked her, too, all the way. She was conscious of being mocked by it and had sat in Florie's lush, pre-revolution drawing-room as a bitter alien in whom the envies burned.

The professional hatchet-woman. How badly the role fitted. She lay now, under that terrible cap I'd never seen off her head, looking a child, a slightly grubby one, weary from the endless chores for which she was too young. She would never catch up with the living round about her, never quite fit in, for she was an alien by inheritance and from secret inclination. She would never achieve a bearable compromise, either, in the way Florie had.

Her breathing grew even, but I wondered if that retreat was only feigned sleep. The snores of the others got louder and no one moved when I stood, not even Mei Lan. She had her hands folded together and resting in her lap, an odd composure, with her body making economical use of the space she had allowed it. Mei Lan, too, was relaxed into the surprise recess from the usual pressures of the totalitarian pattern. There was here suddenly no telephone, no shouting, no loudspeaker to blare out patriotism. And so they slept and were thankful.

I went quietly out of that hot little oven, taking with me a feeling of my own loneliness and, perhaps from this, a pity for the girl and those sleeping men who were not my enemies so long as there was no one around to tell them it was their duty to be. Pity is a weakness. It isn't something the smart traveller carries around in his luggage. It certainly wasn't a sensible thing to have by me now.

In the shed beyond, the Dolphin glistened. It looked almost uneasy about its surroundings, here on a kind of charity visit and not intending to stay long, totally inanimate but still not belonging.

Another door took me out into China, to let me stand

quite alone for the first time since my arrival. I pulled the door shut behind me, realising this, knowing that I hadn't had a moment of this freedom in the long days since landing. Even in my hotel room there was that ear under the grille, but here in the sharp, hard winter air I could fill my lungs unobserved. The sky had a kind of brightness though there was cloud now over the sun, and under it I had a sense of escape which felt real, as though from this point I could go anywhere I liked, in total freedom, keeping always ahead of any pursuit that might spring up. It was an absurd feeling, of course, I knew quite well that I was still on a lead, but I wanted then to test the length of it.

I began to walk away from the hut, not going fast, but not strolling either, as though there was a purpose in what I was doing even if I couldn't identify it. I went first up the canal bank and then over the top of this into an isolated stretch of paddy, a peninsula of tilled soil holding out against the encroachments of new upheaval.

There was certainly plenty of upheaval. Whatever the works project ahead of me might be, it had churned up its corner of China. There were vast dumps of soil, like the bings in a British mining district, and on the one nearest to me was a line of human figures, silhouetted against the sky, a man-powered conveyor belt. All of them had huge lumps on their backs which would be wicker baskets full of earth. They ought to have been singing, these workers, but they weren't. I don't suppose the slaves of the Pharaohs sang much either, as they built the Pyramids.

I stood quite still watching, with no sound at all upon the sharp winter air, not even a cry from some hidden overseer. The line of figures went up their little mountain, pausing for a moment on the top, and then descending beyond my sight. That chain would never stop, it had vast reserves of men and women to draw on.

It was cold out there, I'd left my coat in the hut, and already I'd lost that illusion of being free. It hadn't lasted long in China. I was turning to go back to the boathouse when there was a crack and the whine of a bullet.

I dropped. It's an old instinct. The bullet had dug into the dried mud of the paddy, five feet beyond me. I was near a bank of clay and earth, built to hold in the water during the flooding. I was crawling towards this when the second bullet came, spattering up soil near my right foot. The sniper was getting his range.

Where the hell was he?

I had about two feet of shelter from my mud dyke. It wasn't a very thick dyke, either, just enough to slow a bullet down, maybe even bury it. In the flooded season bullets might just have come through a sogginess of mud, but now the wall had been cemented up by frost and drought.

I began to crawl along under the dyke and the third bullet went very near where I had been, so he couldn't see my movement. He wasn't up on one of those bings, they went out of range anyway, so that meant somewhere near the edge of the paddy area. I crawled five or six more feet and then looked over my wall.

The reaction to that was quick, a bang . . . whining. . . . And I saw nothing.

Two more shots. They both plopped into the dyke just above me, with a sound like a whole box of matches exploding. Very close indeed. The man wasn't saving his ammo, either. Wasteful, for China.

Back in the boathouse they ought to have heard the firing by this time and come out. I listened for voices. There weren't any. There was a great stillness for one sound only, and that sound split open the silence.

An odd way to die, in a little battle in which you weren't returning fire, because you couldn't. Usually when I've been shot at my sole reaction hasn't had to be purely defensive. I haven't just been a target lump of flesh lying on my stomach.

The sniper could come down on me, there was nothing to stop him. He had only to walk over a couple of fields and finish his little job at close range. He might be moving in. I tested that with my head.

Whing! The explosion from the small bore wasn't any nearer. Why not? And then I knew. He thought I had a revolver and was just waiting for close range. That was a small comfort. I liked the idea of that man kept away from me.

I didn't have time to speculate as to who the assassin was. The only thing imperative right then was to get out of this bit of paddy, and in a lull, while the sniper waited, I looked around, but without making my head a target again. The mud wall curved just along from where I lay, which meant that I couldn't wriggle much farther down it and expect to remain covered from the patient killer. But just where the cover ended was a small wooden sluicegate which meant a flooding ditch beyond it. These were usually pretty deep and I could see the line of the ditch, the way it undulated. I blessed those undulations. Once into it I could get up and run, and with cover most of the time. It would mean an end of this earthworm act which wasn't getting me anywhere much. The ditch was worth trying for, even at the risk of being totally exposed for half a minute while I rolled over the mud dyke into it.

Everything was dead still again. Clearly they were playing possum down in the boathouse. Or maybe the stove was roaring so much they hadn't heard the crack of a gun. Maybe. Anyway, no one was helping me, no one at all. I should have asked Kishi for more bullets instead of handing that revolver back to him. Kishi seemed to know what I needed as a business man in China.

The sniper might have seen that ditch too, and guessed what it would offer to me. And he knew I was heading in that general direction. The thing to do was throw him off here. I did a nice little piece of contortion behind two feet of cover, and faced the other way. I made about three yards back on my stomach and stuck my head up again.

Whing! . . . A near miss. This time I could hear the echoes of that shot going on and on. But the lonely killer was having everything his own way. It was my bet that if I could look I'd see that procession of mud-carriers still moving up their artificial mountain, no slowing down at all in the conveyor belt. Mud-carrying had to go on even when there was a bit of shooting in the area. This was a great country, everyone minding their own business. Except when it came to my business. There had been a concentration of interest in my business since my arrival, which was a little hard to work out. I remembered then that when I had last been in to an insurance company for a life risk I had been shown the door, politely, but shown the door. It hadn't been so long ago either. Maybe these actuaries are trained to sniff out non-coronary types who are none the less death prone.

I was moving back again, more earthbound than I ever remembered and not liking it. I was conscious of my rump tending to rise in my efforts, not a bad place to take a bullet, but I didn't want one anywhere. And then the wall was right there, the bit I had to go over.

This was it. I would either die now or not. Usually in action one is spared this kind of opportunity to look squarely at eternity. I had all the time I needed to look at it and I began to sweat.

This fear was particularly unpleasant, killed like a mole surfacing, an easy job for the killer. And no sense in it for the victim. I took a deep breath.

He was just a little bit late, that sniper. He had been looking for me down the line. He put a lot of bullets around the ditch, but none of them got down into the bottom of it, where I lay. I didn't lie for long, I pulled myself up and ran, bent over, in my trench. He may have seen me sometimes, but he didn't score a hit, though the air went on cracking with the noise from his gun.

Then, while I was still running, there was silence again. I was wheezing a bit and leaned against one side of the ditch, knowing that I could only take a few seconds at this rest, that I had to find out what was happening to the hunter. He could be running too.

I looked up, meaning to turn and push myself up the side of that trench. Someone was looking down at me. It was Humbold. He was very tall, standing there well above me, his legs slightly apart. He held a gun crooked in his arms.

"You can come out now, Harris," he said.

CHAPTER IX

WE LOOKED AT each other, Humbold and I. He could see how much I was still sweating. He seemed cool. But he would only have had to run over level ground, and not too fast either. And he was a cool type. He moved the gun a little on his arm. It was a Czech automatic rifle.

"You keep that for duck shooting?" I asked.

"I keep it."

"Is it too hot to hold any other way?"

"It's quite cold, Harris."

"Want me to feel it?"

I was hating him. I can't say I'd ever liked the man, but the feeling had become as warm as I was. Quite suddenly.

"Come on. Climb out of there. You're quite safe. Now."

"Something in me doesn't confirm that."

"The man who was shooting at you quit when I came over that bank there from the canal."

"Oh. What did you do, wave a hanky?"

"Great sense of humour, Harris."

"It's kept me going at moments worse than this. But not much worse."

I climbed up the side of the ditch, there was nothing else to do. Humbold didn't point the gun at me at all. He held it like someone who hasn't played around with lethal weapons much, but it could be a pretty act.

"If you're still nervous go in front of me, Harris. I'm big enough to stop any bullet hitting you."

"Thanks so much. Can I carry the gun?"

"If you like."

He gave it to me. It was cold. He hadn't been firing at me, unless he had thrown away another gun. I couldn't push myself to believe that, though I half wanted to.

I didn't carry the gun the way he had and I didn't walk exactly in front of him either. I kept my head towards him, not liking his face any better than I had. Our feet crunched on the frosty ground, but there wasn't any other sound at all. We went up a bank, perfect targets, and over it to be no targets at all. We were down on to the road by the canal, perhaps five hundred yards from the little boathouse, from which there was no sign of any kind of life. To the right was a little blue Volkswagen.

"I'm taking you back to Peking," Humbold said. "To get you out of this."

"I'd give a lot to know what I'm getting out of."

"Isn't it pretty obvious? I heard the firing a mile away."

"And stepped on the accelerator to my rescue?"

"Oddly, yes."

"It's odd all right. You just happening along a nice remote road about twenty miles from Peking. And you hear firing and get out your gun and come along and scare off the killer."

"I didn't just happen along. I was coming to have a look at your Dolphin."

"Why?"

"Because I think it's likely that the Chinese Government is going to buy your engine. And there's a story in that for me."

"There's a story all right, Humbold, and no doubt you'll stick to it. You're giving me a lift back to Peking?"

"I am. Right now. We'll get to the car."

"Not just yet."

"Don't be a damn fool. This isn't a healthy place for you to be loitering."

"I won't be long. Just a little investigation. Of that boathouse."

"Get in the car!"

"I wouldn't take that tone with me, Humbold. You made the gesture of giving me the gun, remember? And I'm used to this little model. Actually I've bought it from the Czechs myself. By a roundabout route, of course. Our side needed these guns in Sumatra so we could make proper use of captured government ammunition."

"You've got a nerve, admitting that."

"Why? You already know. You told a friend of mine all about it, too. I don't think it's an indiscreet statement out here really. I can't see you with a mike in your breast pocket and recording gear attached to your underpants. I'm going back to the boathouse. Want to come?"

"No! What if I don't wait?"

"That's your business. But won't you be disobeying orders if you turn up in Peking without me?"

He came along, a few paces behind. I didn't look over my shoulder. I wasn't afraid of Humbold now. But I was afraid of what I was going to find in the boathouse, of what was waiting there.

I didn't make any noise going in. The outer shed was empty. I draped the gun along one arm and went into the room with the stove.

They were all in there. For one moment it was a pretty tableau of blank astonishment, of eyes on me, and then on the gun. They had been sitting quietly around the stove, and all of them were a long way from sleep.

Mei Lan was a long way from sleep, too, standing now, pressed back against one wall, her hands out against it, her eyes wide.

"I'm not going to shoot anybody. Translate, Miss Mei."

She didn't say anything. She didn't need to. It was all in those green eyes.

"You didn't expect to see me walking in here, did you? After all that firing. You probably weren't told there was going to be firing. You were only told there was to be a nice social hour, all of us pals together, and then I was to be allowed to stroll out from these protecting walls. Isn't that it?"

She didn't say anything.

"Isn't that it?" I shouted.

"Leave her alone!" It was Humbold in the doorway. I looked at him.

"I thought chivalry was out in China? Chucked away with all the rest of the decadence. But I'll leave her alone. She can't answer my questions."

We walked back to the Volkswagen. A watery sun had come out, turning the colour tone of the canal water up a few points in lightness. But it was still a dismal scene, treeless, bleak, with an over-blanket of snow which had lost its first freshness. At the car he took the gun from me and put it into a hole under the back seat that might have been hollowed out of the metal flooring. When we were doing forty on a road which shook the car like an old can I said:

"Thanks for saving my life."

Humbold didn't look at me, he couldn't on that road.

"You're obviously stuffed with theories," he said.

"No, just one theory. It holds water nicely. Provided you allow for an unscheduled occurrence."

"And what's that?"

"It's not you, Humbold. You were scheduled all right. It's the man who shot at me who wasn't. And right now you're wondering like hell who he might be, aren't you? That's a better reason for haring back to Peking than taking me to safety. To try and find out. But I'll bet you something. You won't. Because the bosses will be surprised too."

"You've been doing a course of Fu Manchu before your China trip."

"No, that wasn't my light reading. It happened to be records of the trials of the British engineers in Russia in the early thirties. Someone gave them to me before I knew about my China trip and I was quite absorbed. I should have been warned, too."

"About what?"

"Well, from the fact that China is now just about at the stage Russia was in the early thirties. Rampant Stalinism you could call it. The age of terror. And to work a terror you need bogeymen. If you can catch a bogeyman and set him up as a People's target you've really got something. I see now that I was elected. Stupid of me not to realise earlier that I was a potential candidate."

"You're nuts!"

"I don't think so, Humbold. I think I'm very far from nuts. And as a Stalinist yourself you're all for bogeymen and burning them up in Marxist Guy Fawkes bonfires. It's feeding the people just what they have to be fed at this stage in the socialist revolution. And there hasn't been one in Peking yet. Not a really big show. It's overdue."

"When you get back to Singapore see a psychiatrist," Humbold said.

"But you boys don't go for Freud."

"All right, we don't go for Freud. What was I doing out there to-day? What was the role assigned to me?"

"Simple enough. You were to drive out to inspect my engine. And then to your total surprise you weren't to find me in the boathouse. Everyone I should have been working with lay about the stove in a heavy drugged sleep. It's easy for a European to lash out drugs. He needs them to sleep every night, he's so worried about the fall of capitalism. I hand around my pills as sweeties to the innocent and stalwart workers who suck 'em and pass out. That would do for court, wouldn't it?"

Humbold laughed.

"Go on laughing," I said. "You find me flown. You go out to search. And where is the imperialist devil? Snooping, that's what he is. I'm willing to bet that those earthworks have something to do with something that has top priority secret rating in the official books. At least enough priority to make it worth looking at for a British agent. Does that hit any place?"

"You've got me doubled over in pain," Humbold said.

"Not yet, but I will in a minute. You see, I think I know what went wrong out there. I know something you don't. A very important something. And that's who was shooting at me."

The Volkswagen did a sharp little wobble then, quickly corrected, but it wasn't any stone in the road. Humbold was sitting a little forward over the wheel now. I didn't think he'd laugh again all the way to Peking, and he didn't.

As we got near one of those wonderful old heavy-roofed gates which have had odd characters passing under them for some thousands of years, I said:

"Do you mind a detour before we go into the city? I'd rather like to go to the British Embassy. Don't worry, I'm not seeking sanctuary. Fifteen minutes ought to be enough. And then you can deliver me back to my hotel."

I was wanting to use diplomatic immunity to get a code message out of China. The Embassy might not play, but it was worth a try.

::   ::

That afternoon I came down from my hotel room to the politest of summons, almost polite enough to be Japanese and not socialist at all. But the delegation wasn't waiting for me in the lobby; it was in one of the private conference rooms which I hadn't seen before. From the point of view of decor there was a lot to be desired in that room, one wall another mural of China rampant in extraordinary chemical pigments and not a vestige of a lost taste for the æsthetic. There were four contemporary chairs, thought about in Sweden, conceived in Moscow and born in considerable pain and stress south of the Great Wall. Two of them were occupied, one by Miss Feng, showing her knees, and the other by Commissar for Trade Chow.

"Ah," said Chow, with great joy at seeing me so fit and well. "Mr. Harris. We have come in haste to see you."

"Well, bustle is certainly a symptom of progress," I said.

His broad smile wavered for a minute but stayed. Miss Feng rustled in her chair. I couldn't look at the girl without wondering just where she had received her training in this continuous sending out of bounce signals. My bet was still Hong Kong, though. She had that stamp.

The only thing that might rid her of it would be a session in a People's volunteer work camp. And this lassie was well dug into safety. I had the feeling that if I were Chow and little Miss Feng ever went missing from my outer office that would be the moment when I'd take off on a quick mission to Albania with the hope of slipping over the border into Greece and eventually getting to Switzerland. She was a new kind of status symbol, you might almost say a barometer. And any cool breezes sneaking into that Ministry office block would be sniffed out by this girl before you could say sabotage. Chow could smile now he had her, but watch, boy, watch! You believe in Stalin, remember?

I must have been grinning.

"You are in excellent spirits, Mr. Harris. I am so happy this is so. After this morning's misfortune."

"Oh, yes, a good marksman."

"Please!" The smile had quite gone. "We are greatly upset. It is to be fully investigated."

"Oh, naturally."

"At the moment no possible explanation."

"It could be a careless guard. Well, not careless, determined. Full of zeal. We have them, too, you know. People who use their trigger fingers first and think afterwards. They're an embarrassment to any democracy."

Chow wasn't quite with me, but little Miss Feng was right there. I got a message saying that if I'd had any future at all in China she would have been enchanted to accompany me up. This girl would always be interesting to have around as the intelligent man's guide to his ascent rating. Down there in Singapore I have an English secretary, extremely efficient, but rather solemnly married to a university lecturer and under the mistaken impression that it is important for a woman to exploit to the full the cultural opportunities of her environment. It's an approach which makes for a certain dullness in the smaller things of life. And really earnest women so rarely know how to do the right things with clothes.

Miss Feng would have looked all right in a one-piece made out of burlap. I couldn't help wondering why such a natural-born pirate should have chosen to operate here in Red China. The outside world would have seemed to offer a much juicier market, but then maybe she saw the future more clearly than I did.

Chow's smile was now just a shade defensive and that pleased me. I knew he must have had a full report from Humbold and it made for a curious state of things between us, him knowing that I knew what he knew. And always the chance that I knew something else besides.

Possibly Chow's Ministry, or another one, was continuing to be just the smallest bit rattled. I had walked nicely into the spider's web, but was managing to shake the corner in which I had landed hard enough to keep old hungry from walking over to its dinner. I wasn't fully assessed as yet. There was some rethinking going on about my case, and they had goofed badly once, to say nothing of having been somewhat baulked this morning by a killer on the loose. The situation was unresolved, to put it mildly, and it was a time for caution, perhaps even go-slow. There was also the fact that some people are better subjects for brainwashing than others. I was out now to give an impression of a high resistance to Red cleansing. A total dope in the defendant's box is a reflection on corrective techniques. The victim has to seem alive up there under the cameras, even appearing to be able to think.   But he must also be extinct, with no threat of residual eruptions.   They had been caught once or twice in Russia by the not quite sterile zombies.   And by now there must be a whole literature of text-books on the subject.   Stalinite text-books, of course.

"I'm a little bit worried about the boat you've supplied, Mr. Chow.   It's on the small side.   So's that section of canal, as a matter of fact.   Do you think we can find a river and a junk?"

"Of course, of course.   I am so sorry about this.   A slip up.   A most foolish mistake."

It wasn't quite that but I went on looking pleasant. Mr. Chow explained at length.   The detailed arrangements for my engine had been left to an underling who wasn't, as yet, sufficiently trained.   I would understand how responsibility had, at times, to be delegated?   The man in question had been severely reprimanded and immediate steps were being taken to find me a river and a decent-sized craft for the Dolphin.   It would perhaps take a day or two.   Meantime would I wait in patience and enjoy China?   I said I would be delighted to enjoy China and Miss Feng put out the tip of her tongue over a tricky bit in her shorthand.   She was distracting me and knew it.

"We are soon having a party for official business delegations," Mr. Chow told me.   "Will you please consider this an invitation?   It will be at the Summer Palace."

"An ideal setting for a party in winter."

Mr. Chow laughed.   He was quite a pal.

"There is an enclosed restaurant.   Also if the weather is fair there are the famous rock gardens of the Empress Dowager."

"And the marble boat with the linoleum floor."

"Oh? You know the Summer Palace?"

"I remember the linoleum floor, yes. I think I remember the rocks, too. I'll look forward to this."

On the way out Miss Feng gave me a look and said: "We will be seeing you, Mr. Harris."

"Won't we? Will you be at the Summer Palace?"

"Certainly."

For just a moment Chow's smile slipped, but he pushed it back again.

::   ::

That night at dinner I had a bereft, deprived feeling. There was no Kishi for company, not a hint of him. I sat alone surrounded by those determined eaters and had, for the first time, to gamble on the food from an unintelligible menu. On the whole the results weren't any worse than usual and I left the room with a replete if not totally contented feeling, settling down in the lobby with *The Rise and Fall of the Third Reich*, which I had brought along for light reading. The chairs out here were more comfortable than the one in my room and I didn't want to go to bed. In about an hour a loudspeaker summoned me to the phone, and it was Florie.

She asked me if I'd had a good day and I said interesting. There was something faintly distracted about our conversation, two people who are going to meet soon and who have been together recently without much happening in between which could be talked about on a telephone. She'd had a busy day, too, with more in-patients than usual. I gathered there had been no attentions paid to her of an unusual kind. She was looking forward to the theatre to-morrow night and so was I. She hoped I'd sleep well and I hoped she would too.

"Paul, you're all right, aren't you?"

"Of course. Couldn't be better."

"Oh. Well . . . good night, then."

I went back to the Third Reich, and became absorbed. A noise made me look up. Kishimura was now inside the glass doors to the almost deserted lobby.

A Japanese can never disguise the fact that he is lit, and they don't really try. Kishi came heaving over to me like a sampan in a typhoon, his face glowing. He bellowed from high living.

"Ah! Harris!"

"Hallo, friend. Had a busy day selling shoes that go chug, chug, chug?"

He sank into a chair and let out a long wheezing sigh. The general air of dissipation about him stopped at the neck. Below this point he was impeccably dressed in a neat almost black suit which was quite unrumpled. He thrust out his legs.

"I am at Japanese Embassy," he announced.

"Oh yes? Quite a party?"

"I drink *saké* from much dullness."

"Indeed."

"Ambassador very dull. First Secretary very dull. All dull."

"It's a kind of diplomatic disease. But we have to remember that they don't really like business men.'"

"So, so, so. Don't like Kishi. Vulgar mans. Not good families."

"Aren't you?"

"I am working boy. Osaka. Embassy all Tokyo. Oh, so good family. Imperial University. Kishi no university. Working boy. Kishi like geisha."

He then gave a rather deft imitation in mouth music

of the *samisen*, plucking empty air with his fingers, after which he sang the words:

> " '*Hana michi no uta ga,*
> *Odori mono kara,*
> *Yoi, yoi, yoi!*' "

He lay back and beamed at me.

"You translate, Harris. You translate."

He sang it again, so I'd get it.

"The flower walk song from the dancing girl is pretty good," I said.

Kishi clapped his hands, very loudly. The sound echoed in the austerely functional lobby which was no setting for dissipations. The man at the desk was looking at us as though they didn't see so many middle-aged party boys these days.

"Oh! Clever Harris. You know Japanese so clearly."

"I'm not bad at nursery rhymes."

I went over to the desk and asked for a pot of hot coffee. Surprisingly, the clerk seemed to get that at once and the coffee came with remarkable speed, brought by one of the waiters from the dining-room who looked at Kishi as though at a nicely-staged demonstration of one of the reasons why capitalism was toppling. Didn't anyone in China get drunk any more? It was a sad thought.

In about twenty minutes I judged that Kishi was ready for the lift and took him over. He was walking better but still exuberant.

"In Japan we have good party . . . eh, Harris, eh?"

He nudged me in the ribs.

"I'm ready for anything you'll pay for."

"I pay, sure. When we come from China freely."

That was a thought, about coming from China freely. It wasn't one I was allowing myself to dwell on. And the party mood hadn't reached me at all, not after that session with the Third Reich.

I shut us into the box and pressed the floor button. Kishi stood swaying slightly, humming under his breath still the song of the flower walk maidens.

"I'm a little troubled about Mr. Obata," I said.

I could have sworn then from the way his head came up that he wasn't drunk at all. There was a complete focusing on me.

"Maybe you've been consulting your Embassy about your missing countryman, Kishi? A bit of a problem, isn't it? It bothers me. What motivates the man? Whose orders is he taking?"

"I . . . I not understand."

"Well . . . yesterday he was on the scene to have me beaten up. But to-day was quite different. He was out for a kill, your Obata. He's a good shot, too. Damn good. Oh, here's our floor."

We went down the passage side by side. I nodded to Kishi and slid the key into my lock. He stood rigid by his door as though he couldn't leave things just like this. But I could. I went in.

There was one soft light burning, the table-lamp by the bed. In the only chair was Miss Feng. She was wearing my Yokohama silk dressing-gown and it suited her better than it had ever suited me. She smiled.

Someone pretty high up, much higher than Chow, had organised this. And Miss Feng had volunteered for the duty of seeing that I really did relax. Just at this moment I couldn't see one little reason why I shouldn't.

CHAPTER X

FLORIE YIN CAME INTO the reinforced concrete foyer of the theatre looking like a fashion plate. But an old fashion plate, circa nineteen fifty or earlier. Three-quarter length Russian sables and an apricot-coloured *cheongsam* to the floor shouldn't date, but they do. The furs were cut square on the shoulders for one thing, which gave even their lushness a quasi-military look. She was wearing a lot of make-up.

Florie came to where I was against a pillar and kissed me, which was quite a demonstration. People have never kissed much in China and I was damn sure it was now on the prohibited list. We were getting a lot of stares, and Florie knew it. This was a performance. She stepped back from me.

"Paul! You look smooth. As though you'd been enjoying yourself."

"I usually contrive to wherever I go. Is there any reason I shouldn't in China?"

"Of course not! I'm glad."

But somehow she didn't sound glad. She sounded just a little like a woman who suspects you may be having fun outwith her careful plans for you. It's a tone men of my age recognise pretty easily.

"What an occasion," Florie said, with a suggestion of slightly breathless brightness. "You know I don't go to the theatre much. I couldn't be said to have a night life at all."

"So you told me. But from the look of things here maybe you're not keeping up with the trends."

"Maybe I'm not."

She looked around then, as though noticing the crowd for the first time. It was quite a crowd, too, a fair sprinkling of women, some of them in their best People's two-piece serge but a considerable number reverting to the older ways and in a best which was pretty good. There were some jewels glittering in ears and rings. And about half the women at least didn't look as though they had ever done a refresher course on a mud-carrying scheme. After all, Comrade Mao was in retirement on a farm somewhere and it might be getting all right in the capital to wash and even put on a face.

There was considerable noise from voices and half-muted loudspeakers rendering a selection of classical Chinese cat torture. There was even laughter. But, of course, this lot could afford to laugh, they were the top of the bottle. I wondered then whether we had stumbled into a Commissars' Night at the Kiangsi Opera or whether the masses hadn't yet been raised up to this level of æsthetic appreciation.

"I'd like a double whisky," I said.

"Well, you can't have it, Paul."

"I know. I was just expressing a wish."

"There are soft drinks. Though we haven't invented Coca-Cola here yet."

"Maybe we shouldn't be taking this line," I suggested. Florie smiled.

"I want to. I'm feeling aggressive."

This was borne out quite clearly about twenty minutes later when we went into the auditorium. Our seats were already occupied by two gentlemen in clean serge with shaven heads and fleshy jowls. Florie held the tickets, checked the numbers carefully, and then launched into

a flow of Chinese which surprised me and everyone
within a considerable radius. I didn't need to understand the words to know that she was putting it out hot
and fast. She stood there with the sables hanging open
and diamonds flashing in her ears, not looking in the least
like one of the world's workers and not intending to be
mistaken for one, either. It was a Yin who was putting
on this act, and it began to scare me. The sensible,
behind one of the totalitarian curtains, don't seek out the
limelight in quite this way.

Florie shoved those tickets under the nose of one of the
shaven heads. Both the gentlemen had coloured up and
were shouting back in parade ground voices, but Florie
covered them. She went up a couple of octaves to do it.

I tugged at the sables.

"There's four empty seats in the row behind. It might
be quite a simple mistake, Florie."

"Those are not our seats! These are!"

Then the burst of Chinese again. It's a wonderful
language for a row, rich in tonal variations, and Florie
was sounding like heavy action on the top keys of a
Wurlitzer with all the stops out. Suddenly, to my total
surprise, she won. The two tidily clad gents just got up
and moved out into the aisle. Florie scarcely gave them
time to get clear before she started to take possession.

"Absolute brass neck!" she said, sinking down.

"Did the Yins used to take the whole theatre when
they wanted to see a show?" I whispered.

"This was a simple matter of our seats!"

"I'd hate to have you on the other side in a war."

"Do I look a wreck, Paul? Anger doesn't improve a
woman of my age."

"You look like a million silver dollars."

She got out a compact, peered into it, and said "Oh, damn!" loudly, then began repairs with an absorbed diligence. I have an old-fashioned thing about hating women to do in public what they've already spent two hours doing before they left home. And this time we were being stared at from all sides. I was very glad indeed when the orchestra started up and the lights dimmed.

I loved the Kiangsi Opera from the moment the curtain went up. At once we were given splendid fantasy from which all austerity had been swept away, glittering embroidered robes and towering, tinsel sparkling headdresses. The accompaniment was a rhythmic thumping through which sneaked the thin squeaking of fiddles and honking noises from tin horns. It was a sudden, enticing shambles of sound and prancing and mime, with human voices squeezed out of deliberately malformed larynxes and colour a kind of delicious lunacy. You could tell who the baddies were at once by drab clothes and the way the paint was put on their faces. Innocence shone with splendour and tottered about the stage in chronic helplessness, waving pale little hands. There were actors in glaring devil masks with dyed horsehair flowing out the top, and wicked old men, and handsome young ones, practically everyone singing at the same time while patterns of stylised, slow, sweeping dances went on in the background. Every now and then there was a lull when Miss Trembling Flower came up to the footlights and told us what a terrible time she was having in a nerve-shattering falsetto. Rudolf Bing wouldn't have wanted to book her for the Metropolitan but I thought she was cute, especially when she was doing a fan unfolding and scarf undulating solo in silence except for the tin horns. The girl had something of the look of Miss Feng, the same suggestion of innocence, a slightly tinkling convention, pretty to play with.

"Do you really like it *that* much?" Florie said.

I hadn't known she was looking at me.

"It's got everything I really need in a floor show."

"This is art!" Florie hissed.

"Okay, I still like it."

At the first interval there were refreshments brought right into the theatre, some kind of orange drink and biscuits. There were also hot towels with which to wipe away all traces of your excitement. I was glad to see these again, a little ball of steaming towel whizzing through the air to a customer in the middle of the third row. You wiped your face and hands and then sent it whizzing back again. The few accidents which occurred didn't worry anyone. There weren't any what you could call elaborate hair-dos about which might get damaged.

"I don't suppose I could buy you chocolates?"

"No," said Florie. "I'll take a cigarette."

Not many people were going out into the foyer. I looked around at the privileged company, with the idea of assessing it. Right behind Florie was Mei Lan.

She was wearing her sponged serge and still had her cap on. I gave her a smile for a gala evening and got the usual negative reaction.

"Enjoying it, Miss Mei?"

"Who on earth . . . ?" Florie began, twisting. " Oh!"

Mei Lan gave me a look which requested that I turn around again. It was the first request I'd had from her and I obliged.

"What extraordinary eyes that girl's got," Florie said,

turning down the volume, but not far enough. "It almost gives you the feeling she could be interesting . . . if she had a chance."

"I find her interesting now."

"Yes, Paul dear. But isn't that your reaction to all women under fifty who aren't wall-eyed?"

We looked at each other. The orchestra started up again and we were down in a little well made by noise round about. The lights went out. I put out my hand and found Florie's. For a moment her fingers tightened around mine but she let go quickly.

We didn't get out of our seats until the last interval. And then we didn't go into the foyer where the mob was, but to one of two arcades designed for summer coolness, which ran down the sides of the auditorium and were reached by rounded arches. Not many other people were out here and we walked up and down smoking. Then we had a look at the crowd in the main lobby. At the edge of it was Humbold. It looked as though everyone who was anybody in Peking came to the opera. He had spotted us, and for a moment I saw him hesitate. He glanced around before he came over. We waited for him, Florie seeing the man's sudden decision as plainly as I did.

"Opera lover, too, are you?" I asked.

Humbold didn't smile.

"The season ends pretty soon. I'd missed them earlier."

"Have you met Dr. Yin? You've certainly talked to her on the phone."

His eyes showed nothing. He bowed. Florie barely nodded her head. She was staring at the man, still in her aggressive mood.

"Thanks for all that putting me in the picture about

Paul, Mr. Humbold. I hope I didn't react in any way useful to you?"

"As a matter of fact you didn't, Dr. Yin."

"Good." Florie smiled. She was suddenly very sweet. "And how is your wife these days? Not with you to-night?"

Humbold had to swallow before he said anything.

"No, she's not with me."

"Still busy with her People's Courts, is she?" Florie turned to me. "I didn't place Mr. Humbold at first. Not until this moment. He is married to Tai Tsao, a celebrated jurist of the New Order. Am I right?"

"She's a judge, yes," Humbold admitted, not liking this.

"A very famous judge."

Florie laughed. Humbold had never appealed to me at any time, but at that moment he almost had my sympathy. It didn't require any unusual powers of observation to see that the man had suddenly begun to sweat, physically and mentally. Under Florie's eyes he was acutely miserable. He was, in fact, being firmly pigeon-holed by a Yin. I wondered what had brought him over, to be stung.

Florie put a hand on my arm, a little signal. I nodded to Humbold and we turned away.

"What's all this?" I said in the passage.

"You mean Tai Tsao? She's a female butcher."

"What?"

"I wouldn't know how many she has condemned to death. I knew she was married to a European newsman. I didn't hitch it up, though, until this moment. Bells rang."

"People's Courts? You mean . . ."

"I meant just what I said. If you go before Tai Tsao you've had it. She's been a bit quiescent recently. We haven't heard so much about her. Her great time was just after the Ten Thousand Flowers Unfolding. You heard about that?"

"Yes. A period of constructive criticism and flowering of the arts."

"Purging of them, you mean. Paul, it was horrible. People I knew. They were shot. Some of them condemned by Tai Tsao."

"What a hellish situation for Humbold!"

"Why do you say that? He's one of them, isn't he?"

"Where on earth did he meet her?"

"I believe at the London School of Economics."

I stood quite still staring at her.

"If you're thinking that's a funny place for a jurist to be trained let me tell you it doesn't matter these days . . . about training. It's just your zeal that counts. Tai Tsao has plenty of that. Plenty. I've never seen her. I don't want to. But they say she is quite good-looking. In her thirties, but still attractive. She went to London on a Chiang Kai Shek scholarship. But she came back to China to climb on the other bus."

It occurred to me then that Humbold's wife might be scheduled to emerge again into the full blaze of publicity at my trial. It was a delightful thought to have hit you before the last act of an evening at the theatre.

The warning bell went. Florie and I were walking towards the arch nearest our seats when Mei Lan came into the passage, bent over in one of her spasms of coughing. She had her hands to her face, palms pressed into her cheeks, as though she was trying to squeeze away the fit.

"That's more than a heavy cold," I said.

Florie paused, looking at the girl. Then she went up to her, saying something sharply in Chinese. Mei Lan's head moved in a gesture of refusal. Florie rapped out the words again. The girl pressed back against the wall as though she couldn't organise herself to resist. Florie was crisp.

"I'm telling your interpreter, Paul, to go to the nearest clinic for a check-up. I would say she is running a fairly high temperature now. She ought to be in bed."

"I doubt if there's anyone to carry trays where Miss Mei has to go to bed."

The girl looked at me. And so did Florie. Florie said:

"There are excellent medical services."

"For everyone who needs them?"

I didn't get a direct answer to that. Florie opened her bag.

"I'll give her a note to a friend of mine in the Peking General Hospital."

"No!" Mei Lan's protest was in English. "Please leave me alone. I don't want your note! I don't want . . ."

It was the first really human reaction I'd seen, or at least which had leaked into words. Mei Lan looked now as though she was afraid of us both. I could have held the power to do her irreparable damage and for a moment, from those green eyes, I had the feeling that I might already have done this. It was as though, all the time, there had been someone else hiding behind that façade of apparent self-discipline, someone totally different and vulnerable.

"If we're going to get to our seats before the lights go out . . ." Florie began.

And then there was someone else beside us. There was a great blare up of music from the auditorium and Mei Lan was staring. In her eyes was a kind of terror, but something else as well.

I turned and saw one of the actors, a villain from the drab of his clothes and the painted browns and ochres of his face. The man was standing there, totally ignoring us, staring at the girl against the wall.

"Mei Lan!"

She used Chinese. She was telling him to go away, I knew that. Instead he took a step towards her. The girl's hand came up in a gesture that tried to be dismissal but didn't succeed.

"Mei Lan!" It was a shout from the actor.

The girl babbled then. She wasn't being coherent, or it didn't look like it. She put up her hands again as though to hide her face and her identity.

"Well!" Florie said.

"What is it?"

The actor was standing close in to the girl. Florie kept her voice low.

"It seems your little interpreter used to be a performer with this company."

The lights in the corridor dimmed and went out altogether in the auditorium. There was the din of voices from the stage, the drama in there rolling again. So was our own little private performance. The actor had his hand on Mei Lan's arm now, pulling her away from the wall, and she was struggling against him.

"Here!" I said.

For the first time the actor looked at me. In the dimness he was completely hidden by make-up, camouflaged under swirls of paint.

"Mei Lan my friend," he said in English. "She must come! She must come!"

"Where?"

"To meet all friend. There!"

He pointed to a door at the end of the corridor, certainly leading back-stage. Florie made the curious yapping noises of Chinese impatience and the actor swinging around, made them back at her. Similar noises were coming from the stage now, though much amplified. The actor let go of Mei Lan's arm and began to use his hands, in explanatory gesticulations which didn't help me much.

"Florie, what the hell . . . ?"

"She was a featured player. Your interpreter."

Mei Lan was crying. Her body had crumpled. She was somehow folded over and much smaller, a child in that terrible drab serge, weeping in a kind of total despair. The actor caught her arms again, tugging her towards him, the girl resisting. It had the slight unreality of mime, with its underscored emphasis, as though the actor simply had to make the most of a scene, even a private one. And he had an audience of two.

"Why doesn't she go?" I asked Florie.

"Don't be silly, Paul. You're her assignment. She can't leave you."

"Then let's all go back-stage."

"What?"

"Do you good, Florie. Broaden your experience. Make you glad you're a doctor."

"I'm not going back there. . . ."

"It might be entertaining."

The actor turned the mime on to me. He stood with one leg a little back, taking his body's weight, and both hands lifted. He might have been holding it for cameras. I rather liked this total devotion to his art. It made you wonder what he'd be like at breakfast, chopsticks descending into rice bowl in the sweep to indicate wind on western mountain. Maybe it bored his wife, but it certainly made a change from the utility world outside this theatre.

"You come?" he asked. "To bring Mei Lan you come?"

"Yes."

"No, Paul. I absolutely refuse to go back-stage. I'm just not interested."

"Well, you watch the show out front. Forgive me if I don't take you back to our seats. And I shouldn't be long."

"This is nuts!" she said.

Florie's English was slightly period, like her clothes. There were a lot of refreshers she needed.

Mei Lan had stopped crying. I knew what she wanted right then, it was to get back into a world beyond that door at the end of the passage, a world she had somehow lost. My curiosity was sharp. It was luck that the actor knew English. I could learn a lot and he looked the chatty type.

"Cheerio," I said to Florie.

"I'll go home, Paul!"

"That would be rather silly. I'm not deserting you for long."

"You don't know what you might be getting into!"

"That's why I've always gone through interesting-looking doors."

Florie came with us. And Mei Lan had suddenly given up all protest. She was totally out of the role which had been so carefully maintained to me, looking now like the child just by the pay desk at the circus, all the reality of being alive funnelled down into the time which lay immediately ahead. It was almost as though she had forgotten what she had become. The actor had her hand and she hung on to him.

"Rather sweet," I said to Florie, who didn't reply.

We went through the door and it shut, cutting off a crowd of watchers. The theatre had clearly been built by the New Order, as something of a publicity gesture, and everything was grandiose, even this concrete walled passage, with distant roof lights. We passed doors set in the walls and then a kind of asbestos sliding one.

This was back-stage. It was a massive clutter, of people and objects, cables about, and scenery ready for the next move. Actors were doing things to their faces in mirrors held by assistants, there were prompt men in the wings, and irritated-looking stage-hands rushing about. The place was like a vast barn, and the stage was a revolving one with prepared sets waiting to be swung around into position. No one took the slightest notice of us for a time, Mei Lan just standing there, still holding the actor's hand in a manner which didn't suggest Chinese patterns at all.

The din from the performance was very loud indeed. All this was a kind of echo of what was happening beyond, a concentration on it. Three girls in vast headdresses, were standing quite still while an old woman, with bound feet, and wearing black, did something to their costumes. I saw the old woman turn, perhaps from something said by one of the actresses. She had pins in her mouth, and a battered face under oiled, jet-dyed hair brought back into a tight bun. She stared. Then she spat out the pins and moved.

It wasn't a hobble she used over to us, just progress delayed artificially, an unnatural impediment put on nature. She couldn't use her feet in any ordinary way but those little twisted pegs in tight silk slippers carried her heavy weight slowly, controlling a sudden eagerness in the rest of her body. She put out both her hands, tottering towards Mei Lan.

The girl ran to her. They didn't kiss. It was as though Mei Lan held the woman. Out on the stage someone screamed a solo and I couldn't hear anything, only see a wrinkled face lifted to a young one. The actor was beside them. The three chorus-girls closed in, too. A couple of stage-hands came over. A male dancer, moving out of the wings, stopped, then ran. The crowd swelled around Mei Lan. The actor put up his hand and pulled off that immovable cap.

Mei Lan hadn't any hair, it was cropped short. She stood amongst them, circled, but still alone, and her hands moved, the red little hands.

"What happened to her?" I said to Florie.

"She disgraced herself on tour. Abroad. In Singapore."

"What?"

"I don't know the details. That's what the actor said."

Florie and I were forgotten. I didn't mind at all, but it looked as though Florie wasn't used to this. She went on standing while I sat down on a packing-case. The amplified speakers were making a hideous row, covering everything that happened back here, so that we didn't hear any of the babble going on about Mei Lan at all. She went on standing, circled, and every now and then the old woman put out a hand and touched Mei Lan's face.

A spectacular number came to an end out beyond us

and back-stage suddenly filled up. So did the circle around Mei Lan. It was a mob now. I heard the thin whining of fiddles and again the voice of the little girl I had liked in the show, Miss Innocence doing her stuff out there right up against the footlights. But suddenly she had a rival, and it was Mei Lan.

I didn't get what was happening at first, only saw a flare up of commotion, a bustling. Someone had a robe, another a headdress, and then the actor, pushed out of the limelight, remembered us and came over. He was beaming.

"We are all greatly happy." He nodded at me. "My name Hang Ling. This Mei Lan's song."

"What?"

"She sing this song. In many times."

Mei Lan was protesting now, but the headdress was on her shaved head, and someone had put a dragon-embroidered imperial yellow robe on top of the serge, enveloping her.

"She sing. You come."

Hang Ling took us over. There was a little clearing about Mei Lan now and she was still protesting. Then she seemed to listen to that chirruping, amplified singing from out front. Her mouth opened and Mei Lan's voice was only a little cheep almost covered by the official rendering. She began to move, as though the music offered her no choice, the weight of the piled up, glittering headdress making its own challenge. Her hands came up. You didn't notice the chilblains any more. Mei Lan was for a time the understudy of Miss Innocence out there at the footlights, and then she was more than that. It was her song and she took it. She began the dance that was part of the act, a feet-stationary swaying of her body.

It didn't seem possible she was still wearing that serge. Then I saw tears coming out of her green eyes and running down her cheeks.

Hang Ling made a noise at my elbow. He was crying too. A nice fellow. Even with the ochre and brown disguise you knew where you were with him.

"She used to do this number?"

The actor nodded.

"Sure, sure. Always she do."

"What's the song about?"

"Ah! Sad she-dragon."

"I didn't quite get that?"

His eyes stayed on Mei Lan.

"Song now saying . . . I am light as feather morals, perhaps, maybe, so it seems. I follow undutiful course in my heart. I follow love. Not good guide."

"The she-dragon says this?"

"Sure, sure."

He wanted to listen and watch. I didn't bother him. After all, I couldn't be expected to really grasp this. Only the Chinese could believe in a she-dragon with a complicated sex life. It brought tears to their eyes too.

It didn't bring any to Florie's. I wasn't greatly taken with her expression then. She was looking more than slightly like the great lady brought suddenly into company which she has heretofore felt it policy to ignore as a factor in the human scene. Florie wasn't the sort who came back-stage at all.

I looked at my interpreter. There was no make-up on Mei Lan's face, but I could see her ready for this act, with hours of work behind her for it; the dead white face, the green eyes framed in black, a red slit mouth and hands that weren't a worker's, probably with gold nail-shields. Little she-dragon. It was possible to understand Hang Ling's tears. I began to feel myself that I might have caught cold out there by the canal.

This was Mei Lan's world from which she had suddenly been cut off. She might even have been with this company from childhood, perfectly safe in it, remote from political upheavals, privileged. And then something happened. I had to find out what. I tugged Hang Ling's sleeve.

"Why did she leave you?"

He never took his eyes off the girl, but he leaned nearer to me.

"She become lover."

"Is that serious?"

"Great trouble. It is Singapore. Chinese Towkay. Mei Lan wish to stay. You see?"

"Mei Lan fell in love with a Chinese Towkay in Singapore and wanted to stay there?"

"Yes."

"What about the Towkay?"

"He rich man. He wish, too. Most greatly. He take Mei Lan for number two wife."

Hang Ling didn't sound as shocked by this reactionary set-up as he ought to have done. But I could imagine how it must have irritated the Head Commissar for Export Culture. They had been to vast trouble and expense to send the Kiangsi Opera abroad to help spread the gospel of the new Chinese way and a prominent member of the cast had been willing to chuck all contemporary ideology overboard and settle for a very old-fashioned type of Chinese domestic nest. Humiliating to put it mildly. An old-style Towkay picks up singing-dancing girl to help maintain the youth he feels to be slipping a bit. The only difference from Hollywood is that you don't put out your number one in order to bring in number two, you let established wife getting plump continue to eat your rice while you add a new wing to the Chinese equivalent of a ranch-type family home. It's quite a humane system, really, and it cuts out the social problem of the ageing divorcée who can't seem to locate herself. In the old China she didn't even have to move her potted plants, only learn to smile politely now and then towards the new version of what she had looked like eighteen years or so ago. A little disturbing at first, perhaps, but women are realists, and it is all so much less painful than upsetting domestic arrangements which habit has made comfortable. Most men continue to want their first wives, too, it's only the conventions of the West which makes her inaccessible by divorce. How often I have longed to say to the distraught spouses of my friends . . . "It's only his glands, dear. Just let him have a little house in the garden and you'll soon all settle down." But perhaps I have too Oriental an outlook.

The she-dragon song went on for a long time, both front and back-stage, and I grew a shade impatient. There were a number of questions I wanted to ask, but Hang Ling looked so rapt I had to invent the answers. It wasn't too difficult. Down there in Singapore Mei Lan must have leaked her plan to retire from public entertaining, possibly to her best friend, and the consequences of this had been immediate. She was pounced on, hustled to the airport, and flown out of the country in black disgrace. Further, once back in China she was sentenced to corrective training which, judging from her hands, had meant heavy manual work. Perhaps mud carrying.

Poor Mei Lan. I could understand her fear now, and that total apparent elimination of all personality which had covered it. She had been on probation with me, in a new job, and had to succeed or the mud carrying was waiting again. No wonder there were still tears on her cheeks, for a life lost, for a known security smashed up all around her. It was cruel for her to get this feel of old security again.

I turned around to Florie. There was no sign of her at all. She must have gone back to her seat. I should have followed her then, and I would have gone with her if she had asked to go back, but now I hung on, with just the smallest hint of being glad Florie had decided all this was not for her. She was probably angry with me. I couldn't help that, I had to wait.

After Mei Lan's song there was a small party. The Kiangsi Opera was privileged, with access to alcoholic refreshment, and little stone bottles of wine began to appear. Characters went off for their turn on stage and then came back in a hurry for a quick one. Hang Ling disappeared at one point, too, and on his return came to break up the solitude in which I had been left. Either applause or the wine had put him in a good mood. He beamed at me, showing wonderful teeth.

"You like Peking now?"

"Bits of it, very much."

He was travelled, was Hang. South-East Asia, Japan, Paris, Vienna and Nasser's Cairo. He told me, waving his hands, that he understood all cultures, that the creative type had to be able to do this. China mustn't hide behind any wall, he said. In Moscow he had been overpowered by the Russian ballet and while in Singapore had attended what must have been an amateur performance of The Wine Drinking Party of Mr. Eliot. That had been a big night too.

I liked Hang. He asked how old I thought him and I said thirty. He told me forty-five. He kept young, under all that make-up, by an ancient Chinese system of muscular bowel agitation. Constipation was something he had never known. I said alcohol was laxative, too, but though we both laughed I don't think he got that one. As that last act moved to its noisy finale Mei Lan held court back-stage and I sat on my packing-case with Hang.

He loved Mei Lan like a brother. Until her misfortune she had been in the company from the age of eleven, first in child roles. Her green eyes came from an Irishman who had sneaked into the Mei family somewhere about the First World War. More than that he couldn't, or wouldn't, say, but the girl herself was a hundred per cent Chinese. What had happened to her down south was just a bad case of getting your dynasties mixed. You acted in one period and had to live in another. It wasn't really surprising that the girl had taken a set of values from classic drama and tried to apply them outside the theatre. A cardinal sin, of course. The old traditions were of historical interest only, and while you perpetuated them in fancy costumes you were also expected to keep upsides with the latest wrinkles in the new ideology, too. Awfully easy to slip, the way the girl had done. And Hang became solemn at the thought of this.

"Will she get back to you one day?" I asked.

He shook his head. And I knew why. Mei Lan was labelled now with that old Stalin tag of bourgeois deviationism. She had become a lover.

I wasn't really looking at the party when it suddenly stopped. There was no cessation of sound, the stage show

saw to that, but a stillness came none the less, a frozen
suspended moment. I saw everyone staring towards the
door behind me, and before I could turn my head Yang
came past, making straight for Mei Lan. He moved so
quickly that I was still on the packing-case when he hit
her the first time. She didn't fall, indeed she was making
some kind of effort to keep standing, perhaps part of the
official punishment patter, that you stood up to it. She
was standing up, a girl with a headdress knocked off,
wide-eyed with terror, wrapped in an imperial yellow
robe. Yang hit her again before I moved. This time Mei
went down. She put her hands up to her head as she
fell.

I caught Yang by the scruff of his neck, but it didn't
do any good. I hadn't half turned him about when there
was something else, sensed more than seen from a corner
of my eye, a rifle butt coming straight at the side of my
head.

CHAPTER XI

THE FIRST THING I heard was Florie's voice saying:

"Well, he hasn't got concussion, at any rate."

I opened my eyes. My tongue felt outsize and furred. I was on some kind of a sofa and Florie was looking down. So was Humbold. Neither of them seemed in any great state of agitation. Florie might have been at the end of a long tiring spell in an out-patients' department, with that look of the professional healer who is badly in need of a long glass of alcoholic boost.

"So you've joined us," she said.

"Who was that . . . with the rifle?"

"A policeman."

"And Mei Lan?"

"We can't tell you."

"What do you mean?"

"Paul, for heaven's sake, stop threshing about."

I wanted to stop right then. My neck felt as though someone had put it in red-hot plaster. But I didn't have to move it to see Humbold. I stared at him, not discomposing the man in the least by that stare.

"Where do you come in on this?"

Florie answered.

"Mr. Humbold did quite a strong-man act. He carried you from back-stage. I only made a gesture with your feet. But he had all the work."

Florie didn't find me endearing at the moment, that was plain.

"Did you see Mei Lan?" I asked Humbold.

"Yes. When the business started."

"You mean . . . you came in with the police?"

"Exactly."

"Somebody must have brought Yang and his bully boys back there. Was it you, Humbold?"

"No. I just followed. I'm a reporter, remember. We make a point of following when we see police clearly bound on serious business."

"Did Yang go on beating Mei Lan?"

"No. There wasn't any need. She wasn't resisting. I think he took her away with him."

"You think . . . ?"

"I was rather involved with you, Harris. That policeman looked as though he was going to use the rifle butt again. Even though you were down."

"You stopped him?"

"I don't expect a medal. I'm not even after a statement from you. But you can forget about the girl."

"What do you mean?"

"It's highly improbable you'll ever see her again. I don't think she qualified as an interpreter."

I shut my eyes. I could see Mei Lan, with that peeled head hidden under towering gilt and tinsel, doing her number. I could also see a line of human mud carriers going up a slope, silhouetted against the sky. I felt sick. I also felt responsible in some way. I couldn't identify my responsibility, but it was there.

"It might be a good idea if you tried to sit up," Florie said. "Only do it slowly. We want to get you back to my surgery as soon as possible."

I took it slowly all right. We were in some kind of private office, very austere, equipped with sofa, desk and straight-backed chairs. Perhaps theatre managers in China are issued with sofas.

"Where are the police, Florie?"

"Mr. Humbold got rid of them somehow. He seems to have influence. With any luck you won't have to explain why you assaulted this Yang until to-morrow morning. That's what we hope at any rate. Though we haven't looked outside this door recently."

"Is the show over?"

"About half an hour ago," Humbold said. Then he added: "If you'll stay with him, Dr. Yin, I'll bring my car round."

Florie stayed with me. She sat in the manager's chair which had her sables draped over it. She didn't look pleased with me at all. She had cause not to be and the enforced relation with Humbold probably wasn't something she liked much.

"Sorry about this, Florie."

She looked at me from her distance.

"Why did you have to go back-stage?"

"I was curious about Mei Lan."

Florie found her bag and a cigarette. She didn't offer me one.

"Oh, I know. Madly exciting. Your drab little interpreter with green eyes turns out to have a past with the Kiangsi Opera. Romantic."

"When did you leave me?" I asked.

She blew out smoke, slowly.

"I got tired of Miss Mei's performance. I didn't think it was all that good. I went back to my seat. Mr. Humbold came and got me out of it, presumably because a doctor was needed. You're lucky not to be locked up now in a police cell."

When Humbold came back his eyes held a kind of flat, studied calm.

"There doesn't seem to be any reason why we shouldn't just walk out to the car," he said.

Florie and I went in the back, with Humbold like a chauffeur in his applied remoteness. We weren't any of us talking, but it seemed to me that our driver was concentrating on his job with a degree of application one doesn't usually see these days. Nothing slap-happy about Humbold at all. He was using that driving mirror like a learner watched over by the official tester. It occurred to me that he didn't want to be followed tonight, and I wondered why. Though I didn't know the city very well any more, Humbold appeared to be approaching Florie's place with a certain deviousness. And he clearly didn't like that parking in the lane by her gate.

But he came in with us and sat in Florie's drawing-room while she took me through to a surgery in the clinic. She was very professional suddenly, dabbing things on the bump.

"Don't put on a bandage or plaster. It'll just draw attention to the bump."

"I wasn't going to. You should be better in the morning, though you won't be moving your head about much for a while. I'll give you something to make you sleep."

"Florie, I'm sorry about to-night."

"It's all right. I'm sorry I panicked."

"Did you?"

"I think so. Inside myself, anyway. Maybe it was the way those policemen looked at me. I've kept myself safe for so long, remember. The Yin bravado suddenly got used up and left me with a cold feeling. But I've got over it."

"Are you thinking about getting out of China?"

Our eyes met.

"Would you help me to?"

"Yes."

"Smuggle me out?"

"Don't be silly. There's nothing I could do in Peking. But Robert's organisation hasn't broken up. If you could get to Canton they would take over. You've only got to say you'll do it."

"I can't give you an answer to-night. And anyway, the way things are you mayn't find it so easy to get out yourself. Paul, I've been thinking about it in the car. If you really get into trouble I'm not going to sit on the sidelines. I couldn't anyway."

"I don't think there's much you could do, Florie."

"I'm not so sure. I'm not without influence. In fact I've got some friends in surprisingly high places."

"You'd use them on my behalf?"

"Of course, you fool!"

She came out with us. Under the bright light at the gate I saw Humbold looking at her as though she didn't spark off a great deal of enthusiasm with him. It wasn't surprising in view of the things Florie had said of his wife. He was probably sensitive about being married to a successful jurist. One of those marriages that have special strains, with hubby playing second fiddle to celebrity. It is not a situation a reactionary like me could have endured easily. There may, of course, be men who like it all right, but I've never met them.

I sat in front this time and we went down the lane.

"It's a clear night," Humbold said. "Like to see the Temple of Heaven by moonlight?"

"Is that a suggestion to make to a convalescent?"

"I want to talk to you. In China you don't just park a car and do that. You have an alibi."

"From a man with sunk roots that's almost a criticism."

Humbold didn't say anything. He just assumed the excursion was on, and in about ten minutes we went under one of the gates and out into the new city, in the direction of the legation quarter. Here the roads were wide, built for parades, and flanked with buildings that had balconies tacked on to them so that party big shots could watch marching hordes in comfort, supported by a room behind them where there would certainly be a selection of soul-sustaining fancy food and drink.

To say that I was curious about Humbold was putting it mildly. In spite of the ache at the base of my skull I wouldn't have missed this bit of nocturnal tourism for anything. I got out of the car with him and we walked up the long, impressive approaches to a white marble pavilion which emperors had used for communion with their near relations, the gods. And that marble somehow wasn't cold looking, it had something of the translucence of alabaster, as though illumined by a faint glow. There was a lot of snow about, but you never lost the marble in that duller shimmering at all.

We walked on its terrible purity, up a long route of designed isolation, with nothing really to lift the eyes, just a great, gleaming wheel laid on the ground, the approach routes the spokes, the temple pavilion its low hub.

One of the sights of the world, probably, and I was conscious of it as that, you couldn't help being, but more conscious of Humbold walking beside me, wrapped up in a curiously awkward withdrawal. It was a little like being with a man who had dropped his old identity and hadn't assumed another.

"What's your assignment?" I said. "To pump me?"

It was the first thing said since we moved on to marble.

"You think I've got a job to do?"

"Yes. Just like you had a job to do that night they murdered poor McVey."

"So you believe it was murder?"

"So do you. And you know he visited me."

"All right! Let's leave it at that."

"I don't mind. The poor devil's dead. But I'll tell you one thing you may have wondered about. Unless they tortured it out of him before they broke his neck. McVey wanted to get out of China."

I noticed Humbold was avoiding the cracks between the slabs.

"I want to get out of China, too," he said.

It was cold. A deep breath chilled you, sinking into your guts. But I took one.

"If this is a brilliant dodge, Humbold, to get me to bare my little heart to you, try again."

"My wife told me to-night she's chucking me out."

"Come again?"

"You heard me. I'm being booted out. A divorce. To clear the decks. Dr. Yin told you all about my wife. I could see her doing it. I was watching your backs. Quite notorious, my wife. People like Dr. Yin wouldn't meet her socially, I'm sure."

"What the hell is this, Humbold?"

"I'm telling you. The skids are under me. My wife is getting rid of a political embarrassment. There had been signs enough before, but to-night I really knew. Just before the opera. My wife was to come with me. But under the circumstances changed her mind. My little wife has made her last public appearance with me."

"What were the other signs?"

"Oh, a lot. Mainly restriction of movement. I used to be quite free. Then last month my pass to the opening of Hupei Dam was suddenly cancelled. No reason. They don't bother to give reasons. Incidentally, that little talk we had the other night about Stalinism didn't help."

"It wasn't meant to."

His head jerked round.

"You knew your room was bugged?"

"I knew I was playing for an audience. Just like you'd been doing. I quite enjoyed my end of the act. It made you sweat. And I'd taken an acute dislike to you."

He didn't comment on that. We were walking slowly. No one, in that whiteness, could have been following us, or hiding ahead. You saw everything under the moon in this great circle, even the low balustrade along the walk providing only the slightest shadow. There was a temporary pulse in the bump on my neck, pounding away. My heart was moving beyond its normal rate. I wondered why, for I didn't feel fear, only increasing curiosity.

The fear was coming from Humbold. He was a contained man, but he couldn't contain this. It sent out curious radiations in the knife-sharp air that was also dead still. I was ready to believe him long before I would admit that in words.

"Why do you want out of China? Is it the thought of waiting around to be condemned to death by your wife?"

"Shut up! I loved her, damn you!"

"It's a bourgeois sentiment."

"Oh, don't be so bloody smart."

"Why do you want out of China?"

"I hate the place!"

"You mean Stalinism under Mao?"

"I mean . . . I don't feel that way any more. I don't believe in it."

"You put on a pretty good act for me, then."

"I could put on that act now if I had to. It doesn't mean a damn thing. It doesn't work, this system. It kills everything. Slowly. I ate my meal every night with a woman who came in from her . . . work. Next day I read in the papers about what she'd done. She never talked about it to me. There's security between husband and wife, too, you know. And the kids if you have any. A watching that goes on."

"None of this is news," I said.

"No. You've only heard about it. You haven't lived with it. I've had to eat and sleep with the thing. To drift with it. That's what I've been doing. Drifting with it. Going through the motions."

"Why are you telling me all this?"

"Because I need your help."

"The last man who asked me to help him is dead now. I might have a kind of lethal touch in that direction."

"Listen, Harris, with my record I'd have difficulty in landing in any British controlled territory out here."

"Yes, you might. Still, I doubt it. Singapore is broad-minded these days."

"I want to work against them. Something positive. In journalism if possible."

"Oh, I see where I come in. With my reputation. Do you think I'm going to get out of China?"

He stopped dead. We stood facing each other in the moonlight.

"Two days ago I wouldn't have given any odds on it. Now I think you may."

"Thanks, Humbold."

"I'll help you. I'll take any risks to do that."

"All right. Let's start now. Tell me all you know about a Japanese called Obata."

I heard his breath going in then, a very deep one.

"Obata? Who's he? The name doesn't mean anything to me."

It was exactly what I had expected. Humbold was lying, of course. And after the recent display of moving candour his lie seemed to me very significant indeed. He was a frightened man. And he certainly hadn't cut himself free. Someone was still pulling the strings which made Humbold jerk and grimace.

:: ::

Christmas morning didn't begin to feel like it until Kishi came in just as I had finished shaving. He stood in the doorway, very neatly dressed for breakfast, and said:

"Christmas congratulations."

"Thanks very much and the same to you."

"In Japan much displays in department stores. And also Santa Clauses."

"You're missing the old Japanese white Christmas, are you? I see it isn't even snowing here."

We went down together, with Kishi determinedly bright, even over a dish of communist porridge. And while we ate eggs which had been held up for six months in a railway bottleneck on the way from Hunnan, he explained, with a bright smile, that the *Hashimi Maru* must by this time have completed its turn around at Port Arthur and have sailed again for Tientsin to pick us up. Very soon we would be returning to God's own country under Mount Fuji, a bit late for their New Year, but still early for the plum blossom. Kishi began to savour in prospect waiting delights, mostly gastronomic. Where else but on a Japanese ship could one hope to sit down to a meal of chilling rice, sour pickles, and horse-radish fermented into decay in a sauce which looked like sawdust diluted with liquid garden fertilizer? Where else, indeed?

"You like *oyakidomburi*, Harris?"

"Don't set my mouth watering."

"I think *sukiyaki* your taste, perhaps?"

"What I really go for is a Virginia baked ham straight from the smokehouse and which has never been near a deep freeze."

"Ah," said Kishi, puzzled. Behind the brightness I was aware of his eyes. Not much of them, but enough. He had been watching me closely for a time, as though something of use to him might come popping out at any moment.

"How's the shoe business?" I asked. "You're not chatty about your triumphs, Kishi."

"No triumph."

"Oh. Are they making their own shoes?"

"They get from Czechoslova . . . vakia. Also, Poland."

"Never mind. There's a Common Market coming up in Europe and that'll give you Australia and New Zealand. Small populations, but they use a lot of shoes. To say nothing of transistor radios. And it'll be a great day when you build all the Australians' ships for them. I see you're already doing it for the South Africans."

"You are suspicious of my people?"

"Very. But I'm prepared to make Japanese friends in spite of it."

"Japan aggressive only in businesses."

"I know. And that's where it matters these days. You'll beat the Americans yet. And won't they be surprised when they wake up and find you're running Asia, like you always meant to?"

He came back sharply. It wasn't quite a game any more.

"You think better to have China run Asia?"

He had me there.

"No. No, I don't."

In the lift Kishi said:

"Bump on neck painful?"

"I'm taking my scars out of China."

"I hope."

He could be economical, like all his countrymen.

I had planned to spend the day in bed with my good book. And I got the morning, but without the book. Mostly I lay and looked at the ceiling, quite undisturbed, except in my thoughts. These refused to smooth out. The continual intrusion was a picture of Mei Lan down on the floor from the second of Yang's blows, covering her face.

It wasn't any of my business. It never had been, but it was something that had interested me. Or perhaps she had provoked me into a partial penetration of her terrible loneliness. If ever there was a little girl lost it was Mei Lan. She had known love and the Kiangsi Opera and been cut off from both. I could hear her coughing as she totted a basket with about fifty pounds of muck in it on her back up an incline. She wouldn't last long at that. She wouldn't want to. The great escape is death, and sometimes it isn't waste. But it would be for her. There were still worlds left that could hear her laughter.

I wondered about the Towkay who had been out to renew his youth. It seemed improbable that he had put off his plans for long over one girl gone missing. Still, you never knew. The heart is a remarkable organ, and grief might have sent him back to the consolations of his number one wife, delaying him there. There just might be a future for Mei Lan if she got out of China.

How the hell could I get her out? How could I even hope to see her again? I lay and thought about that. Florie's friends with influence, perhaps? Somehow I didn't think so. It wouldn't be easy to work up enthusiasm in Florie for Mei Lan's cause. The Yins had probably never believed that the masses, or what happened to them, were very important. Humbold? If the man really was scared for his own immediate future he wasn't likely to work up much heat over someone else's life and death problem. And if the skids were under him his influence was nil. Hang Ling? A hope, but how would I get in touch with him? And even if I did, what would I say. . . . "Bring the lassie to me, I'm adopting her"?

There was, of course, our Embassy, with a whole department to deal with visitors' problems. But I could just see those elevated eyebrows when I presented mine.

The phone rang. It was Miss Feng. Her tones were honeyed still, and I liked that.

"Paul, Mr. Chow asked me to give you a message."

"I'll take your own first."

She giggled.

"I'm very businesslike in the morning."

"When am I seeing you off duty?"

"That's for you to say."

"I thought the Chinese woman was now emancipated? And as a visitor I can only wait for things to happen to me."

"They will," said Miss Feng. "Mr. Chow wanted me

to tell you that everything is now arranged about the engine. It is being fitted into a junk by our own mechanics who appear to be having no difficulty. Mr. Chow suggests that perhaps you would like to go out to-morrow and supervise the final details. Perhaps a trial on your own. Then if you found everything in readiness the demonstration could be arranged for the day after."

"Fine. To-morrow it is. The only thing that troubles me is that I appear to have lost my interpreter."

There was a moment's silence. Then Miss Feng said sweetly:

"I am on temporary loan to serve you in this respect. I hope you're agreeable to this arrangement?"

"I'm charmed. Let's make it a picnic. Shall I ask the hotel to put up a lunch for two?"

"You can leave that side to me. I'm so looking forward to this. One gets terribly office-bound."

She waited for my laugh before adding her own. Then she said:

"To-morrow at ten. At your hotel. Good-bye, Paul."

I couldn't imagine anything more carefully cooked to put all thought of Mei Lan out of my head. Someone was doing a lot of cooking in the background and I didn't think for one moment it was Chow. I was rating attention from much higher authority than that.

After a lunch without Kishi at which the service appeared to be affected by a waiters' go-slow strike, with the Russians looking positively apoplectic, I came out into the lobby to find I had a visitor. . . . Watt-Chalmers.

"I've been sent over post-haste," he said, getting up very slowly.

"On Christmas Day, too. I'm sorry. What have I done?"

"We hear there was a thing last night at the opera?"

"Oh, that. It's all blown over."

"Would an account of what happened be asking too much?"

I told him, briefly.

"Good lord! You were going to hit this man Yang?"

"That was my intention but no one can prove it. Intervention came too quickly. They can't charge me with assault. All I managed to do was take hold of Yang's clothing at the back of the neck. Then I was out of the picture. The whole story is one of their triumph. All I got was a swelling on the neck."

"You're a bit of a problem, Harris."

I thought he was being remarkably mild.

Watt-Chalmers had something for me, sealed with the official stamp. He handed it over, saying:

"It came in code, of course. I did the decoding, as a matter of fact. It seems you have friends in the Singapore police?"

He looked surprised at that.

"Well, we've got a kind of working arrangement. It's grown up over the years."

Watt-Chalmers cleared his throat.

"I think I ought to say that H. E. is most frightfully worried about this."

"Does he want to see me?"

"Oh, *no*!"

"I appreciate your help very much. It may make all the difference. And I'm hoping to leave China on schedule."

"We certainly hope so, too," Watt-Chalmers said.

In my room, with door locked, I broke the official seal. The message was from Inspector Kang in Singapore in reply to my appeal for help. He had a curious job which was mostly security and what he didn't already know he had means of finding out. His dispatch was a masterpiece of economy, and yet positively brimming with information.

"Captain Tada Obata, alias Colonel Zorin. Captain in Intelligence at Jap surrender of Java in 1945. Refused to accept Emperor's lay down arms call and escaped to Sumatra where he went into hiding. Emerged as Colonel Zorin ten years later in 1955, as military adviser and trainer in jungle warfare to Indonesian forces. Then aide and virtual second in command to General Sorumbai during war against rebel forces in Sumatra. Violently anti-Western. Suspected of communist sympathies. But after Sorumbai's death in ambush Zorin discredited and in disgrace with central government. End of career in Java. Returned to Japan as Obata from Sourabaya in 1959. Believed to have entered business. Japanese police unable to give more information at the moment."

My heart was thumping away at speed. Kang hadn't gone in for any deductions, he had left them to me. And there were plenty to be made.

Obata's career in Indonesia had been hitched to the star of General Sorumbai. And it must have been a satisfying career for someone who had refused to accept the Emperor's surrender call, a "bushido" man on his feet again in something that suited him. Sorumbai's death had wiped out that big come-back. And Sorumbai had died in the ambush which had freed me. A lot of people believed that I was directly responsible for Sorumbai's death. I knew that Kang in Singapore believed it. And Humbold here in Peking did, too. It was practically the official version, in spite of my denials.

Obata thought I had ruined him. It was a personal vendetta. I couldn't remember a Zorin there in Sumatra, but he might have been any one of a dozen who had come in to stare down at Sorumbai's trussed-up prisoner. I'd had visitors, all right, most of them gloating.

Obata had taken a festering hate back to Japan and then over to China. Against me. Sorumbai had been on the way to power, perhaps total power as a dictator. And Colonel Zorin would have travelled up with him.

Obata was on the run now, from his new bosses the Chinese. He had suddenly stopped playing the game their way, making it personal. And there was a flap on to get him and to spare me for a slower finish.

How much did Kishi know? A lot. He was probably using me for bait.

It was a pretty situation. I was in a nice warm bedroom with the door locked, and a winter sun shining outside. The wolves were outside, a pack, and a lone wolf, and probably a few mad dogs as well.

At three Florie rang up to wish me a merry Christmas and to ask me to supper. There was something special about her voice, a brightness. She wasn't cooking the meal herself, but having it sent in, so it would be no bother to her at all. Apparently you could still do that in China, or she could.

I wasn't in the mood for any sightseeing that afternoon. I just stayed cosily in my room until seven o'clock when I went down to my hired car. No one followed me out to it, and there was only the driver, no guard. Apparently up on high they didn't think I was in danger here in the city. I couldn't share their confidence.

Florie met me at the gate. She was dressed up, and took my hand after a kiss.

"Imagine having you on Christmas Day, Paul."

"It's a time I'll always remember."

"The meal's Chinese. No turkey, I'm afraid."

There was the glow about her of a hostess who is quietly confident of her arrangements. In the drawing-room were flowers and around the fireplace a little splurge of decorations, a couple of paper chains and some tinsel stars, the kind of thing that could be put up in five minutes and taken down again as quickly.

We had our meal by the fire and the cooking was superb, out of period. We kept out of the period in our talk, too, guided in this by Florie. It was her lead all the way. If I felt we were going somewhere I didn't show it.

The curtain went up quite suddenly, when she was ready, over green tea.

"I didn't sleep much last night, Paul."

"You don't look it."

She smiled.

"I keep the lights low in here. I'm sure you've noticed that. I was thinking about Mei Lan."

"It doesn't do a lot of good, thinking about her."

"You were thinking about her too. I knew you would be. It's one reason why I did what I've done. But only one reason."

I stiffened in a soft seat.

"What have you done?"

"Remember I said I still had some influence? I decided to test out just what that amounted to. I've pulled every string I could."

"For what, Florie?"

"To get Mei Lan to a sanatorium."

I was winded.

"Good lord! Isn't that sticking your neck right out?"

"I had to do it. Oh, not just for your sake. For my own. Part of . . . coming out of my hole. And not hiding."

"Florie, you scare me a little."

"Don't be scared, Paul. There isn't any need. I've had a few surprises to-day. I can't be pushed around with impunity. Isn't it funny? You had to come to China for me to find that out."

I began to get the picture. All this was part of it, too, a Yin testing herself out. The meal had been ordered from a restaurant, the kind of home service that couldn't be looked on with much favour unless you were quite a high up. But it was a service Florie had demanded and got. I could see now a kind of triumph in her manner, and the hint of a new-found power coming from that triumph. She was smiling at me.

"You don't have a guard to-night, Paul."

"I noticed."

"It was something I demanded. I wanted to have you here alone."

"Won't that make them mighty suspicious?"

"I don't think so. They have to rely on some people. It is probably the people who demand special privileges, because they have a right to. And I'm useful. I'm needed. I still have friends. I'm not alone in this country at all. It's why I may not leave it. I may choose to stay here, Paul."

I couldn't say anything to that. Florie provided her own comment.

"To stay and fight."

"Stay as a Yin, you mean?"

"All right, that, too."

"Are they really going to do something for Mei Lan?"

"Yes. She's going into hospital. In the Western Hills. And I'll visit her there after you've gone. I'll look after her. She may even get back to that opera of hers when she's well again. It oughtn't to be too long, with the new drugs."

"Florie, I could send drugs in. Anything you needed."

"Don't under-estimate us," she said, with a sudden hint of frostiness. "Our medical services can provide everything."

I didn't query that.

"Where is Mei Lan?"

"She was sent to a labour camp. This morning. I can't guarantee to get her out at once. I was told it would take a day or two. But she'll come out, don't worry, before being there has done her any harm."

I looked at Florie, remembering the feeling I'd had towards the little girl with a bang who had eaten my jam sandwiches.

CHAPTER XII

Miss FENG wasn't one of those interpreters who regarded herself as a mere mouthpiece, a voice in the background. She was in the foreground all the time, as a kind of combination of tourist guide and high-pressure saleswoman, and she dealt with the rather dismal areas south of the capital as though they were highly desirable Florida real estate and I might be contemplating pulling up stumps and emigrating to stake a claim here.

I'd been a bit surprised as I climbed into the car to see her in uniform, at first glance just another case of a girl hidden away in a blue serge tunic and pants. But on second glance you saw she wasn't hidden away at all, and her serge was no proletarian issue, but something specially woven which turned the new national dress into a markedly personal outfit. The tunic was fitted to her, the pants were tight, and she wore cute little black ballet shoes over pale lemon nylon socks. Almost a home-lounging outfit, in fact, except for that cap on her head, and even this wasn't set in the correct position with the visor strictly horizontal, but pushed up to one side, showing a great deal of sleekly groomed jet-black hair. I couldn't identify to-day's perfume, and it was more muted than usual, but still there.

"I'll have to be terribly correct in my new job, Paul."

That should have warned me. Oddly, I'd thought her a girl who wasted few words, which shows you can never really tell with women. Perhaps the new garrulity was something to do with uniform, a role put on with it. And, of course, she had an audience up front, the driver and his bully-boy-looking handyman. The car was one of the top commissar models, but in service for too long, and every time we hit a deep rut, which was three or four a minute, the rear shock absorbers bellowed for maintenance.

We weren't really travelling fast at all until each time we came to a village when the driver, as though under orders on this, stepped on the accelerator and zoomed through, causing panic to pigs, dogs, children and the few of the adult new citizens who seemed to be about.

Miss Feng didn't think much of the villages. And after about four of them she felt an explanation was necessary. She waved her hand.

"These will soon disappear."

"Why?"

"They are not part of the New China. We have model centres. All the people will live in them." Then she added: "Here and there."

I agreed with the postscript. It was my bet that twenty years from now the model centres would still be here and there and the villages would still be all over the place, with pigs, kids and dogs, looking very much as they did now. That, of course, was just my jaundiced capitalist eye-view.

When we reached the river Miss Feng was still talking, but she got out looking a little like a model girl dumped down in a country setting for an eccentric photograph. It was an ordinary Chinese river, a navigable tributary of something much bigger, high-banked against spring floods, but now, before the thaw, offering only a rather sluggish flow quite a long way down. The car turned and went away, but the bully-boy guard remained. Miss Feng had put on a coat, obviously a rarely worn wool issue, but it didn't weigh her down any, and to demonstrate this she gave a little run along the river bank, squandering energy of which her high-calorific top-people's diet gave her an excess. Miss Feng looked back at the deliberately moving imperialist with a swift smile tinged with compassion.

I thought things just under my breath. Behind me the guard's rifle clinked. He had produced it in what couldn't be called an unobtrusive manner.

"You've got the lunch, Paul?"

"I have, yes."

"Can you guess what's in it?"

"Dead eggs."

"But, yes! How clever of you. Is that your favourite Chinese food?"

I don't care what anyone says, Chinese dead eggs taste like dead eggs, even the ninety-year-old ones you get at a Singapore millionaires' banquet. Maybe they're gourmets as a race, but they've carried this a bit far in some directions. I could remember one surprise heart of lettuce salad which, when you unravelled it with chopsticks, revealed a minute little white mouse which had been stewed in a sugar syrup. Or glass bowls full of moving locusts. The gastronome's trick here was to lift the lid cautiously, nab one locust, pop it into a hot sauce, and then into your mouth. Maybe this kind of thing is a lot of fun when taken in the right spirit, but I'm really a bacon and eggs man at heart. And to-day those Yangtze ox sandwiches from the hotel would have been nearer my kind of protein.

But this was a party. That became much more apparent when we got into the junk. The entire scene was one of total efficiency, in marked contrast to my experience by the canal. There was a wharf flat along the bank, with sheds behind it, and tied up was a craft about sixty feet long, with a high poop, low well-deck and uplifting bow, the kind of little ship the Chinese have used for un-numbered centuries and are still using along thousands of miles of coast as far south as Cambodia. The Dolphin had been built for a job like this, not to send it at speed, but at seven knots all out, which was about a knot faster than most auxiliary engines. The bamboo-ribbed, flat lateen sails were still there and meant to be used when-ever the wind offered no-cost propulsion.

There was just nothing for me to do. Three mechanics had sorted everything out, flat-faced men in overalls who didn't need explanations, even via a good-looking inter-preter. All that was expected of me was to eat my lunch.

Still, I did a check. It took me about an hour, while Miss Feng moved out of the cold into a poop cabin. When I joined her she was alone in a small, square-windowed cell which had been fitted out for a commissars' ex-cursion, which meant very comfortably indeed. There was a wood-burning stove in one corner and Miss Feng was sitting with her knees up on a sofa against a bulkhead.

"Aren't we going out on the river, Paul? I heard the engine on."

"Just a test. We may this afternoon. But I'm not going to need an interpreter. The foreman out there was born in Hong Kong."

"So was I."

"I thought as much. I didn't like to ask."

"Why?"

"Oh, there might have been some horror story about being torn from friends and relations."

"No horror story. I walked out on my family. I came

here because I wanted to. You know what Hong Kong is like. It's going to burst open, it's so full. And it's not a real place. We could take it to-morrow."

"No one's arguing about that."

"I hate it. Anyone with spirit has to get out. So I came to China."

"How long ago?"

"When I was nineteen. How long ago do you think that was?"

"About seven years."

Her ballet shoes made a little plopping noise as they hit the deck.

"Oh!" She stared at me, then smiled. "I could have gone to Singapore if I'd wanted. I thought about it."

"We're crowded, too."

"It wasn't that. I just wanted to be on the winning side. A girl has to be careful about these things. We'll take Singapore too, you know. Quite soon. Will you be waiting for us, Paul, when we come in?"

"I doubt if I'll have survived the fighting."

Miss Feng began to laugh. It was a good laugh, deep in her throat. She brought one leg back up on the settee and set her chin on it. Her body shook a little from deep amusement.

"Poor Paul. Brought all this way and nothing to do for his engine. And you expected a frightful day dealing with Chinese inefficiency. We could eat our lunch now. But I'm not hungry yet, are you?"

"No."

"I told our watchdog to keep out. And there's a lock on that door."

So there was. Miss Feng slid down off the sofa and went over to shove the bolt home.

"Are you tired?" she asked.

:: ::

The next day's demonstration was reminiscent of one of those annual junkets by the city fathers to inspect the waterworks, the same note of conviviality with a very low emphasis indeed on any serious purpose. I had expected all Chinese to be serious at this stage in achieving socialism, but the ones at the top know how to take time off, especially in a boat which can be moved away from any close observation. Chow was there and about eighteen others, all of whom arrived on the scene after I had been waiting for an hour. An interpreter for me had been dispensed with but if I had expected any slight sourness from Commissar Chow I under-estimated the Chinese. They've grown used to sharing everything. He was out for a holiday like the rest of them, with no sign of a thing preying on his mind.

There may have been some technical experts amongst the crowd on the junk but I couldn't identify them. The emphasis was not on my engine but in the refreshment cabin. It could have been the old days really, except for a total absence of sing-song girls who have either been outlawed altogether or kept for very exclusive parties indeed. Everyone was terribly nice to me and the tone of things was almost that of the Anglo-Chinese Friendship Society's annual soirée in a fourth-class London hotel. We all kept off politics by unspoken agreement and talked instead of cultural exchanges. It was the oddest way to sell an engine that I've ever run up against, that is if I *was* selling it.

I made an attempt at patter to Chow, who was beside me in the well-deck.

"We're now doing our seven knots," I said.

"Ah!" He peered down into the oily-looking water to see if it would say I was lying. "See, the wave's hitting the bank!"

There was a decided flush on his cheeks. He looked about, carefully, and then leaned towards me.

"We're buying your engine."

"On . . . this test?"

"No. Our engineers say it is excellent."

"You mean they've run their own try-out?"

"Sure. Yesterday. After you'd come back to Peking with Miss Feng."

He laughed. I didn't.

"And who are all these people, Mr. Chow?"

"These? Oh .. ," he lowered his voice . . . "from the Department of River Waterways. They don't often go on rivers."

That appealed to him. He slapped the rail with the flat palm of his hand. I must admit to being just slightly shocked. It may be my Scots blood which insists that whenever possible business and pleasure be kept in separate compartments. And then I began to have the sharp feeling that it wouldn't surprise me to hear of another purge of top-level party officials coming up. No doubt progressive socialism keeps going this way, by shooting whole departments in one morning. It's one way of toning up the national muscles and as a non-political type I can't bring myself to condemn totally this approach to the problem of a swelling bureaucracy. And anyway China's over-populated.

These boys were eating and drinking while they had the chance, perhaps fully appreciating the hazards of Marxist careerism.

"Come for refreshment?" Chow suggested.

Why not? After all, my own future mightn't be so bright either.

"I have the contracts in my case, Mr. Chow. Are you considering signing perhaps to-day?"

"No, no!" I was a western barbarian. "Not to-day. I telephone you."

"Oh, yes. Well, I could do with a drink."

"Sure," he agreed, as though he thought so, too.

It was because I turned away from the rail at that precise moment that I wasn't killed. The bullet came sizzling past my left shoulder, ripped through the cloth of my coat and then went smack into the mainmast of the junk. It didn't ricochet, it just went straight in.

Chow, staring at me, had gone quite green. Then he let out a howl.

"Down, down!"

But the message had reached me earlier. I was right there on the deck waiting for him. Sprawled behind the rail we waited for the second shot, but the sniper wasn't wasting ammo. The only sound for a moment or two was the gurgling of water past thick wooden sides and tipsy laughter from the cabin. Then the helmsman started to bellow. Chow popped his head up cautiously.

"You're quite safe," I said. "It wasn't for you. As for me . . . I'll crawl over to that door."

But I didn't just do that. I had a cautious look over the rail first. We were about eighty yards from the south bank of the river and had been closing in on it. Chow shouted instructions which rectified this and the junk turned slowly, so that the well-deck didn't present such a good target area any more.

There wasn't a thing to be seen on the banks, just the usual flood dyke which was certainly built up higher than the ground beyond it, which meant that our sniper could be using it as a shield for his movement. There might even be a path just below top level, there often was, along which he could be cycling. Quite simple to keep checking up on the junk without ever being seen, to note course and move on down ahead, choosing the right spot and hoping your victim would expose himself while you were in it. I had stood at the rail with Chow like the answer to a sniper's prayer.

Chow was doing a bit of shouting now. Someone came down from the poop and started to dig into the mainmast for the bullet with a long-bladed knife. I was on my feet again, but Chow didn't like this.

"Keep down, Mr. Harris. Keep down!"

"It's all right. We're not a target any more here. But it might be a good idea if I went under cover somewhere. Not the main cabin, at the moment. We don't want any sensations. And nearly everyone seems to have missed this little incident."

Chow opened the door into what must have been the junk captain's own cabin. It wasn't dolled up for commissars at all, and I sat down on a board bunk. Chow stood in the doorway looking at me.

"Some lawless fellow. An agent."

He was still an odd colour.

"An agent, Mr. Chow?"

"They are still in China. From Formosa."

I laughed.

"I think that's over-complicating matters. Why should Formosa want to kill me? I have some good friends there. And don't let's pretend that the bullet wasn't labelled with my name, because it was. It's the same man who shot at me the other day."

Chow shook his head in a kind of despair. He really looked scared to death, as if my safety mattered an awful lot.

"The matter will be investigated! Most thoroughly."

"That's what you said the last time. But the man has stayed free to snipe another day. Same gun, too, from the sound of it. An armed man, Mr. Chow, wandering around loose."

"A bandit!" he shouted.

"Surely there are no bandits in the New China? I thought you'd wiped them all out?"

"Mr. Harris, I'm full of apologies for what has happened. Believe me, I am most upset. We will now return to Peking. You will have guard, always watching over you."

"While you go on with your manhunt? Since it seems to be a little bit difficult for your authorities to protect me as a visiting business man, supposing we fix up the matter of the engine right away? Say this evening back in Peking? We'll sign the agreement between us and then I'll move over to the British Embassy to wait for the sailing of my ship."

"No! It cannot be done this way, Mr. Harris."

"Really? Why not? You said a short time ago that you're buying the Dolphin."

"Yes, yes, it is agreed. But not finally decided. One thousand engines. This is an important policy matter. Many must be consulted. I cannot arrange for the signing to-night. I cannot!"

"To-morrow then?"

"Perhaps. Only again I cannot be certain. Mr. Harris, believe me. You will be perfectly safe. You will be watched most carefully. Day and night. You will have a private guard."

I could see Chow's dilemma all right. It was a serious one for him. Part of his job was to keep me happy until the final snare had been laid. And their bird, once in the Embassy, would have a fair chance of flying free from China. Not that anything would have taken me to that particular asylum, but Chow wasn't to know this. We were very near the climax Chow and his pals had planned, but not quite there yet. And the Japanese was an unforeseen and completely infuriating intrusion into the situation, unnerving me just when I should be reacting to the various forms of sedation which they had so painstakingly supplied. I began to feel almost sorry for Chow.

He meant what he said about the guard. I'd had one, of course, to travel down with me, the same bully-boy who had been with us on my outing with Miss Feng. But the man was given new orders. All the way back to Peking he sat in front with a gun at the ready, the muzzle of it pointing up. And Chow beside me had a revolver out on his lap.

That night a relief took over in the hotel passage. I mightn't have noticed this if it hadn't been for Kishi. I was getting into bed when there was shouting and I opened the door to find my friend trying to argue an automatic rifle away from his stomach. I had never really seen Kishi looking perturbed, but just at that moment there was a hint of it. The guard didn't know English and it took about five minutes for the word to reach him that I wanted to see the Japanese, that he was an old pal.

I closed the door and locked it, so we wouldn't have a sudden interruption if the man outside changed his mind. Kishi needed some of my whisky, which was what he had come for anyway.

"They love me," I said, pouring. "I'm one of the most valuable commodities in North China. They want my engine bad."

Kishi didn't comment on that, probably thinking about the mike. He had his handkerchief out and was mopping his forehead.

"Any news of the *Hashimi Maru?*"

"Yes. She will arrive again in Tientsin on the twenty-ninth. She sails for Japan at noon on 30th December."

"And when we get on board her again, Kishi, we'll only have been in China for ten days. How long does it feel to you?"

"Much longer," he said. "You will have completed business in time to sail?"

"I think so. It seems to be fairly certain they're going to buy the Dolphin."

"Congratulations. You sign contract soon?"

"Well, that seems to be the snag. It's apparently a big decision involving a lot of people. But I've told them about my return reservation, and that I want to leave China the way I came in."

He gave me a long look, again with the mike in mind.

"A noon sailing means an early morning train from here, doesn't it?" I said. "Are you travelling with your Japanese friends?"

"They are not coming on the ship."

"Oh! Then let's make the journey together? Supposing you book us seats? Could I leave that to you?"

"I will arrange with great pleasure. I have finished your whisky, I fear."

I smiled at him.

"I've another bottle. To see us through the next two

days. I'll keep it just for the two of us. Courage in a suitcase."

He stood.

"Good night, Paul."

I was rather touched that he used my first name. He never had before, in spite of the increasing closeness of our relationship. I had the feeling that he was deeply concerned about me, very deeply. I felt also that Kishi wouldn't be any farther from me than he could help for my last two days in China. I certainly was the object of a lot of attention. But I didn't want to think about that. Right then I wanted to lock my door and get into bed and sleep. I still need a lot of sleep.

CHAPTER XIII

THE TWENTY-EIGHTH was a blank day, or almost. I couldn't arrange to do anything because I was waiting in for some word from Chow at the Ministry. About five I was in my room still at the *Rise and Fall of the Third Reich* when a call came through for me.

"Hallo, Paul," Miss Feng said. "Resting?"

"That's right. I've been stoking up on vitamins all day and lying on my bed."

"Thinking?"

"Yes, dear. About how important I am. I've got a guard on my door. You couldn't get in."

"That's what you think."

"In that case two long knocks and one short."

She laughed.

"I like you," she said.

"Well, don't get too deeply into this. I'm sailing back to imperialism the day after to-morrow at high noon."

"I know. Mr. Chow told me. We're all terribly upset about the shooting."

"What you really mean is you wish you'd been there to see it."

Miss Feng giggled.

"Yes, I do!"

She then inhaled beside the mouthpiece. A deep breath did something for her torso and she knew it.

"I've got a message from Mr. Chow. The contract is cleared and he wonders if eleven o'clock to-morrow would be all right with you for the signing?"

"It would be absolutely perfect."

"Then there's the big reception at the Summer Palace at four."

"I had thought about staying here with a good book."

"Paul! You've got to come! Why . . . everyone will be there. All the trade delegations and everything. There are a lot of people who want to meet you. Didn't Mr. Chow tell you that you were expected?"

"Yes, he did. Almost as urgent about it as you. Okay, I'll be there."

"And I've got a new dress."

"How many of those do they issue you with in a year?"

"I've been a good girl."

"Are you going to tell me your first name to-night?"

"No!"

"It can't be as bad as all that."

"It's absolutely unspeakable!"

"In that case you'll be the first girl I'll' remember as Miss."

"It'll give me a special place, won't it?" she said.

::   ::

The reception for foreign trade delegations was something special. They do these things rather well, with the suggestion of four thousand years of civilised living to draw on and some of it pretty lush living, too, for the minority. This was a minority thing under the new régime, top people, and the setting was one of the Summer Palace's major reception halls on which a lot of tax money had been spent at one time. In fact quite a lot of money had been spent recently, the place was entirely redecorated. It was a bit startling to go into because of this, for beyond were acres and acres of buildings and curved roofed pavilions which had the muted grace of an arrested decay, soft tones from weathered wood and faded paint. In here the dragons curling around the roof joists had all been regilded and everywhere colour had an almost barbaric violence. We went around huge screens about eight feet high, embossed with carving that went straight through to the other side, of pure white jade which looked to me the biggest slabs ever mined. They must have been too big to carry away at the celebrated looting of Peking after the Boxer troubles. Otherwise they'd have been in a British country house or the Manchester Museum of Fine Art. I had to admit privately that it must be a bit galling for the Chinese these days to think about their *objets d'art* scattered over the globe from that particular mass-pinching.

Miss Feng had been entirely redecorated, too. She wore an almost bizarre *cheongsam* in what I can only call pale helio on which was embroidered detail in rampant shades of green, red, yellow, and gold thread. Only a Chinese woman could have got away with it. It would have eclipsed the most divorced Hollywood star, accenting the basic stupidity of her face. But Miss Feng didn't have a stupid face at all. Her intelligence triumphed over the dress, and she had toned down her make-up to test this out. Only her lips picked up the embroidery red.

She saw me staring and took her time about coming over. Then, after I had got through a lot of Chow-conducted introductions and patter about trade with China, she joined me.

"Hallo, Paul."

"If that's a basic design for the new female workers' off-duty playsuit then I like it. It's good to see colour coming back to this country."

"I'm in a special category. Like the dancers and actors. Lucky me."

"Yes, aren't you? I hope you'll be interpreting for the next trade delegation to Malaya."

"Would you be waiting at the airport?"

"With a large bunch of old English roses flown up from Australia in deep freeze."

She sighed, gently. It was rather touching. I found myself looking into her eyes which, though not large, could send out remarkable messages of her own kind of specialised warmth.

"How does it feel to have signed the contract for a thousand engines, Paul?"

"I like doing what I set out to do."

"Yes. But now your only real thought is to get home again as quickly as possible. You know, you haven't told me much about what your life is like down there in Singapore."

"Terribly, terribly lonely," I said.

A waiter brought us Russian champagne. They must have laid in a big supply before the last row with Kruschev. It didn't seem quite the right drink for under gilded dragons but perhaps it had been a bad season for the local raisin brandy.

"I have a feeling, Paul, that we'll meet again."

I lifted my glass.

"In that case here is to cultural and trade exchanges between China and South-East Asia. I promise I'll give a very nice party."

"Tell me about the kind of party you give."

"Oh, flashy and expensive. Capitalist decadent. You know the kind of thing. Everyone has a wonderful time. I'm a great little party-giver. For you I'll fly in an orchestra from Hawaii."

"Is this the way the profits from the sale of engines go?"

"No. Those are ploughed back into the business. I put on my displays from unearned income."

"And you have a lot of this?"

"Enough."

Miss Feng looked, for just a moment, as though she wished she had met me before she had chosen the New China. Her basic simplicity was extremely appealing. I must admit to a great weakness for uncomplicated women who like Cartier bracelets. I wondered then what would happen if I sent her one?

Chow came over and took me away to a departmental head who modelled himself on Comrade Mao and had his tailor-made pants and tunics cut for growth. He was a thin little man lost under folds of party leader serge. He looked jumpy and clearly didn't like the idea of buying engines from abroad at all. Possibly, with all the man-power available, the river junks should have been converted into latter-day galleys. It was odd they hadn't thought of this angle, but perhaps barrelled diesel oil was easier to handle than all the boiled rice which would have been needed.

Mr. Tsung Fa Chew asked me what I had seen of New China and I said the Winter Palace, the Summer Palace, my hotel and a river. I also said I thought they should have left the ancestors alone in their fields, which he didn't like at all. The contract, a fat bulge in my pocket, was making me a bit reckless. I had mailed off a second copy to my partners and sent them a success cable. Everything was being wound up.

"I see you've met Mr. Tsung," Watt-Chalmers said at my elbow.

The departmental head took this as an excuse to nip off at once. Watt-Chalmers didn't seem at all surprised.

"He's the chap I told you about. The one I could get you an introduction to. Has he been useful?"

"Not that I know of. We've only just met."

"Oh. But you've sold your engine?"

"I have, yes. Thanks for all your help."

Watt-Chalmers didn't stay long either. Mr. Chow was engaged elsewhere, Miss Feng was enchanting Indonesians, and I was suddenly alone near the Chinese equivalent to french windows on to a pillared porch. In spite of the time of year these were a little open to let some air into the reception hall which needed it with all those bodies.

A waiter had pity on my empty glass. He came over with a tray and as I was about to take more champagne-type from it he said in a rigid-lipped hiss:

"I am Hang Ling. Take out cigarette. I give you light."

I could only take his word as to who he was. Without the actor's make-up it was just another Chinese face to me. But I brought out my case and he made a very polished little business of striking a match and holding it for me. When the hiss came again I wasn't even sure about his voice. It could have been the man who understood all cultures, and then again it mightn't have been.

The message for me was certainly startling. Mei Lan had run away from her labour camp and was here in the Summer Palace waiting to see me. If I would step out on to the terrace in a moment or two Hang Ling would conduct me to her.

He then bowed slightly and departed with his tray, rather an old-world waiter, not so much a comrade. But maybe at the top waiters are still waiters. I soon lost sight of him in the crowd and began to feel curiously isolated from people there in my window, one of the guests of honour, perhaps, but apparently forgotten at the moment.

I couldn't decline the invitation which had been sprung on me, though I should have taken a few moments to assess the situation, maybe quite a few moments. Instead I stepped through the window and went down about four steps to the gallery.

There was a courtyard beyond, though this wasn't totally enclosed, the galleries ran around it to a gap on the opposite side, and then led through the gap, taking you completely under cover to what was clearly some sort of garden beyond. There was no sign of the man who called himself Hang Ling.

The champagne glass was still in my hand. I emptied it and strolled along the paving, past windows, but considerably below the level of the reception hall. Anyone glancing out wouldn't have seen me. The noise from in there was cut off too. Out here there wasn't a soul, a vast gravelled square surrounded by a cloister roofed in imperial yellow tiles stained by moss. My rubber-soled shoes didn't make any noise, and it was so still I heard pigeons. I was sure that the rooms behind me now were derelict, not yet suitably refurbished for use in a People's democracy. The party was a long way off, I was moving through one of the haunted emptinesses of China, and the silence suggested insulation, as though this vast area of palace and lake and park had been designed to produce a vacuum immune to real living. And, of course, it had.

Hang was suddenly about fifty yards ahead of me. He didn't wait, but began to walk down the north gallery, fast. It was natural that he shouldn't want to seem my guide, but it was also possible that he didn't want to be looked at too closely. A lot of things were possible. It mightn't be Mei Lan who was waiting for me out there in the garden.

It was getting close to dusk. Everything was quite clearly defined still, but shadow deepening. It was also very cold, with that extra bite in the air which says more snow and maybe a lot of it. Without my coat I felt this, though winter Peking is so dry that you can be exposed to sub-freezing temperatures for some time before you really begin to realise just how low they are.

Hang Ling was turning into the opening to the gardens. I had caught up on him a little, but not much. He had shed the waiter's white for the usual padded dark tunic.

I put my empty champagne glass down on the ledge of a railing, wondering how long it would be before anyone would come this way to find it. And I regretted then having returned Kishi's gun. I had no weapon of any kind, nothing I could use. When I was a long way past the glass it occurred to me that it might have been something to hold on to. The ragged edge of a broken champagne glass would have been something. But I didn't go back for it, Hang had disappeared.

I saw him again in the gardens. These were stuck on to the hillside, mostly rocks in the grotesque Chinese tradition, great lumps of them, and paths twisting about between, with few shrubs. I had a dim recollection of having seen all this before, and that it was here that the Empress Dowager had used to play tag with her maids and ladies-in-waiting, probably in off time from a round of political poisoning. The old lady had been quite a Borgia.

Directly below, but half screened by more empty-looking buildings with rampant dragons at the gable ends, was the lotus lake and the marble boat, which is singularly graceless and heavy, with a restaurant on its second floor. But I didn't see anyone about, no movement on that road by the lake, only Hang going down on a narrow path and never looking over his shoulder to see if I was following.

The light was better out here in the open, but I didn't like that garden much. It offered an infinite variety of cover to anyone waiting, standing motionless somewhere watching. I had to watch my feet going down, too, which made me a better target. It was a fool thing to have done, rushing off after a waiter, as though the word Mei Lan would push a kind of button in me. Maybe somebody guessed it would.

There was nothing to stop me going back quickly to the reception except the fact that I don't like going back. And just then Hang disappeared into a pavilion tucked back against a hummock of ornamental rock. The place was six-sided, and looked a little like a carved Victorian sewing box with a pointed lid. He didn't go through it, he was in there waiting.

I went down slowly. The building could have been used as a summer-house, for Imperial tea parties. It had carved marble slabs for walls and rather narrow arched doors between them. Walking into it would have been all right with my hand on Kishi's gun. It wasn't pleasant with a hand on nothing. I had the feeling again of being sucked towards a trap baited for me by the name of Mei Lan. It was highly improbable that she was inside, and the place held deep shadow.

I didn't just walk in. I looked first, from behind the partial shelter of carved marble. Hang was standing in the middle of a kind of symmetrical emptiness, his face half hidden. Five openings were about him, each to little paths through artificial rockeries, but on the cliffside were two massive wooden doors finished in what had once been lacquer, but was now just a chipped surface. They were like doors to a cupboard, secured by a solid drop bar.

"Where's Mei Lan?"

Hang pointed towards the big cupboard.

"Here."

He made a move towards it.

"Just a minute! You're an actor. How did you get to be a waiter here?"

"Waiters come from many places. I ask for job and get."

"After you brought Mei Lan here?"

He nodded.

"When did you do that?"

"This morning. She know you come here."

"Where was she last night?"

"You let her tell!"

He wanted to get away, and fast. I didn't stand directly in front of the doors as he pushed up the bar and they creaked open.

Inside was the most hideous devil-god I've ever seen. The Chinese are pretty good at these little nightmares and this one had been well preserved in its sanctuary. The popping eyeballs glared at me. It was about life-size, fantastic, and yet subtle, too, in that it seemed mobile, about to step down from its niche, almost as though it had been waiting for the doors to open to do that. One arm was uplifted, holding something, I couldn't see whether it was a weapon because of the shadow. The play of evening light in there was a devil's own setting. You could almost smell the evil, a mustiness of rotting wood and decay.

"Mei Lan," Hang called softly.

There was no answer at first. Then we heard a cry of fear and a scuffling.

Mei Lan could just squeeze past the devil and no more. A man couldn't have done it. I saw the point of this hiding-place. Hang helped her down and she stood in front of me, a girl woken from a sleep that hadn't refreshed her, because she had taken fear into it. I could imagine her lying in there, in some foulness behind the figure, her head on her arms to smother the cough, and crying.

It was Mei Lan all right, but as I'd never seen her, not even when Yang struck her down. Now she was crumpled, beaten, and exhausted by terror. The serge she was wearing was filthy. She had, for some reason, perhaps to keep them warm, pulled her cap over her ears. She looked at me, and then turned to Hang Ling, clutching his arm, babbling in Chinese.

He didn't like this one little bit. He kept looking round him, and half trying to shake her off. I remembered that he loved her like a brother and thought him a pretty jumpy brother. Finally he appealed to me.

"She say you not help her. She say that."

Mei Lan didn't look at me. Her fingers were still scrabbling at Hang's arm, and he stood like someone who wants to break off and run. He must have told her to keep her voice down for she stopped talking altogether, releasing him, standing quite still looking down at the marble paving.

"You'd better get back to the party," I said.

He didn't hesitate, not for a second. And Mei Lan accepted his going, as part of her defeat. Whatever had brought her this far she had lost it now, perhaps in the darkness behind the devil-god. She had no hope left. I mightn't have been there, she was so alone. I spoke softly.

"Mei Lan, Hang was right. I want to help you."

She didn't look up.

"You go away," she said. "Quick."

"And if I do, what about you?"

"I stay."

"To freeze to death? It's going to snow to-night."

"I stay."

I put my hands under her chin and lifted her face. Orientals don't like being touched like this, but I couldn't help doing it. I lifted her head until I could see into her eyes, open and empty.

"When did Hang come for you?"

"Last night."

"How could he get into a labour camp? Wasn't it guarded?"

"He steal in. He make a hole in wire. He found me going back to hut. He had been looking and looking. I couldn't believe he find me. Hang has always looked after me. Always."

"Mei Lan, what did he say?"

"I am to come with him. We go through the wire. There are two bicycles. We came back to Peking. In the dark. We went to the theatre. Mother Tsung gave me food. You see Mother Tsung when you . . . ?"

"Bound feet?"

Mei Lan nodded.

"She is my only mother. But I couldn't stay. They would know I go there. Hang said he find you and you help me. So I tell about party here, though I cannot believe you help me. I cannot still. Why should you?"

"I'm going to."

The green eyes met mine, then dropped.

"It's no good. I know now. I can't hide. This time when they catch me they do something bad. That's what I think . . . what will they do now? What will they do?"

"What else did Hang say?"

"He speak many things. That you would take me to British Embassy. But not true. Chinese cannot go there."

"So it was you who suggested coming here? Not Hang?"

"Me . . . I think. I'm not sure. But it's no good. No one can help me."

"Some people back in Peking are trying to help you now."

Her head jerked up. The green eyes weren't empty any more.

"Who?"

"Dr. Yin. She's going to get you to a sanatorium."

"She? She help me?"

"We're old friends."

"I don't believe!"

"But it's true. You were going to be released from the labour camp. I had a firm promise. It might have been to-day if you'd stayed."

"No. Dr. Yin lie!"

"Why do you say that?"

"I'm sure."

"I'm taking you to her now."

Mei Lan stared.

"You . . . take me to her? To her house? I want to laugh! You know what happens? Dr. Yin very kind. Tea and cakes. You must go back to your hotel, and not worry. Everything will be fixed, Dr. Yin says. Then when you go Dr. Yin picks up phone and calls police. Later you get card from Dr. Yin, card to Singapore. With picture of Hatamen gate. Dr. Yin says on card I am so happy now, and coming to good health. And when card comes to you I am carrying mud again."

She began to cry, quite softly. I didn't say anything. I stood looking at her, a girl crying from a loneliness that couldn't be broken down. Beyond us, out on one of the paths through rockeries, a stone clicked under a shoe.

CHAPTER XIV

IT MADE A SMALL sound, that stone. Voices would have covered it, even low voices. But not Mei Lan's stifled crying. Bad luck for the killer coming. I knew which way he was coming, and that he was a killer, coming in stealth. There was prickling on my neck.

He had stopped out there when the voices stopped. It might have been his moving into shadow I heard. There must be voices for him again.

I began to talk, a low mumble. It didn't matter what I said, Mei Lan wasn't listening. She was back against the wall of the devil-god's cupboard, leaning on it. She didn't notice when I turned from her, still talking, my voice inaudible, but going on and on, like someone pleading, trying to break down a resistance. I talked myself against the flat marble of the wall slabs, hard against it, my voice lower still, so that the killer out there would strain to hear and then move again, thinking he had us. I was beside the arch he had to come through.

The gun came first, the barrel of an automatic rifle, already angling for point-blank range before the man behind it could see the target. He saw my hands coming and jerked back, but I had hold of metal, pushing it up, drawn to the killer by my hold and his, looking into his face under the arch, Obata's face.

Lips were drawn back from his teeth. I could see wet on his forehead. He had been sweating coming towards us, even in the cold. He was afraid, too, as I was afraid, and for a second we looked at each other, fear naked in our eyes, before the fury came.

I was expecting the judo trick to shake me from the gun, forward, quick down and up, but it was badly executed. I relaxed when he should have broken the drawn tension of my body, tightened when he staggered from failure. I let go and used my right. The gun swung to stop the blow, but too slowly, too late. The crack on his jaw was real enough.

It sent him back, wobbling, the gun with him. He sagged against rock, trying to bring the wavering barrel up to his hip, to fire it that way. I bull-charged with my head down. He hadn't the purchase for his feet to counter that and went back into rock. His head came up as mine did and we looked at each other again. Then he groaned.

I got the gun easily enough and stood over him with it. The jagged ornamental rocks had done more damage than I had. He didn't move. A voice said:

"Leave him to me now."

It was Kishi with an automatic in his hand, standing on a path for which night was reaching.

"You are hurt?" Kishi said.

"No."

Kishi turned a little towards Obata. The man against the rocks still didn't move. Only his face changed. It became the face of the warrior at the inescapable moment, the mouth turned down at the corners.

"*Owari*," Kishi said in Japanese.

It means finish. Kishi shot Obata through the heart and then through the head. The sound was oddly modest and controlled, as though contained by the rocks about us.

Kishi lifted his head and looked past me towards the pavilion. Mei Lan was standing under the arch, both hands out, holding on.

"You've got what you wanted in China, haven't you?"
I said.

Kishi didn't answer that. He went on looking at the
girl. She turned and stepped back into the pavilion, to
be hidden.

"What are we going to do with the body?" I asked.
"The shots may have been heard."

"The gardens most empty, I think."

"They haven't felt like it, to me. We can put him
behind the god."

When she saw what we were going to do Mei Lan
protested.

"You won't be needing the accommodation," I told
her.

We had to lift the body right up to the level of the
devil-god's head before we could shove it through. We
were both sweating before we were finished. I was
shaking a bit. It was from reaction as much as the effort.

"Obata's gun is no use to me," I said. "But I'd like
the loan of your revolver again."

Kishi didn't seem to want to hand it over. I noticed
he was shaking a little too. The colour was drained
away from under his skin.

"If they find the body . . . and you with this gun . . . ?"

"I know. But I still need it. I'm in a bad enough spot
as it is."

He handed the revolver over. I put it in my pocket.
I had the feeling of all initiative gone from Kishi, of the
man spent suddenly. It wasn't a thing I'd noticed with
him before.

"You get back to the party," I said. "Humbold is
there. You know Humbold, the reporter?"

"Yes."

"Don't rush at him. But get to him. Tell him to bring his car down here. To the road along the front. Near the marble boat. Tell him I want him. Will you do that?"

"Yes."

To give him a moment I picked up Obata's gun and popped it over behind the devil-god, on to the body. I was aware of silence which had come back, and was firmly held in those gardens. The light about us was thinner. It would be dark in twenty minutes, half an hour at the outside. Mei Lan was standing against one of the carved screens now, staring at me. She looked totally beyond all comprehension of what was happening.

I closed the doors to the devil's cupboard and dropped the bar home.

"Kishi?"

"Yes, Paul?"

"I won't be able to travel with you to-morrow to Tientsin. But I'm going to get there, somehow. With Mei Lan. I want you to keep a lookout for us. That's all I can tell you. Just to keep a lookout for us."

He nodded. He was back in control again and didn't waste time.

"Take care, please," he said. And went to one of the openings. But he didn't go through it. He just stood there. In a moment Humbold walked past him.

"I heard two shots," Humbold said. "Very close together. Who was shooting at who?"

"What brought you out?"

"I'm a reporter, remember? I follow leads. I saw you leaving and about two minutes later there was your Japanese friend doing the same thing. Very discreetly, but still doing it. Can you blame me for being curious?

The only trouble was I couldn't get away at once. I was talking to a very important personage. It would have looked odd."

"Were you expecting something to happen at this party, Humbold?"

"I always expect something to happen. And it often does. Especially in China."

"Mr. Kishimura was bringing you a message from me."

"Oh?"

"We want a lift into Peking in your car. Mei Lan and I."

"Before I agree to that one I want to know what I'm in for. That shooting. Is there a body?"

"Yes. In there."

"And who is it?"

"Obata."

Humbold's expression didn't change at all. There was no interest in his eyes. The name might have meant nothing to him.

"There'll be sighs of relief in many quarters about that body," I said. "When they find it."

"You'd better get back to the party," Humbold said to Kishi.

"Paul . . . ?"

"Yes, Kishi, go."

For just a moment the Japanese hesitated. Then he turned and went up the path.

"Will you get your car now?" I asked.

"Yes, I'll get it."

I was quite sure he would, too.

When he had gone I asked Mei Lan if she was cold, a silly question, for it was bitter. I took her hand and it was icy. I began to lead her down stone steps towards the road by the lake. She came with me like someone who has lost all hold for herself, not knowing what she is doing.

::   ::

In the Volkswagen Humbold sat alone up in front. I was in the back with Mei Lan, who was wrapped in a car rug, and keeping her head down low. When we got into the city I made her get down on to the floor. We were going to Florie's. There was nowhere else we could go.

"How are you going to get the girl out of China?" Humbold asked suddenly.

He was driving carefully, not too fast.

"I don't know yet."

"I've never heard of it being done from up north. Unless into South Korea. And you'd never get there."

"I'm not going to try to."

"It's Tientsin you're aiming for?"

"That's your guess, Humbold, isn't it?"

"Had you thought of our Embassy?"

"Not for long. Can you see them taking in a refugee Chinese?"

"Frankly, I can't. It wouldn't be good diplomacy."

He was silent for a minute or two.

"What do I do when we get to Dr. Yin's?"

"Drive up to the gate, let us out, drive off again."

"What about the girl seen going into the house?"

"I'm going to try and arrange that she won't be seen."

But this wasn't too easy. I had forgotten about the light over Florie's gate and a very bright one in the courtyard beyond. Mei Lan was a bundle on the car floor when I got out via a tipped back seat. But Florie wasn't long about opening the gate, and that was something.

"Paul!"

"I've come straight from a very dull party, Florie. Humbold very kindly whipped me away. Let's go in, shall we?"

Inside I said:

"Turn out the lights."

Florie didn't argue. Mei Lan stumbled in from the lane, into blackness. I closed the little door after her.

"Paul? What is all this?"

"Can we talk inside? We're frozen."

Florie kept her central heating at about seventy. It was welcome. Mei Lan still had Humbold's car rug wrapped around her. She stood in that hall looking as though she didn't think this shelter for her was going to last long. I didn't think so, either.

"Some of that whisky I gave you, remember?"

Florie got the bottle. I poured while she poked up the drawing-room fire. This time Mei Lan sat on a soft seat and shivered at the whisky which I made her drink, holding the glass to her lips like medicine for a child.

"I think Mei Lan could do with a very hot bath. Could you run to it?"

She nodded. Florie was practical in an emergency. She was heaping up all her questions for afterwards. She went out and in about five minutes came back to lead the girl away. Mei Lan never looked at her. She was obedient, but there was absolutely nothing between the two of them at all. I waited in that comfortable room, looking about it, remembering being here years ago, when Florie's father had presided over the household. The old man had been a power-conscious Yin all right, a man who had held his family together through all the shambles of China before the great upheaval. Down in Shanghai he had managed to keep his business going even under the Japanese occupation. The world beyond his family hadn't meant a great deal to old Yin. Your ancestors watched over you and helped you to pick your way, no matter who was temporarily in power.

Florie came back. In the doorway she said:

"Paul, what in heaven's name are you doing?"

"I'm taking that girl out of China."

"It's . . . madness!"

"I know. I'm doing it."

"But how? You don't mean on that ship from Tientsin?"

"Maybe. If not we'll walk south."

"I think you're quite out of your mind! I don't know what's happened . . . but she must have run away from the camp and come to you."

"Yes."

"The little fool! If she'd only waited. . . . I had everything arranged."

"Did you, Florie?"

"Of course!"

"Did you, Florie?" I asked again.

"Yes, yes, yes! Oh, you don't have to believe me. But these things take time. I was trying. I swear I was. I heard to-day there was a bit of a hitch. I wasn't going to tell you. Paul . . . if you try to do this, you'll be caught. You're a European. You'll be spotted at once."

"Not if I was wearing some of your father's clothes. Do you have any still?"

"My father's . . . ? Yes. Yes, I kept some. I don't know why. You mean, a disguise . . . ?"

"That's just what I do mean. Maybe it wouldn't stand up to any sharp tests. But it would let us hide in mobs."

"Paul! Your height!"

"There are tall Manchurians."

"I need a drink. Honestly, I . . ."

She poured herself a sound one from my Christmas present to her. And afterwards I had one, too.

"I didn't want to involve you, Florie. But I had no choice. And we won't be staying long."

"That doesn't matter."

Ten minutes later I was in Florie's bedroom, and laid out on the bed were two of old Yin's suits, not the national serge, but old man's black.

"I hadn't thought of playing an old man, too," I said.

"Just a minute. Father did have one of those serge things. I don't think I gave it away. And he was quite tall for one of us. The legs would be a bit short but you ought to be able to get into it."

The outfit was brand new, never worn, clearly the largest issue size. National serge with no smell of moth balls.

"I'll put it on," I said.

Florie went out. But I didn't put on the suit. I waited for a minute behind the bedroom door, before opening it very quietly. Mei Lan wasn't singing in her bath, but she had revived enough to splash a little. I went down the passage, making no noise at all, but I heard a sound from the sitting-room. It was a number being dialled.

Florie had her back to me.

"I'd rather you didn't use that phone," I said.

She turned slowly, staring.

"Paul! I didn't hear you. I was only going to ring

up to see if I could find out what happened about Miss Mei. . . . I mean, the hospital arrangements."

"Really?"

Something went slack in her face then. She had seen my hand.

"What's . . . that . . . ?"

"A gun. And it's loaded."

"You're . . . pointing it . . . at me?"

"You're not dreaming this, Florie. Put that receiver back on the hook."

She did that slowly, half turning her body.

"Don't reach for a drawer. I'd misinterpret the move."

Florie swung round to me again. Her face was tight, showing nothing, but her breathing was quick.

"Can I . . . ask for some explanation?"

"Yes. It's simple. I came to China to find out one thing . . . whether or not Robert got here to see you."

"Robert? Here in Peking? I haven't seen him for fifteen years!"

"I think you saw him a very short time before he was executed. I think he hid here, looked after by his sister. Or so he believed. One Yin looking after another. Get what I mean?"

"No! Paul, stop being a damn fool! And stop pointing that gun at me!"

I lifted the gun a little.

"Robert set out to come to see you, Florie. I knew his plans. He was quite certain he could make it this far north. And I think he did, too."

"Why would Robert come here?"

"You know why. To get you out. He loved you, Florie."

She didn't drop her eyes. She went on looking at me. I could feel the stranger there, withdrawn into the bitter hostility she was putting on a desperate act to cover.

"You're saying . . . I betrayed Robert?"

"Just that. My evidence is circumstantial. Even now I've no direct proof that he ever got to Peking. I'm just damn sure he did. I believe you sentenced your brother to death. You see I know now that I'm under a death sentence from you, too. Admittedly I'm not another Yin and haven't the claims on you that Robert had. But old loyalties are there. You'd kick old loyalties in the teeth without thinking twice, wouldn't you? What the hell does family mean to a dedicated communist of your kind? Absolutely damn all!"

"You're mad! You're raving!"

"You put quite a lot of feeling into that. Maybe because you're badly scared now. You had no clue that I was getting anywhere near the truth, had you, Florie? I've played things the way you wanted them, right from the moment when I first began to suspect you. And that was in the Winter Palace. A nice act. Staged to convince me that you were risking real trouble to stand by me. Very pretty. Like all the other acts along the way, step by step. Bringing me to this."

"What do you mean . . . to this?"

"To coming to you with Mei Lan because I had nowhere else to go. I didn't plan to go anywhere else, Florie. I wanted to see this act, too. And as long as I reacted the way you expected there was a kind of safety for me. That became obvious pretty soon. The only risk was Obata. He was the unknown quantity. You weren't."

There was a kind of calmness about Florie now. She

stood perfectly straight almost forgetting to play innocence outraged because curiosity was operating. She didn't like failure, but she was prepared to learn from it. And maybe she didn't think she had really failed with me yet.

"You think . . . I'm behind everything that's happened to you?"

"Yes. You're a big shot here, Florie. Tucked away, but important. And you wanted the kind of evidence against me which would make the prettiest show trial to be staged for a couple of decades. Spying . . . I was snooping there by the canal, wasn't I? Having a look at one of China's secrets. Since nearly everything is secret in this country it wasn't difficult to plant me in that one. Then I would be caught trying to get Mei Lan out of China. A tidy offence that. The only thing that troubles me a little is who I'm supposed to have murdered? Yang was a bit precipitate with McVey, wasn't he? A little accident during an interrogation, perhaps?"

Florie wasn't even protesting any more. She just stood looking at me. I moved a little nearer.

"Hang Ling was your man, too, wasn't he? The only innocent was Mei Lan herself. You were wise to choose her. You guessed I'd commit myself, that I couldn't help it. You only slipped up on small things here and there. Like laying out a recent issue People's uniform. That could never have belonged to your father, Florie. But what about that murder charge? Who was I supposed to have killed?"

"Me," Humbold said from the doorway.

I spun around, but not quickly enough.

"Drop that gun or I'll blast the side of your head off!" Humbold said.

I dropped the gun.

"Kick it over!"

I kicked it over. Humbold looked relaxed standing there in the doorway. He was holding that rifle I'd seen before, but this time as if he knew how to use it. He had us both covered. We were almost standing lined up for him. He pulled the revolver towards him with his foot and bent for it, but kept on looking at us all the time.

"You didn't expect me to use the key you gave me quite so soon, did you, Dr. Yin?" Humbold said.

He leaned back against the door jamb.

"What's got into you?" Florie snapped, dropping the innocence completely.

"I've been doing a little thinking, that's all, Dr. Yin. It's not difficult for a man who's lived in China for as long as I have to know when someone's had it. Remember I'm a reporter. I've seen a lot. I can recognise the road out for me."

"You're perfectly safe!" Florie shouted.

"I don't think so. I think my future prospects are just slightly dimmer than Harris's here. You know, for a while I toyed with the idea of getting clear somehow and perhaps getting Harris to help me . . . that is if he got clear too. But I've decided the effort isn't worth it. Sometimes you reach a point from which you can't make a new start. That's where I am. I think I knew it when my wife gave me the push. It would have been wiser to delay that, Dr. Yin."

"You're all right, I tell you! You did what you were told. You're all right now."

And then she looked at me. If I'd had the gun I'd have shot her. But I wasn't to be the executioner. Humbold said:

"Take three steps back, Harris."

"Paul, no. Don't let him! No, no! Paul!"

I took three steps back. Florie moved towards Humbold and screamed.

He shot her through the heart. The noise was hideous, even in a big room. Florie kept on moving for a moment, with both her hands out. Then she pitched forward on to a thick, Peking carpet.

There was a cry from the passage. Humbold swung the gun on me.

"Get out in the hall! Keep that kid from coming in here. Go on!"

I caught Mei Lan in my arms. She ran into them.

"Paul, Paul!"

I held her tight.

"It's all right, Lan, it's all right."

The drawing-room door slammed. I found myself wondering where Mei Lan had heard my first name and why she used it like that. Her hair was still wet from the bath.

"Who is it? Paul, who . . . ? I heard voices!"

"No one who'll hurt us."

I had no proof of this, it was just something I felt. The Marxist in there had gone back to sentiment, at least as far as we were concerned. He couldn't get us out of China but he wouldn't stop us trying to do it.

Ten minutes later Mei Lan and I were sitting side by side on the big sofa, the girl with a glass of whisky in her hand. Humbold was opposite us. He had covered Florie's body with a curtain ripped from its hooks, but he hadn't moved it. Mei Lan kept trying not to look that way. Both small hands hung on to the glass, tight around it.

"You've worked with Florie all the way, haven't you?" I said.

"That's right. Number one stooge. They put the heat on me to bring me to heel first. My position wasn't a happy one. It started by a refusal to let me have passes to important things . . . you know, opening of dams, the arrival of some big man from Russia. I had begun to sweat, Harris, long before you showed up. You go on thinking that other people's terror is something you'll be able to watch from a nice safe seat. And then the terror is yours. Like a contagion."

"What makes you certain she was going to kill you?"

"The fact that she told me to come back after bringing you from the Summer Palace. I was to give her an hour and then show up. They'd have found my body here after you'd gone. There's a gun in her handbag."

"Was I expected to use your car?"

Humbold smiled.

"That's it. You wouldn't have been able to resist a ·car, would you? And they could have picked you up just when they wanted. Dr. Yin thought of everything. But she miscalculated on me. There are some things these people aren't good at. They can't really see when a man has spent himself. When he's at an end. There isn't a chapter in Karl Marx on what to do with a man who's spent himself."

Humbold lit a cigarette. After a moment he said:

"How are you two going to get out of China?"

"I haven't had much time for planning."

"Then it's a good thing for you I took time. The Kiangsi Opera is on the move. For a season in Manchuria. Playing first in Shenyang. The place they used to call Mukden. When you were a kid they used to have an Emperor there, remember? A stooge of the Japs."

"I remember. What's the Kiangsi Opera got to do with us?"

"It could have a lot. Moving the thing is a major undertaking. They have their own train. They dismantle that revolving stage and take it with them. All the scenery, too, and the costumes. A long special train. It leaves to-night some time after passenger traffic has thinned down on the rails . . . for Mukden. Get it?"

"The only rail line to Mukden is by Tientsin?"

"It's a good thing to know your geography. That's your fairy godfather's last gift. A special train via Tientsin."

"If we can get on it."

"Yes, a big if. But you might thank me for taking all this trouble."

"I do. I thank you, Humbold. There's one little thing, though. Florie could have been down for elimination and you could have been the elected killer."

He laughed.

"Friend, you've got a real feeling for the policies of the late lamented old Joe. Now de-tombed. It could be as you say. I can't prove that it isn't. You'll just have to take me on trust. If you get out of China you'll know I was playing it straight."

"Even with this train you don't put our chances of getting out of China very high, do you?"

"Frankly no. But I've done all I can. Remember I told you it paid to keep in with journalists?"

Humbold stood. He looked down at us.

"I'm off. I wouldn't advise you two to hang around here too long. But there is no one watching the house. This part of the game was being left entirely to us. Florie was to report when she could. I gather you stopped that. Well . . . dress up warmly. It's started to snow out there. And take some food with you. You ought to find plenty about."

He went into the hall. I had to leave Mei Lan sitting on the sofa trying not to look at the curtain-covered heap on the carpet. She didn't protest.

It was snowing all right, coming down quite heavily. In the courtyard I said:

"Humbold, come with us!"

He turned.

"I believe you mean that. Thanks. But I have some tidying-up to do."

"What?"

"My wife isn't in our flat. I don't know where she's gone, but I think I can find her before they catch up on me. I think so."

He hitched the gun up under his arm.

"I wouldn't leave this courtyard light on if I were you," he said.

Humbold switched out the light before opening the hatch to the lane. I heard that little door slam.

CHAPTER XV

SNOW CAN BE GENTLE in China, too, coming down softly, the blanket piling up, laid easily over ugliness. It was gradually covering the ugliness of that Peking goods yard, floating past the hard white lights set up on high poles, filtering them a little.

Mei Lan and I crouched in a blackness between two wooden sheds. It was bitterly cold. We were padded out with clothes but the cold seeped in. Mei Lan hugged wadding to herself, with arms folded over her breasts, as though she was holding in that cough. I don't know what she had found to wear in Florie's cupboards, but it had been plenty. She knew her climate. I had made her eat plenty, too.

I wasn't too happy in that serge uniform which had never been in the house in old Yin's day. And on top of two stretched pullovers and a cardigan of Florie's it was a bit binding in places. I had thought about not wearing the thing at all, and then had thought again. I wanted to pass in a crowd. The peaked cap pulled low hid a lot of my face.

We had spotted our train all right. For three hours we'd watched it being loaded. There was a drill for this, something done in cities all over China when the Kiangsi Opera moved. It needed twelve dinky box-cars of the kind that looked like a hangover from British influence on these railways, and right in the middle of them was an antique passenger coach. This might be for a guard, though I couldn't see why they would need much of a guard for stage props. We hadn't seen any armed men about and that was something. It was one in the morning.

I wondered whether they had found Florie yet. The answer was almost certainly that they had, even though I had moved the body which Humbold hadn't touched. Bleeding had left a big stain on fawn-coloured carpeting, but Mei Lan had put a small rug over this. They were scattered about the room anyway, little Persian prayer-rugs. All I had wanted to do was give an impression on a first quick search that Florie had, for some reason, gone out. I carried her, still wrapped in that curtain, to a cupboard we found in the clinic. And as I was putting her into it the cloth fell away from her face. At a certain stage after death the face can take on an extraordinarily youthful serenity. Florie's was like that, the lines tautened out in some way, her jaw held up by the angle of her head. She stared at me until I closed her eyes.

We had to get food then, but it wasn't easy for me to eat or think about the need to. I felt I was on the run from something which had once included Florie, an old life wiped out which had wiped her out, too. Florie and I, the kids going to school down in Shanghai, and Robert the older brother who had known all the answers.

If they caught me now Florie's death would be pinned on to the list of crimes they had waiting for me. The evidence would be tailored to fit the victim in hand.

Mei Lan began to cough. She had a trick of swallowing which sometimes worked, but it didn't now. I had to pat her on the back, while she hid her head, trying to smother sound. The sound didn't matter so much here, but it could later. And this cold wasn't helping her any.

When she was resting I whispered:

"Who travels in that passenger car?"

She looked up, stared at it, and then said:

"Hang Ling."

"What? Why didn't you tell me?"

"I forget."

"Does he always go?"

"Yes. He's in charge. Always. When I am younger I sometimes go with him. There is a stove. It is warm."

Mei Lan, even at her age, had something to look back on, a time when she had been able to keep warm, and there had been enough food in her stomach. A time of the she-dragon song. None of these agonies of coughing then.

"Paul, look!"

They were closing the doors of the freight-cars, and heavy padlocks were being clicked in. Those cars almost certainly wouldn't be unlocked again until Mukden. I don't know how long it takes a freight to get to Mukden these days, but I could see us carried out rigid from one of those sealed tombs when they opened it up again. We'd freeze to death. It's awfully easy to do in winter in Manchuria.

"Lan, how many people used to travel in that passenger carriage with Hang Ling?"

"Sometimes train guard. Some actors, too. But not many. I can't be sure. It's a long time ago."

"There's a guard-box in the end van, you can see that. If it was only Hang Ling in the coach . . . ?"

They were locking all the doors now. A steam engine came hissing its slow way back to hitch on the front of the train. I stared at that carriage in the middle. It was lit, but only about a third of it. The other windows looked as though they had been painted out, and Mei Lan told me that the main section was used for storing the elaborate headdresses which were the most valuable part of the company's costuming. Some of them were centuries old, and priceless. Each headpiece was packed separately in its own wooden box and these were stacked up. There was no room to hide, she said.

And yet the carriage was our only chance, unless we were prepared to ride the rods through a Chinese winter night.

That coach was a real antique, with platforms at each end, little miniatures of the things they used to tack on to observation coaches for people who liked to sit out and breathe engine smuts. These two were ornamented with iron fretwork suggesting a Hollywood Western. And one of them was bright with light suddenly, as a door opened on to it. A man came out wearing a leather coat with fur collar and fur hat with earflaps tied up on top.

"Hang Ling!" Lan whispered.

Another man, also dressed for Manchuria, followed the actor down the steps. They took opposite directions, each checking van doors. I let them get about four vans away from the coach before I put my hand on Mei Lan's wrist.

"Come on!" I said, and pulled her up.

She didn't protest. The girl had developed an almost total faith in me which was unnerving. If she had ideas of her own they weren't in evidence.

We ran, through the gently falling snow, over rails and without cover, exposed to the lights from poles. It was nonetheless our moment, the loaders all away now, up somewhere beyond the engine, only the two men doing a final check. And the snow, though it left our tracks splattered across the goods yard, gave us silence to move in. We were all right if those checkers didn't turn.

I pushed Mei Lan, who was panting hard, up steps on to the platform. I opened the door and shoved her into the coach.

"Keep down. On the floor."

Then I went to the edge of the platform and looked out. Two backs still going away. Nice. What wasn't so nice were those tracks we had made in the snow, big feet and little feet, right back to darkness. Anyone coming along this side of the train couldn't miss them. In half an hour they wouldn't be there, but they were now, shouting.

I went into the coach bent down. Mei Lan was beyond the lit end which had seats along under the windows. She was crouching amongst the boxes, in a narrow aisle between them. One look and I knew we couldn't make ourselves a hole behind the headdresses, they were packed with a careful Chinese neatness, right up to the roof.

Mei Lan was looking at me but she didn't ask any unnecessary questions. The coach jarred as the engine was connected, and just as I noticed a walled-off section beyond one side of boxes, a place with its own door.

The carriage had been the last word in luxury once, probably one of the first fitted with a lavatory. We went in there but didn't risk the bolt which would have sent out an "engaged" notice. From behind the opaque window I heard Hang Ling and his pal coming back to the coach, on the side away from our tracks.

::   ::

The freight train was moving at all of twenty miles an hour when Mei Lan began to cough. We were out in the country, well past lights glistening through the glass. It was the cold in there which started her off. She just couldn't control it. I couldn't help the girl, short of smothering her.

There was a voice outside and steps. I didn't snap the bolt, I yanked back the door. Hang Ling was there, a dim shape in the light from the far end of the coach, but I knew him. He wasn't carrying anything.

"Don't move," I said. "I've a gun. We're travelling with you for a little on our way out of China. If you try anything you'll leave China, too."

I moved out on him. He backed away from me. Down the coach I could see the other man, on his feet, but unarmed. Actors didn't carry guns, even on this duty.

"Come on, Lan," I said. "You might as well sit by the stove."

We all sat by the stove. It was a coal burner. Hang Ling's companion was a pretty boy, who looked as though he might be a female impersonator to trade. Perhaps that was why he was along for the ride. I had the feeling we had disturbed something.

It wasn't cold in the back part of the coach at all, but Hang Ling looked as if he was cold. He had no conversation, which was a bit curious from a man who had all world cultures at his finger-tips.

"You made a poor waiter," I said.

He swallowed.

"Does this train stop anywhere before Tientsin?"

"I . . . not sure."

"What do you mean by that?"

"It can stop . . . to let other train pass."

"Pushed into a siding, eh? Is that what happens all the way to Manchuria?"

"It's slow," Hang admitted. He swallowed again.

Mei Lan hadn't been looking at anyone. She was

right up near the stove, on one of the long seats, huddled over. She hadn't much of a reserve left and wouldn't have lasted long mud carrying. I got up, still with the gun in evidence, and made her lie down, putting Hang Ling's fur-lined coat over her. For a moment her eyes were on my face, green eyes, expressionless, save for a kind of acceptance of me. What I did was all right with her. She was just coming along with me. The little she-dragon was a load around my neck all right.

"Go to sleep if you can," I said, and she closed her eyes.

We were travelling towards Tientsin, but it was a long way still to the *Hashimi Maru*, much longer than the miles between.

I lit a cigarette and gave one to Hang Ling and his boy friend. They were a bit reluctant to commit themselves to this involvement with me, but I insisted. I pulled out a flat flask I had found in Florie's house and gave them some whisky, a couple of shots, letting that work, seeing Hang breathe more easily.

"You wanted Mei Lan to die?" I said conversationally. I could have stabbed him with something.

"No, no! You not understand!"

"Why?"

"Please, Mr. Harris, listen! They make me do it. They make me."

He glanced at the youth then, thinking about that, but deciding he had means of keeping the boy quiet.

"You not understand. They would let Mei Lan come back to us. That's what they say."

"And you believed them?"

"In China . . . we must believe."

It was true enough. There wasn't all that choice left.

"They meant to let Mei Lan die," I said. "And now that you know, what are you going to do about it? Report us as soon as you can?"

He looked at the carriage floor.

"We can die, too," he said.

That was also the truth. It wouldn't be easy for this pair to clear themselves of having let us ride to Tientsin. When the boy licked his lips I knew he had picked up some English.

Allies they were not, and probably couldn't be converted to the role. Hang Ling had loved Mei Lan as a brother. And brother was the operative word. The affection may have been strong enough, but this was testing it. I could see the girl's pale face, with black lashes dropped on her cheeks. She wasn't breathing like someone asleep. Fear was still sitting on her chest.

"Listen, Hang Ling, you know what happened to this girl. You saw her growing up. The Kiangsi Opera is a nice safe little world, even in the New China. But she was torn out of it. I'm not saying any of you could have stopped that, though you might have done. Could you have helped her to stay down there in Singapore?"

"No!" But I could see the guilt in his eyes.

"She had a year in a work camp. Think of it, Hang Ling. You've seen them. You were sent to that camp to fetch her. You saw what it was like."

"Please!"

"No, don't go soft on me. I'm asking you to think. To imagine Mei Lan doing that. And getting her cough. Thrown into it from your world. Think, man!"

"They put us in work camp, too!"

The boy cried out then, in Chinese. He was scared. After a moment I said, pulling out all the stops:

"I want Mei Lan to sing again."

The green eyes were open now, staring at the carriage roof.

"Remember the dragon song, Hang Ling? 'I follow undutiful course in my heart. I follow love.' That's all she's done. You want her to die for that?"

"Please!"

The train was up to thirty miles an hour, rattling through the night. We sat a long time listening to it do that.

::   ::

I hadn't been asleep, just lying back with the lids half down on my eyes, when the train began to slow down, in the way a freight train does, the brakes applied without any delicacy of touch. We were jolting down to a quick stop.

I prodded Hang Ling with the gun.

"Out there on the platform. Look ahead and see what it is. I'll be right behind you. If you try to jump off I'll shoot."

He hung on to a hand-rail to lean out. His head jerked back quickly.

"Soldiers!"

"Look out the other side. Are there any there?"

In a moment he said:

"No!"

"This is your chance to tell them," I hissed in his ear. "Cover yourself with glory. You and the ballet boy. Lan!"

She was behind me. We went down the steps on the side away from the soldiers. There were three steps, and we hung on for a moment. The embankment sloped away down there but there was room enough to land without rolling down it. I jumped. Mei Lan followed me without a moment's hesitation, so I almost caught her, but not quite. She fell flat, and was winded. I picked her up and carried her down the bank, then we lay there, with my arms around her, our faces down. The guard's little van with its red light was about fifty yards beyond us when the train stopped.

For a long time nothing happened, though we heard voices. I could imagine Hang Ling in there by his stove talking his head off. The hunt would start quite suddenly. Mei Lan and I would run into the dark of China somewhere about half-way to Tientsin.

But that didn't happen. Suddenly the whole train was swarming with soldiers and lights. They opened every van and the search must have taken three-quarters of an hour, while we lay and watched, hearing our hearts, Mei Lan swallowing her cough.

I blessed military discipline then. Soldiers don't just shamble off when a job has been done, they have to fall in and be marched away. There was shouting to fetch them and it must have been a good unit for the men ran. There wasn't room for the fall-in on our side of the train so they all went around to the place where they had stood waiting. Mei Lan and I got up and crept along the embankment wall, keeping it as cover, until we were opposite the steps to the coach, but the steps to the front platform this time, which was dark. We waited there until the engine whistled and then crept over. I hoisted her up. We hung on, packed down on to three steps, while the coach slid past soldiers not eight feet away from us.

When we went in the dark end of the carriage Hang Ling was sitting with his hands over his face and the boy friend was biting his nails.

"Thanks," I called down. "Time for another whisky all round."

          ::   ::

We stood at the back of a Tientsin crowd, Mei Lan and I, a female worker of the world and a big peasant from Manchuria with his peaked cap pulled rather low over his face. We even held hands without anyone noticing. A crowd collects easily in China and there was plenty for this one to look at. Over across the road was the entrance to the small dock area and beyond a go-down roof were the yellow masts and the black funnel of the *Hashimi Maru*. There were at least ten soldiers on each side of the gates, and every car that went through them was positively pawed over. Even the seats were taken out. No one was laughing over the act, either.

From both sides of the gates a tin fence with a spiked fretwork along the top stretched away and in front of it, and as far as the eye could see either way, standing practically shoulder to shoulder, were more soldiers, all with rifles at the ready. A flea couldn't have got through. It was quarter past eleven on a bright, crisp winter morning and Mei Lan's hand in mine was cold.

I thought about the other bank of the river and then stopped thinking about it. There would be soldiers there, too, spaced along the retaining wall, with orders to shoot at anything that moved in the water. China's a big place, of course, but it was determined to contain us. I couldn't go on playing a Manchurian peasant for long. All they had to do was see that the *Hashimi Maru* sailed without us, down-river to the Yellow Sea, then wait for us to pop up. A lot of things could speed on that moment, and hunger was one of them, hunger in a winter country.

We withdrew gently from the crowd. There was a lot of talk around us as we went, and some laughter. People knew what was happening all right, there was that informed note of eagerness in their curiosity. It was probably all in the morning papers, so that the few million in this area would be on the look-out for the stranger. To catch an imperialist spy and murderer would be the kind of break which could lead to that highly desired goal of Party Membership. It was an exclusive club and you didn't go up in the world without being in it. Once or twice I thought someone was peering at me, but it could have been imagination. Here in Tientsin we were on the road to the north, where big men come from. There were even one or two of them about in the crowd.

And the people we met in the streets beyond the dock area weren't curious at all. They all looked as though they had their own problems. Mei Lan, not holding my hand now, and walking just a hint behind me, as a peasant woman would, didn't ask any questions. I was glad about that. I didn't have any answers ready.

No one tried to stop us going into a People's Park of Rest and Recreation. It seemed quite empty, even of old men practising the national exercises for spiritual and physical regeneration. We sat in total isolation on a stone bench and looked at the depressing prospect.

A Chinese park makes no bid at nature touched-up with deft skill. This was all discipline in ferro-concrete, get tough with capitalism posters planked down where the trees should have been. The place had clearly an incidental use for rallies and there was a rostrum decorated in front with chunks of lava. What shrubs there were sat in cement boxes designed to control any deviationism of excess growth. Everything neat and tidy, with a coating of snow laid over any litter that might be underneath. It would have been a good place to shoot yourself.

I wasn't thinking about doing that. It may have been the strong sunshine which suddenly produced a completely irrational mood of optimism. There was every cause for alarm but sitting there I didn't feel it.

"I think you can ride a bicycle, Lan?"

She looked at me. She lifted both hands from her knees and let them fall back again. Her voice was very small.

"Yes."

"Well, we need two."

She turned.

"Paul, listen please. It's no good. We can't . . . you and me! I have the feeling, you could get away. Without me. Somehow you would do it. But not with me, Paul. You can't!"

"Where can we pinch two bicycles?"

"Listen! Will you listen to me?"

"Why should I? We get out of China together, or we don't get out."

"I'm not strong now."

"Lan, did anyone ever tell you your eyes are beautiful?"

"No. I hate my eyes. I'm ashamed."

"Of your Irish great-grandfather?"

"He was my grandfather. Not so far away. Not far enough!"

"Is that the way your mother felt?"

"Yes. She lived in Shanghai. Sewing. All her life she sewed. Nothing else. A whole life sewing. But she fought for me. I would be Chinese. And I am. I hate my eyes."

"When we get out of here, you'll stop hating your eyes."

"We're going to die," Mei Lan said.

"I've never liked Oriental fatalism. If you're going to be a top people you've got to get rid of it. To-morrow is a bright new day."

"To-morrow the ship has gone down the river!"

I didn't rally to that one. I looked at the commissars' rostrum. The upswing in my spirits was checked, but though I couldn't produce any therapy for myself, I could for the girl.

"Listen to me, Lan. I want you to do something. Alone."

"You mean . . . we separate?"

"For a little while. But don't decide to disappear to lighten my load. Because if you do I won't try to get out of China on my own. Is that quite clear? We're sticking together."

"You have a plan?"

"I always have a plan. They come popping into my head one after the other. It's a gift. Listen, Lan, scout around for bicycles. There must be fifty thousand in this city. It ought to be easy enough to pinch two. All I want you to do is find where. We'll do the deed later. And then buy a torch, quite a big one, strong enough to throw a beam in the daylight. It'll probably be black market smuggled in from Japan and you'll have to pay a lot for it. But here's plenty of money. And remember this . . . no one is looking for a girl on her own. Keep that cap pulled down. They won't see your eyes. Get back here in half an hour. I'll be waiting."

I think the thought came into her mind that I wouldn't be waiting. Our eyes met and held.

"You little fool," I said. "Get going."

I watched her go, a small girl, but scarcely slight, wearing everything she possessed under a uniform, like most of the other citizens. She went through a pair of gates to where a thin crowd moved on the opposite pavement and was lost. She was Chinese and hated her green eyes. I wondered what she thought about my blue ones. I lit a cigarette and deliberately refused to contemplate the future, to give my aching mind a rest.

I was still resting it when two truckloads of soldiers arrived. They would have got me if it hadn't been for that military discipline again. Someone gave an order in a loud, sharp voice before the clattering of boots began. And when it began I was already running, towards the lava-splashed rostrum, ducking behind it, running along, making for a row of those regimented pine trees.

What little guerilla fighting I've done hasn't given me a great respect for the conventional military mind. In our time it just tends to get a lot of people killed who could have been held in reserve. The soldiers moved into the park in a block from two entrances, leaving me a considerable area of unattended wall to jump over, which I did. If, on the other hand, I had been one man dug in with one machine-gun there wouldn't have been many soldiers left. The Chinese have always believed in the mass rush to gain their ends, victory by right of numbers. It didn't catch me that morning.

I wasn't in top training, but I've always been able to run well for limited distances. I ran so well right then that I was two city blocks away before the pursuit abandoned the park. The odd thing was that there was no hue and cry after me from the scattered citizens. Heads turned, but a running man was in trouble, and trouble wasn't their business. A lot of them went into shops.

I turned into a lane, and then another lane, and came out into a square before a perfectly hideous modern block which was certainly some kind of new civic centre. There was a very large portrait of Mao on a pole staring down with a benign smile on rack upon rack of Civil Service bicycles, parked for the day.

At the edge of the pavement, looking thoughtfully at the bicycles, was Mei Lan. Half of them had no lock and chain. Perhaps you lost your ears if you stole a Civil Servant's bike. We stole two very deftly with Mei Lan again asking no questions. All I said was:

"Did you get the torch?" And she nodded.

::   ::

By three-thirty in the afternoon we were by the banks of the Pei-Ho River, some eight or nine miles east of the last outskirts of Tientsin. Our only real trouble had been the roads and the village dogs. The roads were frozen, which was something, but frozen in ridges, so that you had to choose your rut and ride down it. Mei Lan fell off more often than I did, but after the first few times she insisted on remounting without help. For the last mile or so I had a punctured tyre and rode on the rim, but it didn't seem to make much difference.

The dogs were something else again. I had noted before that during the day a Chinese village seemed remarkably unpeopled by adults, and this was the case in the half-dozen we passed through. The old women who were about looked at us with a lack of interest which seemed to suggest that they neither read the papers nor listened to the radio. But the dogs were fascinated by visitors. I was behind and took the full brunt of the packs, developing a technique of kicks from the saddle which was moderately effective. Yet those dogs never yelped in pain, they just snarled and came in again. The kids, watching, laughed. I wouldn't like to be a door-to-door salesman in China at all.

The dogs always came with us to about a hundred yards beyond the last house and then packed up. Even the yelping died away quickly as though on a signal from the boss dog. Mei Lan and I reached the river with shredded trousers and minor bloody lacerations, about which she made no fuss at all. If I'd been at home I would have howled for the doctor and immediate medical attention.

This was a good way from home. When I worked it out as we sat on the bank I made it to be just about that point on the river where, coming into China, I had turned away from the rail with Kishi and gone below to play chess. Ten days ago. In that time I had acquired a contract for a thousand engines, a professional singer-dancer, and was wanted for murder, as well as spying and probably kidnapping.

We were a long way from any house, and that was a comfort. There was one tree in our area in which three crows sat on a bare branch looking at us. They were absolutely immobile, unthawed by the sun, and looked stuffed, except for their eyes, which were hungry. They were carrion crows, being Chinese.

"Paul, where is the ship?"

"It hasn't come yet."

"But . . . it sailed at noon."

"It was scheduled to sail at noon. That's something quite different again."

"Or it has gone down-river!"

"Lan, we'd have seen it doing that. This country's as flat as a pancake. Besides with the twists of the river it must be ten or twelve miles to Tientsin. And they have to go slowly."

"Why do you think ship will stop?"

"Because I'm going to ask it to. Now, Lan, stop worrying! Let's eat something. And drink the last of the whisky. Are you cold?"

"No."

As a matter of fact she didn't look cold, she was looking a good deal better, as though that bicycle trip was a bit of long-needed exercise. There was also the fact that I had been making her eat quite a bit since I took charge. We had been well rationed. It was a state of affairs which would end very sharply if the *Hashimi Maru* went by us without stopping.

I had told Mei Lan that there was no danger of it doing that, because my friend Kishi was on board, whom I had warned to keep on the lookout for me. What I didn't tell her was another little fact which I tried to keep light and bouncy in my own mind, and that was that in this river all ships had Chinese pilots and were virtually under the control of Red China until the vessel had passed beyond the Taku Bar.

We drank the rest of the whisky and ate a whole tin of Portuguese sardines from Florie's store cupboard which was the last of several I had squeezed into my pockets.

At four-thirty one of the crows flew off. It stayed away for about twenty minutes and then came back with another crow, so that there were four of them sitting rigid on the branch looking down at us.

::   ::

It was pitch dark when Mei Lan began to cry. Just a few minutes before the dogs in the nearest village had

set up a terrible yowling, which just might be a patrol
coming through. I went up on the bank to look for lights,
but there were only a few visible, very dim and small and
distant on the vast plain. China had gone neutral about
us, bitter cold and indifferent, as though she could take
her time, and there was no hurry at all. We couldn't see
the crows but they hadn't flown off as dusk closed in.

I put my arm around her shoulders.

"Lan, it's all right. The ship hasn't come down yet."

"Why? Because they hold it! Until they find us. The
ship must stay in Tientsin until they find us. You hear
the dogs, Paul?"

"Now stop! Lan, Lan, you'll lie in the sun, I promise.
Not in Singapore. Up in a place called the Cameron
Highlands, where the air is a bit like Switzerland, though
not so cold. And your cough will stop."

"All this for me, Paul?"

"All this for you."

"I am nothing."

"You're my she-dragon."

She made a hiccuping sound which was a bid for a
laugh.

"Why you say that?"

"That's the way I think of you. What's your hair like
when it's long?"

"It's good hair. Thick."

"I'll bet."

One dog began to bark, much nearer this time. From
a farm by the road, maybe.

"Look for lights," Mei Lan whispered.

I went up the bank but there were no lights. I put my
arms around her again when she began to cough, and I
held her. It was horrible, but she didn't shiver so much

after coughing, the spasm warmed her. It wasn't snowing, but the air said it was going to.

"In the river," Mei Lan said, "it's easy to die."

"Ssh!"

"What can we do, Paul? We can't stay here. Not in night cold. We have to find house. And that . . ."

"We'll stay a little longer."

"The ship won't come. Oh, I'm coward. But . . . I would not fear to die. Truly. If we choose, you see? If we choose!"

"We're not choosing yet."

But I had no plan now. Mei Lan and I were alone in an icy emptiness I couldn't fill with any action. The windless night was a vacuum sealing us away from all living. Living went on somewhere over beyond hard fields, in the yellow houses about which the hungry dogs roamed.

I thought the throbbing was my own heart at first, a quick pulse. Then I lifted my head. It was a sound in the night, starting to fill it, a vibration that seemed to come out of the earth on which we were sitting. Big diesels!

"Lan?"

"What? Oh, Paul, I nearly sleep."

"It's the ship. Look. The lights."

"No! Those lights not right. It's something coming, Paul. On land!"

"It's the ship. The river bends, remember. It's a snake. Those are the ship's lights. They're moving, Lan."

The diesels were a drum. I held her and we watched. I took the big torch from my pocket, not to test it, just to have it in my hand. I tried not to think about how difficult it would be for a ship to stop in this river, with the current, and sandbanks. It could be done. Kishi was on board.

And what could Kishi do about a Chinese pilot on the bridge? They might have sent soldiers with the pilot, to see the ship out of China.

There was a straight of about half a mile up-river from us. It was why I had chosen this point. As soon as the *Hashimi Maru*, moving very slowly, at about four knots, swung into that straight, I began to use the torch. Mei Lan gasped at the brightness of the light. I sent the message in morse, but in Japanese.

"*Tasukete-kure, tasukete-kure.*"

I had never asked a Japanese to save me before, but I did that night.

The ship loomed and glowed down on us. We could see it as a little world, contained, comfortable, safe. The glazed observation deck under the bridge was bright with light. But there was no flickering helio answering my cry for help.

The *Hashimi Maru* came abreast of us, rows of glittering port-holes, bright square windows on the decks, but no answering light for us, no sound of the engine bell for a stop, just that pounding throb in our ears and below this the hiss of the stern wave against the river bank.

I turned with the torch in my hand, sending that message now to the wall of decks behind the bridge. I thought I saw a huddle of people on the promenade deck, and certainly a door opened, a figure standing in it for a moment. Passengers might be mildly curious about a flashing light from a bank that was China, but that was all, no answer from the bridge. My torch was flashing towards the poop now, and the rising sun flag hanging limp.

"Paul, Paul! Stop using light! They've seen us. Stop!"

"Who? The ship?"

"No, no, look there!"

I looked back up-river. Just about at the bend, on our side, perhaps half a mile away, were other torches.

"Run!" I said.

"Where? Where to?"

"With the ship!"

It was all we could do, run along the bank behind the *Hashimi Maru*, which was pulling away from us. Soon it would go into another curve.

And then a bell rang, sharp, piercing. I saw the froth of the propeller as I pulled Mei Lan along.

"It's stopping! It's stopping!"

Even at four knots it takes a while to stop four thousand tons. And we didn't gain on her at first, then we did. On the fore-deck a floodlight was switched on, shining down over the plates. And against the plates was a rope ladder.

"Lan! Can you swim?"

"No."

"Never mind. I can get you out. But get rid of that uniform. We're wearing too much."

Mei Lan didn't protest. I shed my Chinese wool skin, too. The only thing I snatched from the inner pocket was my contract and wallet. I shoved them under the tight sweaters. It was just as well they didn't shine a light on us from the ship. We must have made an odd sight running down the bank.

We went into the river opposite the stern of the ship, while the propeller was still churning. The current caught at me before I was up to the waist and I had to grab hold of Mei Lan, pulling her with me. I pushed her through the water, using my legs in a crawl stroke, letting the current sweep us down as we fought across it.

I shouted to her.

"Catch the ladder. Hold on. I'll . . . have to hold on to you."

She caught the ladder. She held on. I had to pull myself up her body until I got the ropes myself. Then I made her slide under me and climb.

"Don't look down."

There were faces peering at us, a row of them, until the first bullet hit the plates with a metallic ping, and a whine of ricochet. Then there weren't any faces.

The firing came fast, but they hadn't got range. They just seemed to be firing at the ship, in a kind of frenzy. I heard the propeller start again when we were only half-way up the ladder. Once Mei Lan swayed out above me and I had to catch hold of her.

"Only a little more, a little more!"

Hands came down and pulled her up. They pulled me up, too, a moment later. We both fell on the deck. I could feel the ship swinging into a bend of the river, and the firing was astern, and patchy now. I was on my knees and wanting to stay there for a little. But I wasn't allowed to. A voice said in English:

"Come at once!"

I looked up into the barrel of a revolver. And then beyond it to a man in a civilian suit with a Japanese face. Mei Lan was already being led away. She looked back at me before she was shoved through a door.

They locked me into my own cabin. I sat down on the bunk knowing that for some reason Kishi wasn't on board the *Hashimi Maru*. Our rescuers wouldn't be interested in my story, they probably weren't going to give me the chance to tell it. We'd be locked up until we reached Taku and then handed over to the Chinese to go ashore in the pilot-boat.

After a few minutes I pounded on the door and a guard told me in Japanese to cut that out.

   ::   ::

When I woke the diesels were at slow again, and the sound of the engine bell rang out. I had pulled off my wet things and climbed naked into the bunk. There was nothing else to do. The porthole wasn't big enough to squeeze through. Anyway I needed rest. If I was going to think, I needed rest. Maybe I could contrive to talk to the captain before they put us off.

I'd left the light on in the cabin, but now I got up and switched it out. The door was still locked on me. But I could see the Taku Light, swinging around, putting its beam out to sea.

The engine bell again! And the diesels beating up to power! I unscrewed the porthole and pulled it open. The moon was out and almost full. It glittered on the sea and on China and down there on the swells was the little pilot-boat, bouncing back to land. It seemed very full. I could hear the chugging of its engine even as we gathered way.

The knock on my door was polite. When it opened I had the light on and was wearing a towel. Kishi bowed in the doorway.

"Hallo, Paul."

"Oh, God," I said. "You! Kishi, how did you work it?"

"Very difficult. I am now retired pirate."

"What? Kishi, I love you like a brother."

He bowed again.

"Great compliment. There is also great feeling in this heart. But you are much trouble. Often so with younger brother, I think."

"How did you do it, Kishi? What's this about a pirate?"

"Very difficult. Please go to bed. Keep warm."

I got into bed, still staring at him. He took the one small chair. And then I bounced up again.

"Mei Lan?"

"Quite safe. Japanese lady stewardess in full attention. Much kind words and soothing treatments. Leave young lady to these ministrations."

I sank back against the pillow.

"All right, I'll do anything you say from now on."

"Please put in writing. I blackmail later."

He took out his Kyoto cigarette holder and fitted it up.

"Lung cancer very dangerous," he said. "But not so dangerous as China, I think."

"Supposing they send a gunboat after us?"

He laughed.

"Japanese build good fast ship. Engine now all out. China, *sayonara*."

"Those lovely words."

"Sure. Now we have a party, Paul. At Lake Biwa."

"Blast you! Tell me about your piracy!"

It was the Chinese who delayed the *Hashimi Maru*. They searched every inch of her, and then she was ordered to sail, even though neither the captain nor the Chinese pilot liked the idea of the river in the dark. Kishi had taken one look at the precautions around the docks and decided that I couldn't possibly get to the ship there. He paid me the compliment of believing that I would see that at once and not waste time. I was still free in China according to the morning papers and he believed that if Tientsin was impossible I'd try somewhere else. He organised a little posse of Japanese on board to keep watch and then went to see the captain.

I would like to have been at that interview. Kishi explained the situation. The captain was perturbed, to put it mildly. His line had a tidy monopoly of the somewhat scant passenger trade to China on this run and it would be highly embarrassing, both to himself and to his company, to be involved in a little matter of helping fugitives out of the country. In fact he refused. Kishi became a little vague here, but it was plain enough that he then revealed to the captain just who he was, and the captain must have ordered tea and served it with hissing noises.

Kishi's plan was simplicity itself. Of course, if it came to the point where it was necessary to embark fugitives from the Reds, neither the captain nor his company must be involved. A great face-save had to be arranged. It could easily be done by a little outrage of piracy. The captain was requested to provide Kishi and his friends with guns, together with a few of the crew dressed as civilians, and if an "emergency" arose the pirate gang would immediately seize the ship, holding up the captain in his cabin, while a party went up on the bridge and held up the pilot and his Chinese guards. This provided the captain and his company with a most splendid out when the Reds complained, as they certainly would. The ship, at the time of the incident, had been in the hands of a batch of bad Japanese. And the pilot and his guards, when sent ashore, could testify that this had in fact happened. The *Hashimi Maru* could then sail back to Japan, leaving everyone happy except, of course, the Chinese. If the incident swelled to international proportions the Japanese Government could then issue a statement that the pirates in question had now all been rounded up and received punishment.

"Did you hold up the pilot and his boys?" I asked.

Kishi nodded.

"Yes. I see '*tasukete-kure*' come flash, flash. It is moving to my heart. I think Paul is making appeal to Japan. It fills me with wish for prowess. But capture of bridge most easy. Chinese guards look at us with mouth open. And pilot has wife and large family, I think. Domestic responsibility makes courage damp. But I am sorry you must feel the ship is to pass you. You will understand piracy is not accomplished in one minute."

"I understand, Kishi."

He looked at me for a time.

"It will be most difficult on this ship, Paul, to find suitable clothes for you. Only little Orientals here."

"Kishi, you belong to the Japanese Secret Service, don't you?"

He stood.

"I think now time for you to have long sleep. But before I go one thing. . . . I am not interested in Nishin engine."

"I apologise. What about Okura Shoten Trading Company?"

"I am chairman."

"I see. It gets you about."

He was opening the door, but he shut it again.

"Before you sleep, Paul, there is question in your mind of Obata?"

"Yes. I know his history in Java."

"On his return from Java I employ Obata. To say I not know of his past is untruth. But he is exceptional man. Very few Japanese speak foreign language well. Obata could speak Chinese, three dialects, like native. Also Malay. Also very courageous man. I think he is useful for us."

"As a shoe salesman?"

Kishi removed the cigarette from its holder and stubbed it out very carefully. Then he looked at me.

"When Obata disappear in China we find out he has joined Chinese, for training as terrorist in South-East Asia. He is at a camp near Peking. He is traitor to us. Therefore he is for punishment."

"You went to China to kill him?"

"Of course."

"When did you tie me into this, Kishi?"

"As soon as I hear you go to China. I know what General Sorumbai means to Obata. I know what Obata thinks when he hears you are in Peking."

"Why didn't he kill me at the Winter Palace?"

"Maybe my revolver stop him."

"Bait, that's all I was," I said.

Kishi smiled.

"In this case bait survive dead fish."

    ::   ::

I did a lot of resting as we moved fast over the shallow, bumpy Yellow Sea, but not as much as Mei Lan. The stewardess had one object, to keep her charge in bed. She had my full support.

Kishi promised to help me when we reached Japan about Mei Lan's passportless state. She could apply officially for sanctuary there but he thought we could work out an arrangement whereby she was shipped, in a plane with me, under a kind of bond to Singapore, avoiding Japanese immigration arrangements. I was quite certain that if Kishi thought he could work this, he would work it.

The day before we reached Japan we passed through the little islands at the southern tip of Korea. A lot of people have pretty grim memories of that peninsula, but I don't think anyone who has seen those islands under sun could ever forget a beauty that is totally of the East. They are as remote from anything in the Western world as the mountains of South China, or the approaches to Haiphong, or the Inland Sea of Japan . . . a frivol of islands, scattered down in deep water, so that the paths of ships is straight through them, sometimes very near. They are flat and they are pinnacled, all of coloured rock, and over them, set with a kind of grotesque formality, are little miniature pine trees which look as if they had been taken from a nursery and just dropped down. Some of the islands have tiny shrines or Korean pagodas, and the mind boggles at the idea of people coming for miles off shore in boats to erect little useless trinkets of buildings which only sea-birds can possibly use.

I looked down at a sea which was jade from a sand bottom, and the wind was mild, a sudden warmth which could be from one of those brief false springs that come before a winter storm. I was thinking of Mei Lan when she spoke to me.

"Hallo."

The stewardess had fitted her out with a nice warm padded dressing-gown that almost certainly came from an Osaka department store. Round her head was a Japanese *furoshiki* or carrying cloth, in a rather sombre shade of brown. Lan had also used borrowed make-up with a theatrical feel for plenty. I couldn't tell whether she was feeling well or not under all that applied colour.

"You oughtn't to be out here."

"I'm tired of bed. All I do is eat, and I'm like a pig." I could easily have put my two hands around her waist.

"How's the cough?"

"I don't cough now. I'm cured."

"You're rushing things a bit. But you'll live."

"Like you said by the river, Paul? In the sun?"

"Like I said. Like any way you want."

"Why are you good to me?"

"Do you mean, what do I get out of it?"

The green eyes were looking straight into mine.

"Yes."

"At my age it's real fun to play uncle."

"Oh."

"Mei Lan, I haven't mentioned him before, but what about this man in Singapore? Who is he?"

"Wang Fa Lin," she said, and as she used his name a light came into the green eyes I hadn't seen there. "You know him?"

"Yes."

I knew Wang Fa Lin all right. Quite a boy. We had a club in common. He was no chicken, even by my standards, with a rice-eater's face like a moon over Eastern Hill. All that sex appeal and a number one wife as well. Yet the light in Lan's eyes was for love, pure and simple, love that had survived a year's mud carrying and a lot else. If Wang had taken a number two I'd see to it personally that he pensioned her off.

Maybe I sighed, I don't know.

"Paul, what's the matter? You don't like Wang Fa Lin?"

"What? Oh, sure I like him. We've had some great times."

"You and Wang Fa? Great times?" She was delighted.

What do you do with love? I don't know. Tell them it doesn't last, that you should go for the durable object like the kind of man who only wants one wife at a time? Mei Lan's mother had turned the daughter into a Chinese all right. It wasn't a thing I could monkey with.

"You take me to Wang Fa?"

"Of course I will, Lan. By the hand."

She began to cry then, in little bubbling sobs, and I held her on the boat-deck, while the tiny islands went by and a useless pagoda seemed to nod at us.

"Go back to bed, Lan, and get better. Go on."

"I'm so happy."

"Sure. Go on back to bed."

I watched her go. At the door to the companion-way she turned and lifted a hand on which the small, pearl-coloured nails would grow now. Like her hair.

Then I looked at the sea. Probably I was meant for the Miss Fengs of this world. And there were quite a few about.